Richard Bradford

Conjuror's Journal

Conjuror's Journal

Excerpts from the Journal of Joshua Medley
Conjuror, Juggler, Ventriloquist, and
Sometime Balloonist

A NOVEL BY

Frances L. Shine

DODD, MEAD & COMPANY, NEW YORK

Printed in the United States of America

1 2 3 4 5 6 7 8 9 10

Library of Congress Cataloging in Publication Data

Shine, Frances.
Conjuror's journal.

I. Title.
PZ4.S5563Co [PS3569.H495] 813'.5'4 78-17869
ISBN 0-396-07598-3

For my mother

Author's Note

Neither Josh Medley nor any person except well-known historical figures described in his journal ever existed outside the covers of this book. But Medley himself owes much to Richard Potter, the mulatto conjuror who was America's first native-born magician. Potter was born in the Frankland mansion at Hopkinton, Massachusetts, in 1783, of a slave mother and unknown white father. Unlike his fictional descendant, he was slim, graceful, and by all accounts a man of great charm. He was also a master prestidigitator.

He had but one wife, who outlived him by two years. Their graves may be seen at Potter Place, New Hampshire, the site of the mansion Potter built and maintained with the considerable wealth he earned by conjuring.

A debt of thanks is owed, first of all to Mr. Robert Olson, Assistant Director of the Old Sturbridge Museum, from whom I first heard of Richard Potter and who gave me much helpful information; also, to Mrs. Jeanette Ellsworth, Librarian of the Public Library at Hopkinton, Massachusetts; the Public Library of Andover, New Hampshire; the American Antiquarian Society; and to Mrs. Brenda Joziatis and Mr. Ralph G. Chaffee, both of whom generously shared with me the results of their own researches on Potter.

Conjuror's Journal

November 4, 1793

Oated and dined this night at Dunbar's. North of Greenfield we had a sorry journey of it: above six hours in darkness and rain—something windy—the gullied roads foul with mud and snow. It was, "Now, gentlemen, to the right! . . . Now, gentlemen, to the left!" from our driver; and we poor shivering cattle throwing our penned weight away from the deep ruts, in a kind of seated dance.

The fellow next me, being full of rum punch, found sport in feigning helplessness. He came down upon me with boisterous roarings, the whole of his weight behind. He was full, too, of sorry jests—"Here's the oak, come down upon the oak gall," and the like—that he flung about as freely as his bulk.

At the first, I bore him in silence; but at length demanded he cease his d—d rudeness. He seemed much surprised that I should take offence—called me *Sir Pepperpot,* until I offered to teach him his manners when next the coach should stop.

The other passengers here grew alarmed. Soothing

words were spoken; and an elderly clergyman with the face of a benignant goat undertook to pour oil on our stormy seas.

"Be patient, good Sir," says he aside to me. "Let me beg you to subdue your choler in charity. The man has stewed his brains at dinner."

Thus appealed to, I restrained my impetuous tongue. We contrived to finish our journey with no more rumors of war; for my loutish neighbor soon after fell (prudently) asleep.

Our peacemaker was a Reverend Mr. Jedadiah Smith, returning to his congregation at Alstead Center after a visit to his daughter in Greenfield. He and I had much pleasure in each other's company at dinner and after, with our pipes. He expressed an intelligent interest in conjuring and deemed it a pity he would not be here tomorrow for my performance. "For," says he, "I have no doubt *your* feats of natural magic, Mr. Medley, are a curiosity worth seeing."

I bowed my acknowledgment of this good opinion, which came, I thought, rather at the expense of my profession. We be honest tricksters all; but do charlatans abound amongst us more than amongst lawyers, doctors, merchants, or even (God save us!) the Congress? Too often comes this well-bred surprise that I should show—in speech, parts, &c.—as something better than your mere mountebank. Always it sets my pride to burning.

But my old gentleman was innocent of offending. We toasted each other in flip, and I won him to an account of the great houses in the neighborhood. There is but one that sounds at all likely to my purpose. Tomorrow I shall hire a mount and ride out for a look at the front door of the place. God grant I find at last the knocker with the serpent's head!

November 5, 1793

A fine, large crowd this night. The inn is full of drovers; also of farmers travelling to Troy with frozen hogs, pelts of fox and fisher-cat, homespun cloth, splint brooms, &c. The board of inns comes too dear for their country purses, but they are welcomed nonetheless, to sleep by the kitchen fire and to cook their suppers of frozen bean porridge (called tuck-a-nuck) that hangs in chunks from the sides of their loaded sleighs.

So close upon me did the spectators press I feared my sleight of hand would be detected by the sharpest—but no. Wonderment and loud applause were mine. Fired by the response, I presented the new *scientific experiment,* so long practised, of the handkerchief.

Self: Can some gentleman in the audience favor me with the loan of a handkerchief?

Offerings from a number of drovers I contrived to pass over, they being none of the cleanest. Instead, I accepted a fine cambric handkerchief from a small gentleman in spectacles and a snuff-colored wig. I then produced my lead ball.

Self: Gentlemen—I propose to pass this lead ball through a candle flame, so that the *caloric* in the flame passes into the ball; this, mark you, without damaging the handkerchief.

A look of dismay appears on the face of my snuff-wigged friend. He eyes the handkerchief with a rueful air, as he would have it again if he might. The drovers, whose own handkerchiefs are safe, take an unseemly joy in his dilemma.

I set my candlestick upon an inverted wineglass to magnify the dripping sound of the melting lead; and thrust the ball, wrapped in a fold of handkerchief, into the flame with the point of my knife. My hours of practice have profited me well—the exchange of handkerchiefs went totally unobserved. The drippings rang clear, and soon the handkerchief was in flames. Much commotion, from the audience.

"My apologies to the gentleman," says I in my most careless tones. I displayed the large charred hole in the fabric's center. "You must take care, from now on," I blandly told him, "never to place your nose in the exact middle."

An explosion of guffaws from the drovers, and my poor gentleman, ruffling like a turkey cock, trying to make himself heard. Taking pity upon him, I called the crowd to order, balled the ragged linen in my fist, and with a flourish *produced* the undamaged handkerchief from the air above my head. Bowing, I returned it to its glad owner, and the demonstration ended in laughter and huzzahs.

My first-night audience being so well pleased, I am in hopes I may extend my stay in this place. 'Twould be a welcome respite from the road—the hard seats of the stage wagons; the early risings and joltings after meals. At thirty-seven, a man loses the freshness of youth that laughs at such discomforts.

My ride this morning bore no fruit. The roads to the mansion-farm, through some pretty country, were muddied still from yesterday's rains. Both I and my mount were bemired before we reached the stubble fields of the place. The house stands upon the upland nigh to the road, its knocker plain to see: lyre-shaped, and of brass.

So much for the neighborhood of Keene. I scarce hoped to find the serpent knocker this far to the north. But Lord, Lord! How I yearn over this Connecticut-River country! As I behold the sloping fields, coveting them all, I am my father's son with a vengeance. E'en more, mayhap, than when I ruffle at slights from some drunken passenger in a stage.

November 8, 1793

Came to this place, a handsome inn with a pillared portico, in the town of Hancock, New Hampshire. Again this day our travel was through rolling country, with a pretty November melancholy to the blown stubble fields. Many oaks have shed their leaves; clumps of larches show upon the dark hills, like clouds of golden smoke.

The fair weather has dried the roads, and we came along merrily. There will be no mire, if this weather holds, to hinder folk from coming into town. I hope for three days of profits in this place.

The usual group of idlers drifted by the inn step to watch the arrival of the stage. When I stepped down, my trunk following, there came a flurry of nudgings and winks among them. A number of little lads and lasses that had run shouting in the dust of the coach whilst we rattled down the street fell in behind me. One chubby rascal, bolder than the rest, demanded, "Please, Sir, be you Mr. Medley the conjuror?"

"Yes, my lad," says I. "And I have a wand with magic fluid in my baggage yonder, to turn your ears to butterflies." For two butterflies they quite resembled as they stood.

They all shrieked out aloud in fear and delight; and I heard one say, as I entered through the door, that he had not thought I could be the one. *For,* says he, *he is not big enough. He might be anyone. He looks quite the fine gentleman.*

These words, I fear, inordinately pleased me. Heaven amend our vanities!

I must cease to write and put my fingers to flexing; to be ready in an hour's time for my juggling turn. And I must send for hot water. Last week, I dropped a plate, the first for near eight months. More and more the pesky cold starts the rheumatics in my fingers. Poll, poor lass, would nightly rub them for me, with thoroughwort ointment. The loss of her has made me neglectful of such measures.

November 10, 1793

Here is presently a great hubbub and to-do downstairs. The spit-dog has escaped from the kitchen and is being hunted through the house. These little creatures lead wearisome lives of it. I have oft observed one of their number trotting in his wheel nigh to three hours, to turn on the spit a roast weighing near thirty pounds; tantalized all the while by the smell of the meat he dare not approach. This one heard the hostess directing the cook, and at mention of "the wheel" astutely disappeared. I fear the wretch will smart for it, when found.

There is a great expense for candles at this place. Receipts of last night amount to eighteen dollars.

Once again, during my performance here, I had occasion to note that *manner* is as telling as *matter.* Wit, used sparingly, is useful. But I care not for the extravagant airs of an actor. Always I strive to present my turns with that brusque civility peculiar to the physician. Indeed, to rattle or declaim is not my nature, which inclines to silence.

But I digress. (You are too prone, O Medley, to these profitless fits of self-appraisal.) I was about to set down the effect on the populace of the *Philosophical Paper* trick. 'Tis the least of my skills—indeed, it requires but little skill once the requisite paper is variously folded to pattern. The rest is manner.

"Gentlemen! I propose to demonstrate that in truth we are every one of us wealthy. To make us so takes but one thing—Imagination."

With the proper air and delivery, their attention is caught by the puzzle. Last night I knew them in my hand. Then 'twas but a question of the proper swiftness, rhythm, and grace with which my arm swung the paper into its various shapes.

"We see a fan . . . a fireplace screen . . . the rosette for a lady's shoe . . . a shoemaker's knife . . . a curry comb . . . a Palladian door on a house . . . Ah, and the wicket gate at the rear! . . . an Italian couch . . . a lawyer's desk . . . a dark lanthorn . . . a farrier's knife . . . a vase . . . a wine glass . . . a costermonger's hat!"

Since I have won them at the first, they are quick to *wish* to see the object named; so that their eager fancies mend every deficiency of my paper's artifice.

In especial I love to observe the children. Watching the wonder of these little ones, I grow half convinced myself that the wand of "magic fluid" possesses all the powers I claim for it.

November 12, 1793

'Twas Providence, as I think, that led my strolling steps to the graveyard on the hill nigh to this village. Therein I found as striking an epitaph as ever I read, and one peculiarly chastening to me. I doubt not I have lately shown myself in need of such chastening—indeed, as I cast my memory back I find the old faults cropping up like weeds.

Pride, vanity, worldly ambition, with the fierceness of resentment that swift follows in their wake. I am as far from Christian humility as ever.

To continue: I climbed the hill, finding the way wooded, desert but for the jay's screech in the bushes. Toward the summit, the prospect widened: pastures bounden by stone walls, and an apple orchard much fallen into neglect. To the right stood a farmhouse, all empty of life. The family graveyard lay in the corner of the orchard next the road.

I mused for a space upon the stones, which bore the surnames of Stevens and Dearth; the latter signally in keeping with the air of the place. But this vanished household must once have known prosperity; for in the rear of the plot a family slave was interred. His epitaph, composed by no indifferent hand, so struck me that I at once committed it to memory.

God wills us free; man wills us slaves.
I will as God wills. God's will be done.

CUFFEE BILLS

A native of Africa, who died
March 1778, aged about 60 years.

Though born in a land of slavery
He was born free.
Though he lived in a land of liberty
He lived a slave.
Death, the grand tyrant
Gave him his final emancipation
And put him on a footing with kings.
He practised those virtues
Without which kings are but slaves.*

*I have since found these lines to be copies from a longer epitaph, of somewhat earlier date, at Concord, Massachusetts. *J.M.*

Upon reading this, I was much affected. The obscure slave was my brother (or quarter brother) in blood, though more lightness of color than is due my mixed blood is mine from my unknown father, and my mother herself shows more Indian than Negro in feature. Through no merit of my own, I have known only freedom. There upon that hill, as the wind stirred the orchard boughs, I clasped my hands and humbly thanked God for't; asking His pardon for my misuses of it. Given my advantages, what might not this virtuous Cuffee Bills have become? Is it not incumbent upon me and every free *gentleman of color* to prove by our enterprise and virtue that our enslaved brethren in the South should likewise be free? The founders of New England thought by prospering to prove themselves of God's Elect. I must succeed for other cause: to cast their lie in the teeth of all who claim the black has not the capacity for freedom. God will condemn my fierce worldly ambition, unless it be from this noblest of motives, to instruct my country—so erring, yet so dear—in the injustice of her ways.

I left that hill abashed at my angry craving to find out my father.

As I drew nigh the tavern, I heard frantic yelpings. Next moment comes a whitish object hurtling over the gate straight onto my chest. Staggering, I caught and held the thing, which proved to be that same wretched spit-dog that failed of his duty two days before. He seemed to find my arms commodious shelter enough.

Up comes panting a kitchen maid, bearing a hazel switch.

"Oh, Sir," cries she, "if he has not muddied your waistcoat and linen with his muckied paws. —Fie, Socrates, wicked beast! Do but give him here, Sir, he shall smart for it, I promise you. Mistress sent me—" And here she breaks off in wonder at hearing her sullied gentleman whoop with laughter.

Indeed, I could not restrain my mirth at hearing such a pied, knobbed sausage of a creature laureled with the name of Socrates. These spit-dogs are all of a long-bodied, short-legged build. This one had an inordinate large bullet head and one ear torn askew. His whitish hair, freckled with black, was coarse like a terrier's. He kept his eye with judicious attention upon that hazel switch, as one who knew well its uses.

"Spare him this once, lass," says I. "Heaven requites the merciful."

"Oh, Sir; but I cannot, indeed. My mistress would so scold me . . ."

"I will speak to your mistress myself," I said shortly, and stalked off to the kitchen bearing the dog in my arms.

In truth, I know not what possessed me. Fresh in memory was that hillside grave and the thought of those enslaved. I fear I began to upbraid my hostess as if she were some grand tyrant, even King George himself.

"Mr. Medley! Sir!" cries she, affronted. "The beast has stole a hare."

"Then he operated quite upon American principles," I told her, smiling somewhat. "Taxed by his physical labors, he found means to represent himself at table."

"You are pleased to be humorous, Sir," cries she. "You must see my husband—I shall have naught to say to you more, on the matter." And she swept me up and down with her glance like any Duchess before she bustled from the room.

I followed to the taproom, the dog still pendant in my arms. It appeared I had done the beast no favor by interfering with my lamentable lack of tact. Indeed, I before all, who move from tavern to tavern about these New England states, should be aware of the esteem these landlords (and their wives) are held in by their communities, leading them to high notions of their own dignity and of the respect due them from all comers. Most landlords are prominent citizens, Colonels or Captains, often selectmen in their respective towns. More than once I have seen the astonishment of English travellers in our country, who, expecting to be met, as at English inns, with smiles, scrapes and servility, have their first peremptory words put down with awful wrath by their affronted host.

By good fortune, the landlord here is not unmindful of the brisk business my presence has brought to his bar each night. He received me loftily, it is true, but with good humor.

"I well understand," says he, "a man's taking a fancy to a dog. I myself once fancied a pointer bitch, Sir, that no man could see good in, but me; for the creature was of no account in the field. She was gun-shy, Sir, but a handsome bitch, and I fancied her for that." (He here gave an incredulous shoot of the eye at Socrates.) "So if you have a liking for the animal, I shall be pleased to let you have him for a trifle. To be honest, he is more trouble in the kitchen than he is worth, be he ever so strong in the legs."

I plainly saw that will-he, nill-he, Josh Medley must buy the dog or leave him worse situated than he found him. This idiocy has cost me six dollars. Now the beast lies by the fire in my chamber, doubtless revelling in this unaccustomed leisure, but keeping a wary eye on me the while. *There is some trick in all this,* his look seems to say; *this man cannot be the fool he appears.*

November 20, 1793

The old dream, come last night.

One reads of men and their recurrent nightmares, but my dream is no such matter. 'Tis of brief duration, as it seems; but brings unbounded peace and joy. I doubt not 'tis a memory, like my waking memory of the serpent knocker with eyes of green stone; but buried deeper than can be plumbed by the rational mind.

'Tis not in philosophy that so simple a thing should bring such quiet sweetness: naught but a cleared pasture sloping upward, to a line of trees stirred by the wind. Never have I seen more than this. Since first commencing this journal I have noted the dream on some fourteen occasions, at intervals of from three to eleven months. But indeed, I have dreamed it all my life. If the knocker memory is an early one (as its height above my outstretched hand and my great yearning for the *pretty thing* would indicate, as well as the sensation of being whisked away from the spot by one presumed to be my mother) then doubtless the dream field with its trees dates from the same early days. If I find the one, I am convinced, I find the other. Then will the mystery my mother is pleased to make of my birth be solved.

When I awoke, Socrates was at the window attending to the call of the watch passing below.

> The clock is three! The three in one above
> Let body soul and spirit truly love.

I murmured an *Amen*, listening to his footsteps fade. A heavy mist had risen at the valley's foot, obscuring like a curtain all the stars to southward. I heard the call of the watch a second, then a third street over; followed by unbroken silence.

My fire was sunk, and I was disinclined to climb from bed to feed it. I called Socrates, patting the bed with my hand, and willingly he joined me. With him at my feet, I slept the warmer, till the cocks began their exchanges at the first light.

November 22, 1793

Arrived at Portsmouth this night, late. Stavers' a fine inn.

Our breakfast halt this morning was at Bustard's—a meagre, inhospitable, rascally place! Having expounded in this journal upon the respectability and pretensions of our American landlords, I am constrained to note this sorry exception to the rule. Here were six of us passengers, our breakfasts paid for, seated at the long table; awaiting with sharp appetites our corn cakes and creamed salt fish, which were almighty slow in coming. From the western approach to town our driver, with six blasts on his horn, had apprized the landlord of the number he must seat for breakfast. There seemed no excuse for the delay.

Whilst my companions fretted and stamped, I sat still, thinking. Two years back I had passed this way and met with the same creeping pace of hospitality. I recalled too, how the driver had summoned us unconscionably soon, forcing us to rush off just as our breakfast appeared smoking from the kitchen. Most profitable for our host—to be paid in advance for a meal there lacked time to consume! As the minutes passed, I speculated whether the same game was not being played upon us, with our driver privy to the scheme and rewarded for his dispatch in the yard.

Just over the bar was hung a painting on wood, of a dead cat; with the words:

> Care killed the cat.
> Trust kills the landlord.

I could see the host's red face as he bustled with a great show of business between the kitchen and his post behind the portcullis of the bar. Now and again he peeped out at us through the spokes. He might have been in a gaol; and in my temper of the moment I thought it a frame most suited to his rascally head. Sure enough, at the very instant when our breakfasts (with enticing aromas) appeared from the kitchen, in pops our driver in a prodigious steaming hurry. "Gentlemen, the coach! The coach is leaving!"

Cursing and complaining, my fellow-passengers stamp from the room, unwilling to lose their places. I remain at table. The girl with the hotcakes, about to whisk them into the kitchen—no doubt to cozy them for later guests—catches my eye; hesitates; then brings them to the table.

"Coach is leaving, Sir!" the host calls out. I return no answer, but commence eating without hurry. He shrugs; a trifle discomposed, as I think, by my silence.

Crack, rattle, and to-do from the yard, as the coach drives off.

I fix my eye on the painted cat over the bar; and, chewing busily, summon my back-throat voice.

"*Meerrowr?*"

"*Mee-urrower?*"

The landlord looks sharply at me; but my mouth is closed, my gaze fixed hard upon his painted cat.

"*Meer, Meerauer.*"

His eye perforce follows mine to the sign; then casts about the room for some livelier feline intruder. My chance made, I neatly slip from their holder a dozen silver spoons and conceal them under my coat as I rise. By the writing desk stands a large coffee urn, and within it I deposit the spoons; covering the slight clatter with an *ahem.* I take up an easy stand before the fire and spread my coattails. The landlord, still puzzling for cats, moves to clear the table.

My one fear is, that he will not at once observe his loss; but trust a greedy cheating rascal to look well to his own. His back is turned toward me, but I see him stiffen.

"My spoons!" His fist thumps the table, and he swings toward me a face of rage and consternation. "Sir, Sir," he cries, "my silver spoons are clean vanished. Have you observed . . . ?"

I seat myself and take a pipe from the drawer.

"If that coach were here again, Landlord," I remark placidly, "I fancy I could point out the man who took your spoons."

He stares hard a moment, then turns and runs to the kitchen, from whence his frantic shouts drift back to me.

"Dick . . . ! Dick! Throw a saddle on old Deb and off after that coach. Tell Elihu to turn her back, nor let any man climb down on the way! Ride along beside and look out sharp, or the thief may try to throw my spoons from the window!"

After a minute, Dick is heard taking off at a gallop, and mine host returns. With something of a hard eye he stands looking down at me where I smoke.

"I am obliged to you, Sir," says he at length; in no very grateful tone.

I bow acknowledgment, puffing away.

"... Yet your good word might have come more timely," he adds, with something of a sneer. "Before the thief got off."

"You are safe, Landlord, you are safe," says I. "Your good friend Elihu will bring all snugly back to you, I have no doubt."

He takes the shaft, and glowers. "... You are certain you know the thief," he says after a pause.

"I did not observe the theft," I remark. (This was true—I had used a handy side motion, my eye upon him the while.) "But I doubt not I can help you to their recovery."

He began to rail at the thief, the low vagabond rascal who had taken them, stamping to the window to peer out.

"—Come, Sir," I called after him. "Another man might say it was but justice. Did you expect them to get nothing at all for their money?"

At this sally, he swung toward me. But the noise of the coach returning interrupted us. I heard Elihu's "Whoa! Whoo-oof!" and the wagon creaking as it was emptied of its angry cargo. Like a small whirlwind, the passengers broke into the room, scolding and expostulating.

Our host proved to have splendid lungs. He shouted over them all. "My spoons are stolen!"

A shocked silence fell. One of our number, a Mr. Geer of Kittery, was the first to speak.

"Sirrah," said he dangerously, "do you dare accuse—"

"—This man knows the thief!" the landlord cried, pointing his finger at me. "Sir, Sir, will you speak?"

I laid by my pipe and arose. "Yes, gentlemen," I said. "I know which man of us took the spoons." From their peg I took my cloak and clapped my hat upon my head. They watched me like so many owls. "I am that man," says I then. "You will find the spoons inside the coffee urn yonder. —Driver!" (And I spake this loudly.) "I have now finished my breakfast. Let us be off."

Leaving stillness behind me, I walked out to the yard, whistled Socrates from the stable, and was into the coach before driver or passengers emerged.

Only Elihu grumbled at the delay. Satisfaction in the landlord's discomfiture reconciled the others to my ruse. Indeed, they ended by laughing heartily and clapping me upon the shoulder. Mr. Geer in especial was delighted with me. He pressed upon me a complimentary ticket to an upcoming assembly ball at Portsmouth (for which he serves as a committeeman) and would have the story from me in detail.

"Well played, Mr. Medley, well played!" cried he. "You were sharp, Sir, to see what was afoot. I myself was struck with the slowness of his kitchen and the speed of friend driver; but it did not dawn upon me we were being cheated."

Having read over this entry, I cannot but note the glee with which I record my small triumph; the basking in others' admiration of my cleverness. All this smacks of worldly pride, my besetting sin.

Indeed, upon a second reading, my prank strikes me as a childish come-uppance upon an object who better deserved my silent scorn. Did I not lower myself to the level of Bustard and his Elihu, by such a mountebank trick?

No, not so far; for the rascally knaves are not even honest. Should an honest man allow himself to be cheated by rogues in order to maintain a spurious dignity in the eyes of the world? This would be a worse sin of pride than the other.

So does a man who strives for virtue find pitfalls dug

everywhere for his feet. Indeed, I suspect all my blushes at past actions, my agonized craving for revision, are but one more manifestation of *Pride.* So farewell, introspection, for this night! I should cultivate the philosophy of Socrates, who is anything but enthusiastical toward abstract virtues. To him, the greatest virtue is found in a bone. (How he toothes that one from my supper.) Lecture him on obedience or gratitude, and he will yawn.

November 24, 1793

Have been about the town, prettily situated along the bank of the Piscataqua as it meets the sea. Near the bay's mouth lie several islands. A spire peeps from the pines across the river in Maine province where lies the village of Kittery.

I walked out to view Whidden's Assembly House in Vaughan Street, a most imposing structure, painted white. Here, I am told, all of Portsmouth gathers. Indeed, the local citizenry enjoys a splendor of social intercourse equal to Boston, New York, or Philadelphia, for there is much merchant wealth in this place. The streets are full of fine equipages, and I have counted an amazing number of ladies extraordinary handsome.

Two lads are to distribute my broadsides. I hope to make an extended stay here; a prospect not unpleasing to my tastes.

Socrates learns to tolerate my commands. His compliance depends upon what interest he may feel in the alternatives. He proves inordinately fond of cheese. If I toss small portions to him, he snatches them from the air with great cleverness.

"Aha, Sirrah," says I to him. "Are you so accomplished

a juggler? Then we shall contrive to put your talents to better use than wheedling me out of my cheese." I must see what I can make him do to please the public. The landlord will perhaps let him share my sleeping quarters so we may rehearse together. Yet I gravely misdoubt the beast will be easy to train. *Independence Forever!* is his motto.

But I like the rogue too well to deprive him.

November 24, 1793 (Entry continued)

Forgot to record my attendance this day at morning and afternoon services. The minister discoursed on the manifold blessings bestowed upon our land—not only in the triumphant end to the War but in liberty with order under the new Constitution. He prayed most affectingly for President Washington.

Betwixt services at noonday had a most sinful feast here —pumpkin pie, roasted turkey, chicken pie, with vegetables, raisins, citron, walnuts, popcorn, apples, and cider. I felt dumpy for hours after; scarce able to stay awake during the second service.

Noted again the large number of handsome lasses in the congregation; one with a complexion the freshest red and white that ever I saw.

November 25, 1793

Disaster this night, during the cake-in-the-hat trick. I blame myself; for much of our art lies in selecting from the audience those who will follow the conjuror's lead. I have long prided myself on my ability to distinguish, at a glance, those suited to the part; and, in especial, to detect any spectator the least in his cups and give him the go-by. But last night I badly misjudged my man—a long fellow in his twenties, respectably dressed in smallclothes of black serge. He showed a fresh honest look and appeared quite sober. Indeed, I still am doubtful whether the fellow was drunk or suffered from some constitutional unbalance of the brain.

In an unlucky moment I borrowed his hat for the trick. All went smoothly, at the first—my finished cake stowed within my coat, the whole egg on the plate with the three eggs previously blown. The wax plugging their holes was invisible, unless to close inspection.

I thanked the fellow for the use of his hat; and holding it against my waistcoat, I called attention to the plate of eggs whilst quietly transferring the cake to the hat's interior. To further the illusion, the one good egg next was dropped *accidently* and smashed upon the table top.

I saw how sadly I had mistook my man when I cracked the first blown egg within the hat as if emptying its contents therein. "These eggs are very fresh," was my remark. "Mark how the raw white clings to the shell and to my fingers." Here I wipe my fingers elaborately along the tricorn brim. But last night as I made the gesture, I was startled at the change in my volunteer. Such a malignant look of fury came over that complaisant face, I at once foresaw trouble ahead.

Quickly I *emptied* the second egg within the hat; and now the audience, noting the man's resentment, began to laugh at him. This, together with my second wiping of fingers along the brim, seemed to render him mad. Leaping from his place, he snatched the hat from my hands and dealt me a blow upon the nose that produced a gush of blood.

My fiery temper o'ermastered me. I plunged across the table, seized him by the throat with my left hand, and commenced belaboring him with my right. He fought back; and we rolled from the upset table to the floor in a welter of squashed cake, blood, and broken eggshells. (Our thrashing about proved the ruin of his precious hat, hitherto unscathed; a fact in which I take enormous satisfaction.)

Many hands pulled us apart. One of the men who held me, feeling me struggle to continue the fight, admonished me. "Peace, Mr. Medley—Hold, Sir, hold. The fellow is twice your size and but half your years." (This was a calumny.)

"David and Goliath!" a second man roared. "When roused, our conjuror is a fighting cock, by G-d."

"You may let me go," I cried, lowering at my enemy. "You have my word. I should never have stooped to strike him." (A metaphor—the man towered over me.) "He is a fitter object for pity than for anger. But let him heed well, lest I close his other eye for him."

"How you strut it, damned mulatto rogue!" he roared. (Knowledge—guess—or mere intent to insult?) "You shall pay for my hat. You should be rode on a rail . . . You shall pay!"

In silence I lifted the crushed hat and displayed its interior, dry and clean, to the company at large. Already they were on my side, annoyed at the interruption of their pleasure. One seized the hat and jammed it on the head of its owner; and half a dozen hustled him from the premises.

With the aid of a cloth from the kitchen, the bleeding from my nose was stanched at last. Socrates had found means to improve the time and was devouring busily the fragments of smashed cake upon the floor. Ignoring my blood-bespattered linen, I addressed the crowd.

"If I might request the loan of a hat. . . ." At which words they roared. A sea of hats moved toward me, but I lifted a hand, slightly smiling. "Unfortunately, I have no more eggs." A second roar, and I produced my pack of cards. "I will endeavor instead to entertain you with these," says I. "The devil's pasteboards, some call them; but I say, judge a man by his conduct, not his toys." A cheer arose that continued till I was forced to call for quiet. Thereafter, every trick was received with near tumultuous approval.

'Tis strange, how a display of pugnacity ingratiates a man with a tavern crowd. Christian humility, meekness, the world does not admire. I can easier forgive myself for my slip—I was, after all, infamously provoked—than for the satisfaction I took in my enemy's downfall and the plaudits of the crowd. I fear I strutted it like a gamecock indeed.

November 26, 1793

My fame (of doubtful sort) fills Portsmouth since the battle of last night. Judging from the ticket sale, the crowds at my show will tonight be doubled. Even in the street I am stopped by persons wishing to speak of my valiancy—by which they mean my skill at fisticuffs.

This is scarcely the kind of repute I would see attached to my name. When thus accosted, I respond shortly and with dignity, meaning to warn the speaker just how little I relish such praise. Most are surprised by my coldness; a few seem amused by it.

But the noise this affair makes, though mortifying, has benefited me much in one way: it has led to one of the gladdest reunions of my life.

I came back about four to the tavern, much put out by my encounters with the public; and was making for my chamber when the hostess called to me.

"Mr. Medley," she cried, "there is one waiting in the bar to see you."

I had already refused toasts to my fighting blood from total strangers. "You will give the gentleman my excuses," says I. "I must rest before tonight's performance." Then as I mounted I heard one call out, "Josh! Josh Medley!" and a fellow followed to the foot of the stair.

Something in his voice struck me, though at the first I could not see his face. Then he moved, and the glow from the candle in the hall bracket fell a little upon him.

Will Poole! And 'twas downstairs in one leap to clasp his hand. We clapped each other upon the back, laughing like madmen; as if our meeting after so many years was the joyfullest kind of joke.

"Will, Will!" I gasped, holding him off at last. "Let me look you over, you rogue!"

The same steady grey eyes and large-toothed smile casting more radiance than ten pennyworth of candles. But he was no longer the gaunt, hollow-faced soldier I had known.

"Look me over?" he slyly repeated. "What, with the evil eye, you necromancer?"

"Conjuror . . . conjuror," says I. "The divines have no call to denounce me from the pulpit, Will."

"I was sure you were the Medley all Portsmouth talks of," says he. "The choleric conjuror—mighty Hector in a brawl."

"The town will have me a roarer," says I with a groan. "Come into the bar. I want all your news—and to feast my eyes upon you, old friend."

"Both of us older than when last we were together," he agreed, passing his hand over his oddly cropped hair. Its black was grizzled o'er. "Mind you that forced march to Princeton?"

"The frost is in my fingers yet," I told him. "It plays the devil with my juggling, on damp days."

"You have marched too little of late," says he with a poke at my waistcoat. We seated ourselves in a corner.

"Come, tell me of yourself," says I. "Do you reside here at Portsmouth?"

He shook his head. "I stay but the night here. I'm off to Falmouth tomorrow, then on to Court at Pownalborough."

"You follow the law?" I asked him.

His smile flashed, sudden and gone. "And a sorry chase she leads me—from Nantucket to the Kennebec. Josh, there be so many lawyers now. I must swim hard to keep my head above water. And my family's back at Rowley."

"What, married and a father?" I exclaimed. My voice must have rung out something wistful, for I saw his face soften.

"We have four now, Betty and I" says he. "I thought you would have been before me in marrying, Josh. You were always talking of it—and of that farm of yours."

"I have been wedded," I told him. "I lost my wife in '89." 'Tis always hard for me to speak of Polly. "The farm I shall have, some day. A wife and family, too—a round score of little ones! God grant I may enjoy them soon. I'm thirty-seven, Will. I weary of the road."

"Then wait not too long," says he. "The best lands are taken up, and more and more new folk seek what remains. We be the older generation, Josh, looking back to the War our children never knew. —I saw President Washington at a levee in New York four months back. Our General has so aged, I scarce knew him."

"Small wonder," says I, "what with this business of the French—of that rascal Genet! . . . *The World Turned Upside Down* . . . How we blessed the name of France, in those days! I can remember cheering her till my throat was hoarse . . . ay, and with the water standing in my eyes! — Did you speak to him?"

"There was a crush of people," says Will. "I gave my name and bowed; and he bowed in return most stately, but a trifle wearied by the press of so many strangers. Then I added, 'Of the 8th Massachusetts.' And at once his whole countenance so lighted . . . ! I had started to move on. But he reached out and seized my hand in both of his and held me to the spot. He inquired how long I had served and then presented me to his wife. She has not aged so much as he."

We both fell silent, remembering over-much for speech. At last Will gave a little laugh.

"We scarce dreamed," says he, "in those starved frozen years, that a decade thence would see us sitting fat and wistful in a tavern, yearning toward the past as for long-lost joys. . . . Is it the hard times we miss?"

"You have hit it," says I. "Heark'ee, Will—when times were hungriest and darkest, when no rational being would give *that* (I snapped my fingers) for our chance of winning through—then was it I was most hopeful. Most happy, indeed! Nights I recollect when I saw clear in the camp fire our cause and the worth of it. I could not believe Heaven would allow it to fail. The thought of freedom was like the thought of the sure spring coming."

"I mind me," Will says. "Your spirits never faltered. You were a pillar of strength in those days, Josh; to many besides me."

"The salt has lost its savor, since," I said; and I spake with bitterness.

"'Tis great pity," Will says, watching me. "But the Southern states could not be brought in and slavery kept out."

"Ay," says I. "So have we now freedom to enslave to boast of, along with our other liberties. We will pay for it yet, Will. We, our children, or our children's children. We were led out of bondage through the wilderness, to our Promised Land. Now we turn from the true God to idols —greed, injustice, expediency—we shall pay for it, both north and south; as did the Israelites."

Will was silent for a moment. "Old soldiers all find sweetness in memories of war," he said then; striving (I could ever read Will like a book) to lift the shadow from me. "Beware, Josh, that when you have your farm at last you look not back to regret your days of wandering."

I shook my head. "Were I still twenty-seven, perhaps. But I cannot juggle forever. —'Tis true, my Aunt Deb still is off with her gown and on with her blanket and away north—the devil knows where she wanders to—each fall, regular as the flocking geese pass to south'ard. But she is pure Nipmuck blood; the Hassanamiscoe tribe."

"Well, we must get you a wife," Will exclaims, throwing himself back with an arm over his chair. "You must come to us at Rowley, Josh. I doubt not Betty can turn up one among our local lasses to suit; although you once flew high in your notions."

"I am as good as any man," I retorted, something fierce.

He laughed. "Then you bear yourself more humbly than you did," says he, "for you used to think yourself better."

"Never have I concealed my mixed blood," says I, still high with him. "Nor hung my head for it."

"No, Josh," says he, sobering. "You flaunted it like a banner and fiercely, although with your ruddy looks there was no need. Judging from Portsmouth, 'twould seem no barrier to your success. Is not your mixed blood generally known here?"

"So I would guess," says I. "The d—d rascal who tackled me last night called me a *mulatto rogue.*"

"Yet you have won the populace to you," says he.

"Ay, for I entertain them" says I. "They graciously allow a *gentleman of color* to provide them with amusement. Yet how many would have him to dine? I am doubly barred: by birth and by profession. So I go into company but seldom; and when I do will find or make occasion to declare myself *mulatto* for good or ill. —But mark ye, Will, in business I mind my business. Let others mind theirs. I fought for freedom, 'tis mine, by right. There be those that would deny it me—or limit it at the least. —'So far you may pursue your notions of happiness, no farther. This much money you may make, but no more. Here you may not walk, nor there. From this place to the other you may not go without a pass.' —The D—l!"

Will heard me with a troubled face. "These things be not in Massachusetts law now, Josh," says he. "Our Constitution treats as equals the white man and the free black."

"Ay, the law—but not custom," I retorted. "'Tis why I chose to be a conjuror, not the doctor or clergyman my mother hankered after. I would grow rich, Will. —So would I not be a fool to blab what may become a weapon 'gainst me, to rob me of my rights? Though indeed, I answer truly if asked and with no hangdog air. For, of my three bloodlines, 'tis only that of my white father's I feel aught of shame for. Nor will I assume, as some do, a Spanish or East Indian name to account for my shade of skin. Were I to call myself *José de Medleo*—"

Here Will, the dog, gives a great laugh, throwing himself back in his chair. "You would make a find grandee, Josh, I swear," says he. "Yet would I wager, in the battle 'twixt Pride and Policy, Pride proves more often the victor. I mind you of old. Indeed, I ever honored you for it, old fire-eater."

"'Tis true I am something impetuous of tongue," says I. "If I hear the Negro (or the Indian) slighted; if I witness some public persecution, be it petty or grave; then am I apt to blush for this physical envelope, this one gift from my father, that exempts me in the main from persecution—and to tear it open in the World's despite."

"Have you found out your father?" Will asks. "You were used to wonder much about him."

"I think less on that now," said I, and fell silent. I confess I was ashamed to have him see how sharp the craving yet is, to *know.* Indeed, just hours before, I had heard tell of the fine seat of one Hamilton, said to be eighteen miles up-river. Already I had appointed in my mind a day when I might ride to see the knocker of the front door.

Will is to come to my performance (in an hour's time) and we will gossip and make merry together after, until late.

November 27, 1793

Will off for Pownalborough this morning, in a light fall of snow.

We said our farewells at his inn, to which I made my way before daybreak through silent streets crossed by the grey slanting flakes. I had thought to bear him company as far as York; I had hired a horse for the ride up to South Berwick. But the weather prevented. Instead we snatched a few moments by the fire, with scarce a word between us. We were both downhearted and scarce awake. Last night Will came and cheered my magic, all the louder for our several flipdogs together at dinner. Then to my chamber, where we talked and talked of old travails, whilst Socrates dozed and whimpered at the snapping of the logs.

The stage wagon stood ready at four o'clock. Together we stepped out to the yard where the horses steamed and stamped and the driver shouted at the sleepy coach boys shivering through the dark, their lanterns wavering before. One last time Will shook my hand, smiling wanly in the lanterns' gleam. He clambered to his place and shoved his valise beneath the bench; before he had settled himself, the last man was in. The driver cracked his whip. "Order, whope, *git!*" The wagon rattled down the silent street toward the river.

Many a promise we made, to meet again soon; he to write me in care of the Grapes in Boston; I, to come to Rowley in the spring. Yet I know 'tis the world's way that none of these is like to be. I sorely envy Will his wife, his children, his farm in Rowley—even his December circuit ride to Pownal Court House; rattling north on the snowy roads, blowing on his fingers as he peers at his legal brief in the half light; with the cold fire of dawn coming out of the sea. In his shoes (frozen though they may be) I should be well content.

I am glad I saw Will. But our meeting has given me a distaste for my own mode of life and the flummery by which I earn my bread.

My head aches manfully as I write, doubtless the result of all that flipdog. Will is likely in the same state—viewing the world today with as bleak an eye as my own. D—l take flip and all this fruitless melancholy! I shall take a nap.

November 30, 1793

Audience noticeably smaller last night. The time approaches when I must move on. If the roads stay clear, I shall head for Davenport's in Newbury for three nights, and on to Gloucester town.

In this place I now compete with a showman in Daniel Street who boasts a Tyger-Lion and a Learned Pig. Yesterday I found there a line of people outside—it took me near an hour to get in. I thought the Tyger-Lion a poor thing. But the pig proved both diligent and clever; neatly told the hour with his hoof, squealed tunes to the beat of a drum, &c. &c.

I share a bed now with a Mr. Richard Collie, come over from Durham for the assembly ball on Monday evening next. The affair fills all the inns with folk from outlying villages and causes an agreeable stir throughout Portsmouth. These many newcomers may fill the parlor for three evenings more.

I confess, I hanker mightily to attend the assembly myself, having been presented so opportunely with a ticket: to dance, hear the music, and see the elegance of dress and appointments that all assure me are the mark of Whidden's. Since Mr. Collie is a bachelor, I suggested we might go together to the affair. He was most civil in his regrets, but is bidden to dine with friends that evening and then to attend the ball in their company.

Well, well, perhaps I shall go. I had out my embroidered waistcoat and my black plush breeches and the blue velvet coat. The nap of the latter is a trifle rubbed, but not, as I think, very markedly. The waistcoat is something tight under the arms and across my back. 'Twould be a silly extravagance to outfit myself all new for this one affair. The old shall do very well.

If, indeed, I go.

But I must have silk stockings and kid gloves. And powder to my hair.

December 3, 1793

My mind is a-whirl with impressions after Whidden's, yesternight.

It turned cold by afternoon, with a northwest wind blowing the lying snow in clouds. Still colder at early dark: the mercury at 8°, ice on the Puddle Dock, and a sky stuck full of stars, rich and round as plums in a pudding. From six o'clock on, the streets (blown pretty clear of snow) racketed with the clatter of horses and wheels. When I walked to the Assembly House around half past six, carrying my pumps under my coat to keep them dry, I found already fifty or sixty chaises, carriages, &c. lined up before the place; with hostlers chalking figures on the dashers to prevent confusion. Scores of people in elegant dress were moving through the doors.

Upon entering, I gave my ticket, received my figure for the draw, and went to a dressing room to change. But in pulling on a pump I felt my waistcoat split quietly up my back. *Medley, woe betide! Must ye beat a forced retreat and farewell to revellings?* But after alarums the damage proved invisible from the front.

Three large parlors, a kitchen, and a great hall on the first floor were filled with strolling, chattering, laughing crowds. The flow of people passed up the staircase toward the assembly room, and these I joined.

This room runs the entire length of the building and like the drawing rooms, is decorated in most elegant taste: window-frames carved and gilded, deep cornices, an ornate balcony over the entrance for the musicians (already tuning to play). The whole was lighted by clusters of wax candles in glittering chandeliers, and pulsed with flutter and buzz. Two powdered managers, hats under their arms, were busy escorting ladies to seats. I stationed myself near the door to watch as the fair ones swept by, consciously unconscious in their low-cut velvets, silks, and satins. I teased myself with speculation: Which of these charmers was destined, by producing the matching figure to mine (I had drawn *eleven*), to be my partner?

The gentlemen strolled about, greeting acquaintances. I noted a number of faces from among my tavern audiences; a few spoke to me or bowed. I was greeted most heartily by Mr. Geer of Kittery, to whom I owed my ticket. He presented me to his wife, who (I thought) seemed less than eager for the privilege.

He next commenced to recount the tale of Bustard and his spoons so loudly that I was thrown into great confusion; being mortally afeared he might demand a demonstration of my talent for *meowing*. Eyes commenced to turn in our direction and my face to burn—when in good time the orchestra struck up a fanfare. After a manager conducted the most recent bride among the company out to lead the head set, the call of the figures began.

Earlier I had singled out six or seven handsome lasses whom I felt 'twould be the height of good fortune to draw as my partner. But when my figure was called I grew exceedingly rejoiced; for I perceived my partner to be the very damsel of the fair and red complexion I had observed at meeting on Sunday last. E'en more youthful did she appear now, scarce seventeen. Her gown, of a soft dusty rose, spoke finely with her cheeks and brown dressed curls.

Presented by the manager, I was Mr. Joshua Medley, she was Miss Dorothy Reade. I made my duties, she curtseyed; with a heightening of color and a smile that spoke of mortal embarrassment. I feared she was in no wise as pleased as was I with the partner her *eleven* had brought her. Doubtless to her eyes a man of my years, something stout, seemed fitter for shawl, stick, and chimney corner than to cut capers upon a dance floor.

In pity for her shyness (and perhaps as my own pride felt fitting) I did not force my talk upon her. After the very first we danced in smiles and silence the draw dance and the cotillion. At length, in the midst of the latter, she spoke.

"You dance with great gravity, Mr. Medley," says she, peering at my face. "I fear our assembly is not to your taste."

"You mistake me, Miss Reade," says I. "I find the music excellent, and my partner dances . . . excellently well."

"I would not dare do otherwise," says she, "in the face of your silence. 'Tis something awesome to dance with a gentleman who appears to be thinking so many thoughts."

"My apologies," says I, "I thought you did not care to talk. —Do you reside here in Portsmouth with your parents?"

"With my aunt," says she. "My parents are dead. Aunt is my guardian. —Now for you, Sir. You are from our neighbor Commonwealth?"

The dance parted us just then, but I had time to bow an affirmative. She continued peering at my face and screwing her lovely eyes in a way that made me suspect spectacles at home.

"And where in Massachusetts is your home, Mr. Medley?" says she next.

"I was raised near Deerfield," says I. "But for many years I can scarce be said to reside anywhere, Miss Reade. My residence is at inns the length and breadth of these New England States. I am a conjuror by profession."

"You announce your profession with great fierceness," says she, ducking her head with a laugh. "Quite as if you were casting down a challenge. I shall not fight you for it, Sir."

"That you may choose to despise me for it," says I, "I am well aware. But such opinions cannot touch a man whose consciousness of rectitude is firm; whose character is fortified with a shield of innocence and honor ten thousandfold stronger than brass or iron . . ." &c., &c. I believe I was continuing in this vein when she interrupted me.

"—La, Mr. Medley, do not strike out before you are hurt," she cries. "Far from despising your calling, I quite envy you. O, to be always travelling!" She said this childishly, ducking her head again. "I should like it of all things; and yet I have been no farther from Portsmouth all my life than twice to Boston."

Her life was scarce ended I told her; doubtless she would find ample opportunities for travel. "Meantime," says I, "find solace in the word of one who knows the best and worst of it. Travel, in constant doses, grows wearisome. In summer, stage wagons are hot and dusty; in winter, cold and damp. At inns one dines with strangers or chance acquaintances of the road. A few days ago I encountered here in Portsmouth an old friend and fellow-veteran I had not seen in ten years. Our time together was but a few scant hours, and it may be ten years again before our ways cross."

"Yet you chose a wanderer's profession," says she, after a pause. "And you do well, indeed. Your fame is great in Portsmouth. The word is all of your juggling skills, your prowess in—" And here she broke off.

"—In brawling, I suppose you would say," I cried, "only you fear to offend. I assure you, Miss Reade, I am no such tavern bully boy as rumor will have me. The fellow attacked me without motive or warning. 'Twas defend myself or be thrashed."

"Forgive me," says she hastily. "I see I have touched upon a topic painful to your feelings."

Indeed, her interest struck me as unmaidenly in one so young and (apparently) so gently reared. But I was glad my calling seemed not to offend her. 'Tis an awkward thing, to declare my profession at the start of any acquaintance; but honor demands it. I wish to know no man (or woman) who scorns me for't. Conjuring requires honest skills hardly mastered. Well done, it gives every man his just due of pleasure for money received; and it delights the hearts of little children.

But back, my Pen, to Whidden's and that most delightful ball!

We danced till ten, with great pleasure on my part, and then Miss Reade presented me to her aunt, Mistress Atwell, a tall, spare lady with a high Heddus roll and cap perched a-top it; who was all politeness and absence of mind. She refused to come downstairs with us, but graciously agreed I might bring her a cup of chocolate and a small plate of . . . *something.*

My partner and I descended to where the supper was laid out on large waiters; a most elegant spread of ham and tongue sandwiches, thin biscuits, and nuts; besides sangaree, lemonade, and chocolate. Miss Reade showed an excellent hearty appetite. 'Twas "just a morsel of that excellent tongue" or "some of those delicious-looking glazed almonds," till I was kept so busy helping her I scarce had time to fortify myself, after; which was something hard. 'Twas astonishing how heartily she ate—although indeed, she is a sturdy lass. The impression she gives of dainty delicacy stems largely from her pointed face and the natural grace of all her motions. Her form is one of glowing good health, as attested to by her fair red and white.

During our repast she displayed a candid curiosity about me, that I dare hope was genuine.

"Mr. Medley," says she, setting her teeth firmly into an almond, "you puzzle me. If you so detest travelling, how did you ever come to choose your profession?"

"Indeed, Miss Reade, it is nearer the truth to say it chose me," says I. "And I have not always hated travel."

"Ah, when you were young . . . !" she cries.

I own, I felt this artless comment keenly. "Miss Reade," says I (and stiffly), "I am not yet forty."

"Gentlemen will not be thought old," says she then, with something of slyness. "But they wish all to be considered wise. Our books tell us that wisdom is not a virtue of youth, Mr. Medley, so you may not eat your cake and have it."

"I make no pretence to wisdom," says I. "Nor to youth. Something weatherworn I may be—yet never have I felt so aged as now, since meeting you."

She laughed. "Come, Sir, you shall not grow old—you can conjure an elixir of youth. When I am white of hair and toothless, you shall be dancing still at assembly balls."

"I should like better, as I think, to grow old along with you," says I.

She has not yet the art of receiving compliments with

grace. She rolled her eyes and giggled; then said again I puzzled her. "You will think me very forward and saucy," she says, growing suddenly earnest. "But—you have the speech and address of one with education. Pray, where was your schooling?"

"In my early years, from Mistress Betsy Small in Deerfield," says I. "Since then, though a man who travels can scarce acquire a private library, I read what books I can lay hands on. Just prior to the War, I had the opportunity of studying for a brief space at the college of Mr. Wheelock in Hanover."

"One hears good things of that place," she says. "—An outgrowth of his Indian charity school, is it not? And yet it boasts more graduates than Harvard College."

"In 1770, there were but thirty of us," I told her. "Amongst us two Indians, and myself, who have Indian and Negro blood from my mother."

I confess, 'twas with unusual reluctance that I *flaunted* (as Will puts it) my mixed blood-lines. All the same—from no man or woman created will I tamely suffer condescension. I was ready, should Miss Reade evince the slightest distaste for my company, to resign her to her aunt without another word. But she only squinted up at me in her queer way; searching, perhaps, for traces of bear grease and feathers, but with no dimming of her animation.

"You were fortunate," says she. "My sex can attend no college."

"Indeed, Miss Reade, I have always considered that year as a special grace of Providence in my life," says I. "And yet I recall no period (save the War) where I lived harder or suffered more."

"Was it such a Spartan place?" she asked.

"Before we could begin our studies," says I, "we had to

build our college. We had to chop a road through the woods for Mrs. Wheelock's carriage. A hut of logs without nails, stone, or brick was our first building; oiled paper our window glass. We students boarded around at neighbor farms, where we slept in rooms without fires and dined on leftovers from poor meals. If you have never eaten gander for dinner, Miss Reade, cold gander for supper; and come shivering down to a breakfast of more cold gander and swamp tea . . ."

"—It has a heroic sound," she cries. "But I daresay I should not like it at all. But, for Latin and Greek and Logick and English letters—I would try to endure it. As for the War, I was born two days after the Declaration was signed, making me something young to enlist, even had I been a boy. But I should dearly have loved to fight under General Washington!"

"And dearly would we have loved to have you," responded I, with perhaps excessive boldness. Her words kindled a pretty picture of a fresh-faced lass a-soldiering.

She blushed; and the music striking up again, we hastened upstairs, bearing Mistress Atwell's chocolate.

We found her in talk with Mr. Geer and his wife. Indeed, this gentleman from Kittery seemed acquainted with every person in the hall. He was forever hailing friends in a voice that bade fair to make the candles waver. He pounced at once upon Miss Reade.

"Here is your aunt declining to come to my Tuesday turtle frolic," he cries, "though I promise a sleigh to whisk her off from her very doorstep. Persuade her, Miss Dorothy, I must have you both, I must have you both."

Mistress Atwell, smiling, shook her head and would not be moved. "I take cold so easily, I dare not venture," she explained repeatedly to Mrs. Geer.

"Well, you will come, Miss Dorothy," he insisted. "It will all be gay as may be. The Parson and his wife and girls are coming—the Whitmans, the Prys—my Guinea cook is the best d—d hand at turtle in the country. —Your pardon, ladies.—Mr. Medley, Sir, are you fond of sea turtle? Will you make one of us on Tuesday next?"

My intense surprise was reflected in the face of his lady, but if she felt the same gratification she concealed it famously. I cared not for her; my eye was upon Miss Reade. A diminution of her eagerness to go, any dimming of anticipatory joys, would have led me at once to decline. But she turned to me smiling.

"But do come, Mr. Medley," she cries. "If you have not been before to a turtle frolic, you must come. You deserve to taste of such a delicacy after your *cold gander and swamp tea.*"

Mistress Geer now put in a word. Perhaps Mr. Medley was engaged before the public upon Tuesday. "You should warn him, Mr. Geer, he is not like to get back to town before midnight."

At once I said I need schedule no performance for that night, and so the thing was settled. Our arrangements made, Miss Reade and I returned to the floor in good time for our call to dance *Clinton's Retreat.*

She is a merry lass indeed. She whispered that our master of ceremonies, a stiff, straight old gentleman with an eye fiercely blue, was a Colonel Babson, who had been with General Lincoln. "You shall see how seriously we take our dancing here in Portsmouth, Sir," she murmurs. "—Like a military drill, indeed." And forthwith she makes as if forgetting the figure and goes right instead of left.

At once the Colonel bends upon her a fierce glare. "Give over talking, Miss!" he roars out. "And mind what you are about. —D'ye think you are come here for your *pleasure?*" A question that gave us food for mirth for minutes after.

I would gladly have danced with her until the late winter dawn. But at half past one, her aunt beckoned her to leave. I escorted them home (a handsome house situated over the river east of Puddle Dock) and then walked back to my lodgings through the silent streets, not one candle showing, and a fine wilderness of stars overhead.

Mr. Collie was not returned, so I was able, after undressing by the fire, to plunge into the sheets and bolster and to wallow them warm to my heart's content. Socrates showed signs of wakefulness. After rousing to greet me, he fetched his ball, and after mouthing it suggestively at me whilst I undressed (in vain, needless to say), he next shoved it beneath the bed with his nose. I settled beneath the goosedown and bade him lie still. Instead, he crouched where his eye could glare in upon his escaped ball, and commenced growling at it, low and fierce. I feared lest he bark and disturb the household, a crime that would surely banish him to the stables. The landlord has already impressed upon me how singular a privilege I enjoy in keeping a dog in chamber with me.

Be quiet, Sir!

More growls, and an impatient scratching of claws toward the inaccessible ball.

"The D—l take you and your ball," I groaned. I needs must leave my warm covers to retrieve the wretched toy.

No sooner did I stretch out my length on the cold floor and start to reach in toward the ball than the maddening beast pawed his way in past my hand and got it himself; a feat he could have performed, had it suited him, at the very first. The display of frustration had been all a ruse to lure me onto the floor. Triumphantly, he mouthed the ball in my face, wagging his tail the while; convinced that once brought safely down I would prove keen for a romp.

Still half under the bed, I was delivering hot opinions of his dastard slyness; when into the room comes Collie and stops short on finding me sprawled on the floor. He made sure I was ill, or else very drunk. I muttered some explanation, hastily climbed again into bed, and pretended to slumber. He was peskily long and noisy about his undressing; and Socrates again rolled his ball beneath the bed and then growled at it. But I remained deaf to the pair of them.

Such a thing as this bid to the turtle feast has never before befallen me. Mr. Geer is hail and huzzah with all he meets, that is plain.

And so shall I go to his turtle frolic? Since accepting, I have had burning second thoughts about going where the lady of the house showed so little good will to have me. Betimes I have on this score regrets so bitter I contemplate sending word before Thursday that I am indisposed.

Yet would I meet again with Miss Reade . . .

Perhaps my faring this afternoon may settle Thursday's matter. For etiquette demands I call upon my partner of last night.

December 4, 1793

A poor crowd last night. Profits only eleven dollars. I shall certainly leave this place.

Called upon Miss Reade and her aunt but was told the ladies were not at home. I know not whether to believe this.

Tomorrow I ride off early to South Berwick to view the Hamilton country seat. This feverish madness costs me unconscionable sums for hiring horses where'er I go and wastes a deal of time more profitably spent at juggling. Instead of stiffening my fingers by grasping reins for hours on end, I should keep them limber for the night's performance.

December 6, 1793

I have a seat on the stage departing at three Monday morning.

Rode back to Portsmouth today in time to call again at Miss Reade's. Not At Home. I shall not go again. Nor shall I attend Mr. Geer's turtle frolic. I know not why ever I accepted a bid to such a vain frivolity, amongst people I know not, *nor care to.*

A fine brisk journey of it, to South Berwick. Once across the bridge, the road winds up the tidal Piscataqua. Scattered farms, men cutting ice in the river, and the smoky breaths of self and horse clouding the crystalline air. There was a fine chill and sparkle to the day. I met a late farmer or two driving to Kittery; but for the most part the way was solitary, my only companions the gulls that hung mewing and crying above the river.

Arrived around one o'clock at the Hamilton house. The place stands on a rise, with lawns sloping to the water and its shipyard at the shore. 'Tis a handsome square edifice of four chimneys. Its knocker? Plain, and of silver.

Another fruitless journey. Never have I heard my mother say aught of the Province of Maine. Yet was I drawn to inspect the place.

What of the sinking of the heart I felt upon again being told Not At Home? Am I so foolish, so doting as to lay my happiness at the feet of a flighty Miss met but the once? Was I flattered by her curiosity toward me? Twice, on my ride to S. Berwick I found myself in imagination improving tracts of good ground o'er which I travelled; building my castle in air (a stout New England lean-to) on every likely eminence overlooking the river. This has long been my habit—the urge to settle, the wish to own a portion of the country, bites deeper as one grows older. But today a rosy face peeped from the window of each chimerical dwelling.

I cannot believe myself in danger. Pride and our disparate lots in life forbid the softer feeling. Indeed, she is too young and unformed for a man like me. —How she would roll her eyes and laugh, did she know my thoughts!

Perhaps, after all, I should assay the turtle feast—set my mind to go and cease this endless dithering. Indeed, why should I care? If she mislikes it, let her stop at home.

December 10, 1793

Returned late from Mr. Geer's turtle frolic.

I am mighty pleased that I went, though I fall to nodding over this journal. I am an old dog to stay out gallivanting, frolicking, feasting, and dancing till such hours.

A pung full of rollickers came round to the inn door at nine-thirty o'clock. 'Twas the best sort of weather—one of your fine, clear, windless morns of winter; the air cold on the cheek, the sun painting the back warm; the whole world a loud dripping. Even the birds, quickened by the light's false promise, chattered of spring about the eaves.

Miss Reade was there, burrowed into the straw with a black bearskin about her. I could see naught of her but her nose, but that looked charmingly indeed! under a hood of beaver.

The Reverend Mr. Gooch, our preacher on Sunday last, was of the company, with his two daughters; the elder near eighteen, a young lady of wise and worldly airs wearing a spatter skirt; the younger a hoyden of fifteen, with many black curls. Then there were three young fellows of twenty or so, presented to me as Mr. William Lovell, Mr. James Powers, and Mr. Likely Bassett. They already had ensconsed themselves by the three girls—it at first appeared, the Reverend and I were fated to converse exclusively with each other, an arrangement not at all to my mind for a *frolic.* Mr. Geer had a fiddler in our sleigh, and once the horses were well away for the river he struck up a lively air. Soon we were singing all, making a sorry hash of *Wayworn Traveller, Twins of Latma,* and *Selim's Complaint;* whilst the harness bells chimed, the fiddle scraped, and folk along our way stopped to smile or wave. At the bridge, the wind swept down the river to meet us. We needs must burrow deeper into the straw and pull our wrappings to our chins.

'Twas my distinct impression that beneath the blanket and straw young Mr. Powers was holding the elder Miss Gooch's hand. I saw her color and laugh, with a glance at her father; who, all unconscious or uncaring, went on intoning *Ma Chere Amie.*

Once into Maine Province our driver swung right and followed the Kittery road seaward. Not far ahead moved a sleigh crowded with more guests (from Eliot or one of the Yorks) bound for the frolic. Ere long, Mr. Powers and Mr. Bassett were urging our driver with shouts to pass them.

Off we went at a gallop, to a chorus of squeals from the ladies. I marked Miss Reade's excitement; meeting my gaze, she laughed and cast her eyes skyward, making that expression of merriment a kind of friendly confidence between us two.

"Fear not, ladies!" shouts Mr. Bassett. "Our driver is springing them! He drives like Phoebus Apollo across the face of Heaven!" and other like extravagances; with tags of Latin or Greek designed (as I think) to show off his learning, he having been but lately at Harvard.

The folk in the other sleigh, hearing us come up, shouted to their driver, who touched up his horses and strove to put distance again betwixt us. Our fiddler, and theirs, must cling to their seats, so that the mad chiming of bells on the harnesses made our only music.

The road through the village scarce gave room to pass. A pair of geese, shingle-yoked, fluttered and scrambled squawking from out of our way. Dogs barked and ran snapping at our horses' heels. Children leaped up from their play in the snow to shout for joy of us.

Mad with excitement, young Powers sprang to his feet. Unwinding his red woollen-worsted muffler, he brandished it like a banner to the wind. "Charge the line!" he bellowed. "Charge the line!"

Suiting action to the word, I slipped into his place 'twixt Miss Reade and Miss Gooch, settling snugly into the straw. Observing too late his loss, he gave a rueful laugh.

"A pretty maneuver, indeed, Mr. Medley," says he, "and executed like an old soldier," from which I gathered they all had had something of my history from Miss Reade.

"I have as good a right to this place, Sir, as yourself," I called, as he lowered his woollen pennant, crestfallen. "An inalienable right to the pursuit of happiness. —But my pursuit is ended," I added to my two fair companions. "Happiness is now within my reach."

"*La*, Mr. Medley," says Miss Gooch.

"I assure you, Amelia," says Miss Reade, "it must be to you he refers. I danced the whole assembly evening with Mr. Medley without winning one quiz, one flirtatious word. So, 'tis either you or the fresh air has stirred him to such language—he danced all night with me, as solemn as an owl."

"I cannot believe it," says Miss Gooch. "The gentleman has too bright an eye."

"That is your fault, Amelia," says Miss Reade.

"—Ladies," says I. "If you talk across me as if I be not here at all, I shall think my victory a poor thing. You will force me to take further steps to draw your notice." Then it was *La!* again, and we were most merry. The other sleigh held ahead of us, and both drivers slackened speed. At a brisk trot and to fresh tunes from the fiddlers, we passed again into the country, on our right hand now the dark blue water of the open bay.

The farm of Mr. Geer stands nigh to a sea beach; a goodly yellow house with a lean-to roof, set somewhat back upon the slope of the land. Toothsome odors pervaded the neighborhood; and as we turned in, we saw Mr. Geer in shirt-sleeves and apron being active about the barn doorway. There, too, stood his Guinea cook at the trestle. Wooden tables were set up in the sunny shelter of the woodshed wall and blankets strung, further to shelter from the wind. Mrs. Geer and serving girls were hurrying to and fro between house and barn, with much slamming of the kitchen door.

Our host holloaed out welcomes, hastening up to hand the ladies from the first sleigh. (The culinary activities behind him seemed to slacken not a whit for his desertion; making me to guess his apron and the ladle he brandished were more for show than use.) He was a genial host indeed, made more so still by his sampling of the excellent punch prepared for the frolic.

"A keg of limes," he boasted, "and tea, arrack, sugar, lemons, nutmeg, with the best of Barbados rum—'twill warm your bones, if they be stiff from riding. Or there is *mimbo,* if any prefer it. And I believe Mrs. Geer is cozying some of her best India tea against your coming."

His wife had already greeted us, smiling, but something distracted; casting a glance slightly wearied at her exuberant spouse. In her company, the ladies departed for the house to prink and to sample the tea; and Mr. Geer led the way to the punch. It proved to be all he had claimed, and soon heated our blood to a fiery glow. The area, enclosed as it was on three sides, was hot almost as summer. The smoke, wafted to and fro in the light airs, was fragrant with applewood and cedar.

Mr. Geer told me he attributed the good weather to my magic art. "You have produced this, deny it not," says he, gesturing at the sky. "We could have dined within doors, but 'twould make a tight fit." Another sleigh full of guests arrived just then, and off he rushed to greet them, calling to us as he went that there were poles and bait a-plenty behind the barn, should we care to try fishing from the beach rocks.

Mr. Gooch went off eager to test his luck, but I chose to linger by the fire. The young men began a snow fort in the meadow, with an eye to snowballing the ladies when they should come out; such being the violent attentions with which youth is prone to favor youth.

With one eye indeed upon the house door, I engaged the Guinea cook George in talk. He is saving his wages with an eye to opening a catering business in Portsmouth or in Boston. Many blacks go in for this line and do prodigious well; some I have heard of, in New York and Philadelphia, are become tyrannous social arbiters of what is best in gracious dining; no dinner being considered up to the mark that has not felt their guiding hand. Yet that same Society that meekly follows their dicta when entertaining will scarce admit them as guests at table!

This George seems a promising candidate for the business—he went about our turtle with skill and artistry. The terrapins were already boiled some time and the shells and outer skin taken off. I watched as he searched out the sand-bag and gall with the liver. The gall he held up roguishly for my inspection.

"Do but squeeze that, Sir, for a bitter garnish," says he. "A mouth-drawer, that." I noted he carefully set aside the masses of turtle eggs before cutting up the meat. The entrails, too, he opened and drained, suspending them in a cloth bag. All the blood and juices likewise were caught and kept. I was wildly curious, and as he cut up the meat and liver I asked what steps would follow.

He would next add the blood and juices, he said, and half a pint of water with a sprinkling of flour. "Stew slow, almighty slow, for ten minutes' space, adding salt, black pepper, and cayenne; then a blade of mace, as small as maybe. Then," says he, "plenty of Mr. Geer's best brandy and sherry wine. It must simmer easy on that slow fire yonder. Ten minutes to the hour of two, in goes the cream, the butter . . ." He smacked his lips. "Three minutes to the hour, I peel yon eggs and throw 'em in whole, with the clean guts cut up small . . . Two o'clock, Lord, we all eat!"

"Master George," says I, "you are a poet of the pot. My stomach yearns toward the hour of two. If your turtle tastes as good as it smells, I shall be happy to recommend you in your first advertisements. —My name, being known," I added, "may be of some service to you."

He thanked me very civilly and became of a sudden tremendous busy over his meat slices. With head bent, he asked, "Mr. Medley . . . is it true what they say . . . that you be yourself a gentleman of color? That your father or grandfather was that same?"

"Indeed," says I, something impatient. "'Tis no secret, nor should either of us hang our heads over it." (A strange thing—always I feel at a disadvantage with one whose skin is duskier than mine own, as I must apologize for my lightness.) "My mother's grandfather was black as yourself, her father (on the other side) Indian. I am constituted like a fine American stew, with many flavors blended."

He looked round at me. "Yet they say, you do well . . . that you bid fair to be rich," says he.

"I do very well in my line," says I. "As you will, in yours. —Mark you, Master George, we have a duty to do well. For our faults and failures will be e'er blamed upon our black blood. Our every faltering in diligence or in virtue forges new chains for those enslaved. The finger of interest is swift to point: 'Behold—they are not fit to be free citizens of a great nation. Let the mass of them rest in their bonds.' "

"You speak as well as Schoolmaster Harker," says he with a hint of bitter mockery. "—'Tis almighty hard, that we may not be lazy betimes with a free conscience, like white folk."

"Indeed," says I. "And e'en though free men be happier when diligent, 'tis d—d unjust, beside.—"

Then out come the ladies from the house, and I forgot all else. The fort builders in the meadow let fly a barrage of snowballs that fell short by twenty feet. The ladies shrieked and squealed, though in no danger; at the same time tripping closer so as to provide a better target.

But up to me came Mistress Reade. "Will you show me how to fish, Mr. Medley?" says she.

I could scarce believe my good fortune. "Do you truly

wish it?" says I. "'Twill be colder upon the beach."

"I shall not be cold," says she. "But you must bait my hook for me, I could never abide to do it."

From the barn I secured two poles and a bucket of clams. Together we two crossed the orchard for the shore, well out of the way of the combatants in the lower meadow.

"I should have thought you would wish to join your friends at their frolicking," says I.

"Poh," says she. "James and William will forever be acting like children on holidays such as this. No, Sir, I mean to tackle fishing as a serious thing. When shall I have such a chance again?"

'Twas plain, she had chosen me as her assistant from no motives of coquetry; fishing was in truth the eager desire of her heart. This makes me like her the better. Never have I seen a pretty Miss so free of affectation or sly consciousness of her powers over men. Truly, I believe her to be the honestest lass that ever I met.

Discreetly I steered our course away from the Reverend Mr. Gooch at the bay side. He was at any rate wholly engrossed in his casting and scarce noted us.

I handed her up the rocks and together we stood above the suck of the water, the slimy, barnacled sides of rock dark-draped in weed, upon a kind of granite table-top, sun-dried and clean, but for broken remnants of crab shell left by the gulls after their feasting. The tide was fallen low. There was a smell of salt, of sea moss, and of cold, wet sand. The sea made but the slightest heave and stir. The broken ice afloat at its edge lent to the ripple a clear tinkle like tiny bells.

I showed her how to bait the hook and cast her line. At her first attempt (for she would assay the cast herself) she came near to taking a header into the sea. Had I not caught hold of her, she would have followed her line down.

I drew her back with something of a firm hand. "Miss Reade," I exclaimed, "if you do not promise to be more cautious, we will fish no more."

"Never fear, Sir," says she. "The water is not deep. —I knew you would be a strict, stern, scowling sort of schoolmaster who would make me toe the mark. I am glad you prove me in the right of it; for I will, I must, learn to fish."

"The mark I would have you toe is this crab claw well back from the edge," says I. "Keep to it, pray. Were you in this weather but to wet your feet, you would take cold directly."

"Ah," says she, "you sound like my aunt," putting me quite out of countenance and causing me to feel a fleeting pity for that much harried lady. But Miss Reade did retreat to the crab leg. Whilst she swung her pole oftener than need be—she gave the poor old ocean a worse thrashing than ever did King Canute—she performed her casts with greater care.

I baited and cast my own line, and we talked. The blue sea was wide and empty. One solitary pinkie moved slow as a cloud near the harbor mouth.

When had I learned to fish, Miss Reade inquired. It must have been as a boy? So I told her of my early years in Deerfield and of fishing with my friends in the Connecticut River.

"You were born in Deerfield, then," she says.

"Nay," says I, and again felt my face grow hot. "We came there, my mother, my sister Josie, and I, when Josie was six, I scarce three. We lived on the farm of a family named Lamb where my mother was servant and cook. Before that—" I watched the pinkie's sail move out of sight behind the arm of the bay. "Before that, I know not.

There is a great house and little else, in my memory; but the owner of that great house, as I think, was—is—my father."

"But has your mother never—?" she begins; then bites her lip. "I am too forward," says she then. "The subject is one that distresses you. —Quick now, 'tis gone. Tell me of all your travels, and where go you next, after Portsmouth?"

"I wish you to know all of me that I can tell," says I, looking into her honest eyes.

"But I have no right—" she began.

"The right of friendship," I told her. "I would be your friend, if I may."

Lord, what a brilliant smile was mine for reply. So I up and told her the story. Till that moment, only Will of all the world had heard it.

She was silent, listening.

"Perhaps you concern yourself overmuch with your beginnings," she says at last, turning to look after her line. "Is it so important, to find out your father? Half the people of my acquaintance would as lief forget the lowly beginnings of their forebears in this country. My own great-grandmother was a bonded servant—many others must say the same. There are few great houses or great coats of arms behind Portsmouth society, Mr. Medley. What would we do with pride of ancestry now, in America?"

I had not, I told her somewhat drily, noted family pride to be as yet quite vanished from our new Republic.

"Of course you are right," says she. "Even I am proud of my forebears—but for their wit and pluck and diligence that made them their fortunes in the Indies trade. —O," cries she, "were I a man, I should do and do and do."

"You be a patriot," says I.

"As I told you," says she. "I would have served faithfully

under General Washington."

'Twas at that moment she hooked a fish. Or perhaps more than one . . .

Her fish (the finny one, I mean) once landed—'twas a cunner, not six inches long—she won me into more talk of myself. Looking back, I greatly fear I talked overmuch. I told her of my early life, of working on the Lamb farm; and of going on winter morns to the schoolhouse to get the fire up when the mercury might be twelve below. I talked of *making our manners* to the schoolmistress, and how our ink (compounded of soot and vinegar) froze in the leathern inkbottles. I spoke of tending and fattening the stall-fed cattle throughout the long winter; of the proud spring day in my twelfth year when first I was allowed to help Roger the drover drive the herd the long road to Brighton. In vivid fancy the brightness of that long-ago spring morn rose about me. My mother, proud and tearful, waving us out of sight; the leaders of the drove bearing our portmanteaux strapped for safety's sake behind their horns; my excited sense of the whole world opening for me upon the hilly horizon. I talked of the sights and sounds of Brighton market, the spending of my hoarded pennies on gauds and gewgaws for Josie and my mother, and the triumphal return—my first journey by stage—to Deerfield.

"For five months after, I had no higher ambition than to be a drover," I told her. "But my mother had early noted I was a bookworm. She urged me on to wider study; she enlisted the aid of the Lambs and my schoolmistress who found me books. Some instruction I got in Greek and Latin, though not even at Mr. Wheelock's did I clamber much past Beginner's Grammar. Always, she spurred me on. From her I won hints of my father's worldly greatness, but no word of his name. —I know it not, to this day. That ignorance is either a hollow in my heart that must be filled or a sickness that must be purged; I know not which. Only this I know, Miss Reade; the contrast of my mother's life of labor and her hints of him and his wealth behind, smoulders in me. I have long prayed for the new heart of a sinless babe, but the old anger lives on. I feel I shall never lose it more, till I confront that man as the son whom he neglected—and show him we do well without him, my mother and I."

She was about to speak when comes of a sudden a cow-bell's clangor from the farm; and other matters were forgot in our haste to get back.

At the foot of the orchard we came up with Mr. Gooch. Miss Reade proudly displayed to him her catch. "I shall have it for supper tomorrow," she declared.

Mr. Gooch laughed uproariously. (He had four fat cunners on his string.) "Mistress Dorothy, when head and tail are off, you will have scarce fish enough to taste between your teeth."

She pouted, then laughed into our faces. "I care not for that," says she. "I say, I shall have my fish for supper. 'Tis the first that e'er I caught and very like to be the last. Indeed, I have you, Mr. Medley, to thank for it. No doubt 'twas bound for your line, but you by your magic generously steered it to mine."

The winter light had fallen blue in the orchard. The sun, low and up-river, was kindling the higher rocks to fire. As we neared the house we were met by a merry clamor of voices (over which Mr. Geer's boomed without stop) and most tantalizing odors.

'Twas a sinful feast. How we managed to move a step after, I know not; but foot it we did, right merrily on the barn floor, whilst the fiddlers made the rafters ring. We had going six sets, all the barn could hold. Indeed, once or twice I found myself near partnered to a cow—the gentle beasts watched from their stanchions with deep, unwondering eyes, and the horses rang their iron shoes upon the floor as if they too would foot it, if they might.

We danced till five, took tea, and danced after, till near midnight. I would take oath I dropped ten pounds from the exertion. As for my wind, it grew better as the hours passed.

"Mr. Medley, Sir, you dance fiercely," cries that saucy minx my corner, a Miss Debby Sharp of Eliot. "You take my breath."

"Tis so I make my mark on the dance floor," I cried. "I may lack grace, but, Miss Sharp, I dance *strong!*" And off again. *Tum-tump a tum.* The fiddle beat is in my feet still.

Then at last we bade our host and hostess goodnight; into the pung, a high white moon overhead, and back through Kittery where no window showed a light. Our music now was the beat of hooves and horses' white snortings and the harness bells a-jingle. Tree shadows swooped upon us, only to fall behind. On our cheeks a fresh cold air blown straight from the stars. I did not get a seat by Miss Reade on the return trip. I could just see her as she spoke and smiled; but that contented me.

Close by the bridge one of the other sleighs was stopped. They had let down one of their number at a house there and were lustily serenading him (or her). There was nothing for it but the lads with us must have serenading at each stop. Mr. Bassett was the first to leave us. We let him down at his cousins' house by the river, and sang him in the door (I know not what his cousins or the neighbors may have thought of it), then finished our chorus while he cut capers at us from the front window.

Then came my inn. I was serenaded up to the door and Socrates set to barking in the stable. I tried to distinguish Miss Reade during the general farewells, but there was too much noise. I could but wave my hand, laughing, and in reply she waved at me her silver fish.

'Twas two by the clock when I closed the front door and tiptoed up the stair.

A Golden Day.

December 11, 1793

Not at home. So much for bonds of friendship born of turtle frolics. This, the third time I have exposed myself to humiliation. There shall be no more on't. Early next week I depart this town.

December 14, 1793

Tomorrow, the Sabbath and my last day in Portsmouth. I have determined to go again to meeting. I have been wrapt, of late, in worldly desires and pursuits and neglecting things of the spirit. To my Maker I owe a debt of thankfulness—He has indeed prospered me in this place. Some few tender fancies He has not seen fit to move toward fruition; but, for that, should I repine or grumble? Rather I should say, as did Cuffee Bills' epitaph: God's Will Be Done.

December 15, 1793

Walked to meeting in the bitterest east wind that ever I felt. It cut through cloak, coat, waistcoat and shirt, slashed the aching face and filled the eyes with water. In a happy moment I thought to whistle Socrates with me. On Sunday last, I had noted several gentlemen in their pews with their feet warming on their recumbent pointers and shepherd dogs; as, indeed, one sees at many winter meetings. But never before have I possessed a live footstove. In such weather it seemed wise to overlook my Socrates' manifold defects in appearance. Of body heat I knew him a veritable furnace.

Service, despite the weather, was well attended. I paid the dog's fee and took him up under my arm, his long freckled sabre of a tail hanging down behind, and was seeking for the pew frequented by the town bachelors—when open flew a pew door to invite me. I could scarce believe my eyes. Miss Reade and Mistress Atwell were seated within; the face of the former dancing with invitation. She wore a pink ruffled calash with green rosettes, and looked charmingly.

I made haste to accept and ensconsed Socrates on the floor at my feet. Both ladies eyed him with some intentness. I had feared for his manners when grown aware of the other dogs about us—but after settling himself with a sigh something more windy than needful he showed himself the soul of discretion. In my mind I promised him a reward of cheese after service.

When we rose to sing, Miss Reade, with a sweet motion, offered to share with me her hymnbook, and we moved a step nearer together. She made some difficulty with the words which, by her bent head and her peering gaze again screwed small, were plainly all but lost to her sight. She sang with a clear, loud voice, but falteringly where memory failed her for the verses. (I think she must be a vain Miss indeed to put herself to such trouble for want of her spectacles. I wonder in what hour totally shielded from company do they see the light of day at home?) For my part, I sang like a mother to a sleeping child, for I was more disposed to listen to her than to lift my own voice. Her aunt made the roundest noise of us three—the rich sort known as *contralto,* but something through her nose.

After the opening hymn we had prayers. I looked forward to the preaching of my fisherman friend Mr. Gooch, having been much edified by his discourse on Sunday last. He is indeed one of the best preachers for matter and pithiness that ever I heard; only a trifle mannered and chanting in his delivery.

Mounting to the pulpit, the preacher cast a censorious glance at the little boys of the congregation, shuffling in their seats upon the stair to the gallery. At once they fell silent and most grave. Casting deliberate eyes about the pews, he cleared his throat and then sonorously gave out his text.

> And when the living creatures went,
> The wheels went by them; and when the
> living creatures were lifted up from the earth,
> The wheels were lifted up.

My footwarmer stiffened. Too late, I saw his head come up. Ere I could seize him, he was off in a yelping scramble to the other end of the pew. Finding no escape there from the fatal call for the *wheel,* he raced across the lap of Mistress Atwell, who shrieked and dropped her hymnbook.

Wily even in panic, he avoided my clutching hand by leaping into the pew behind, across the laps of the family there, and so to the aisle.

The preacher faltered in amaze. The verger with his stick tried to head the dog, but Socrates neatly dodged him and raced to the closed door. Finding no egress, he swerved and tore down the side aisle to the front. A number of gentlemen grabbed at him as he passed, but he only flattened himself to the floor and increased his speed by a contemptuous little to elude them; to the utter delight of the little boys, silent and grave no longer, upon the stair. As he came again down the middle aisle, the verger in flagging pursuit, I myself grabbed for him; to no avail. But by good fortune, one of the young men in Pew Nine had the wit to throw open the door to the street; and Socrates, still yelping, vanished.

The whole church was a-flutter, and buzzed with sensation. I felt my countenance to burn, and cursed the day I first set eyes upon that monstrous animal. Never, never have I felt a like confusion. I dared not look toward my companions.

Somewhat falteringly, Mr. Gooch resumed his address. I ventured to glance at Miss Reade. Her hands were decorously folded, her eyes fixed upon the speaker; but there was a pucker about her lips and a tremor to her flushed composure—she was not far from losing it. Her eyes were bright with suppressed laughter.

At seeing her great good nature, all my chagrin melted away. My own mouth began to twitch, and I dared not look again. But, from calling down maledictions on the head of my rascal dog, I was tempted to exclaim, "Praise to thy Wisdom, O Socrates!"

Mistress Atwell looked as she had eaten of a bad oyster.

After meeting, Miss Reade, when told I had called thrice to wait upon her, was most cordial in her expressions of regret. "I am sorry we were not at home," she said. "I hope you will call again, Mr. Medley—and bring Socrates with you. We shall promise faithfully not to mention the word *wheel.*" For I had explained to them Socrates' history, by way of apology for his mad behavior. She was most diverted by the story; but her aunt would scarce smile. Miss Reade, as I think, does as suits herself, without much reference to her aunt.

I shall, as I think, postpone my departure from this place.

I found Socrates skulking about the inn yard. He knew himself disgraced, but I was swift to pardon him. Indeed, I saved him a portion of roast lamb from the dish I shared with my host, his wife, and the other guests of the inn.

December 16, 1793

Waited today upon Miss Reade; found her and her aunt at home, and one Mr. James Emery, presented to me as a cousin of the young lady, recently returned from travelling in Europe. I fancy the relationship is a distant one.

I thought the young man a puppy; one of your sneering, supercilious windbags, full of himself and his great affairs. A fop and a rattle. A sly snob.

To please Miss Reade I brought Socrates with me. I had thought we could be merry about him. But this Emery's incredulous airs turned all pleasantness sour. He made a show of admiring Socrates, thus imputing to me an eccentricity that must be humored; and spoke with a lazy scorn that maddened me. "I was present at one of your performances, *Sir,*" says he to me. "Most amusing." In contrast, his manner toward his cousin is insinuating soft, with all the studied consideration of a lover, the which I doubt not he aspires to become. D—l take him!

I must confess, Miss Reade seemed to like him and his ways very well. As for the old lady, she triumphs in him endlessly and dotingly. There is nothing in him of America; from his dress to his manners to his . . . idleness . . . he is all Europe. The aunt let slip that he has spent his small fortune and incurred debts faster than even a partisan like herself deemed proper. Indeed, he impresses as one who would rather marry wealth than amend his style of living.

The rogue had the audacity to suggest that I favor them, during tea, with a few turns of the cards.

"Sir," says I, "you would scarce think it mannerly to introduce the activities of your own occupation—if so you have one, other than idling—over the tea table in a lady's front parlor. Are doctors asked to demonstrate the use of a lancet, or lawyers to argue a writ? No, Sir! Nor yet clergymen to preach a sermon. My assumption is, Sir, that I am present here on the same general footing as yourself."

He began to turn angry; but Miss Reade interposed. "Caution, James, caution!" she cried, laughing. "Mr. Medley is a gentleman of great fierceness—I have myself felt in danger, once or twice, of being called out. —Sir," she then said, addressing me with a more serious mien, "my cousin meant no offence. Indeed, I own I have much curiosity towards some small display of your talents; only I see the idea is offensive to you. I would not for worlds have you feel any slight."

Her glance so disarmed me, I owned my words higher than called for. I said, since Miss Reade desired it, I would perform a turn or two that I hoped Mr. Emery would accept by way of apology.

To this, he bowed with (I confess) a better grace than I looked for. Miss Reade ran to fetch a pack of cards. (My first offer, to set the flowered china saucers spinning in the air, was piteously cried down by Mistress Atwell.) Lacking my own cards, I was limited to a few simple turns. Miss Reade, at my invitation, selected a card and returned it face down to the spread pack; I shuffled the lot and produced her eight of spades, &c., &c.; which made her clap her hands.

I next procured from Mistress Atwell a paper of the requisite size and performed my philosophical-paper turn. I then made a cone of the paper, with a few paper balls, and tossed the balls into the cone while balancing it upon my nose. Both Miss Reade and her cousin clapped at this, whilst Mistress Atwell cried, "Mercy!" repeatedly, in tones of great astonishment. I ended by setting the cone aflame at the fire, and returning it to its place upon my nose.

This trick brought cries of real alarm from the ladies. (Miss Reade's fright was, as I think, for my nose; her aunt's, for the carpet.) Since flame burns upward, the risk is less than appears. I danced a few steps about the room—taking care not to approach the wall hangings—and then, with a toss of my head, shot the charred and flaming cone into the fireplace.

Bowing acknowledgment of their applause, I seated myself again by Mistress Reade, who poured me a second cup of tea; to refresh me, as she said, "after such heroic exertions."

"I understand, you can throw your voice about the room," she said. "And make clocks and lanterns to speak."

"Yes," says I. "In a large room or hall. But in a private parlor ventriloquism would seem but a poor illusion."

"I have oft wondered how 'tis done," Mr. Emery said then. "I saw in Paris once a fellow who had the art—he could drink a glass of water, while at the same time making a doll favor us with a song."

I explained how it is largely a matter of tongue placement and muscular control of the diaphragm. Miss Reade demanded to know more, and soon was on her feet before the mirror endeavoring to say *ah-ee-oh-ay-oo* without moving her lips.

"The most difficult sounds to make," says I, "are B, F, M, P, and V. They demand untiring practice. In my younger days, to perfect the consonants, I would perform drill exercises in my room for hours upon end. At Hartford, once, I was besieged by my hostess and a handful of fellows with sticks and ropes whom she had summoned to subdue the madman in her front chamber. She knew I was alone; yet she overheard me talking on. She put her ear to my door and grew worse affrighted, for the words she heard me speak were like the disjointed ravings of fever. *Very few folk forget the view. Very few men named Michael. Find every man a violent manifesto. Try to pick ten peaches. Don't be difficult, bide your time,* &c. The poor lady was sadly scared. —I was hard put to persuade her and her servants I was no lunatic."

"I have heard men of your trade referred to as 'Gred and Gutter Merchants,'" Mr. Emery says, with a return of his early objectionable manner. "Why so?"

"Because, Sir, we often substitute the sound of G for the more difficult B," I told him quietly. "So that Bread and Butter, for instance, becomes as you have heard."

After some minutes more, I tucked Socrates under my arm and rose to take my leave. Mr. Emery remained lounging upon the sofa. As she accompanied me to the parlor door, Miss Reade inquired again how long I should be staying in Portsmouth.

"My plans are uncertain," I told her. With much complaisance in her manner she asked me to call again. But as I went out at the door and she turned back toward her cousin, I glimpsed her gaze at him—Alas, alas, 'twas one of softness and most tender dazzlement.

I entered the street in utter gloom of mind. That look decides me—Socrates and I shall be on the morning stage for Newbury. She will wed that fellow, and he will spend what money she brings him. Pray God, he may do it kindly.

December 17, 1793

Breakfasted and baited the horses at Hampton. A black departure from Portsmouth in every way. 'Tis hard at any time of life to climb from warm bed to cold floor in dead of night; to dress shivering by the candle's light and hasten out into a frozen innyard; to jostle for a wagon seat with six other passengers as sleepy and out-of-sorts as yourself, who bark your shins with their portmanteaux as they stow them under their legs and who grumble when you with your luggage bark theirs. It is hard, I say, at any age; but when a man feels winter chill his bones in a new way and senses that Time has o'erreached him; more especially, when he has glimpsed a better part of Earth, only to have it snatched beyond his reach—then 'tis indeed hard to bow the head before God's Will and say, *Amen.*

To add to my gloom, my fellow-passengers were a surly, ill-conditioned sort. Not one of them could offer a pleasant word to his neighbor. At Hampton, after we had breakfasted and climbed again to our places, a stout matron attempted with her portmanteau to join our number. There came cries from the driver, of, " 'Blige the lady, gentlemen, 'blige the lady"; but not one of the *gentlemen* stirred a foot. They did but grumble or utter unseemly jests as the poor lady attempted to crawl beyond them to the one empty place in the rear.

I stopped her. "Madame, take this place of mine in God's name," says I. "For myself I choose to have fresher air."

And I clambered up to the seat with the driver, leaving Socrates to run beneath the wagon.

I had chosen well. The early sun soon was gilding the patches of snow in the fields and warming the bare stubble to a mellow hue. The horses' bells jingled merrily. With the sky ever sailing o'erhead and my breakfast coffee warm in my stomach, my spirits a little rose. The driver talked amiably on, with no pause for breath. Often, his talk was of interest to me. He knew every inch of our road, the local politics, the history of each house we passed, with its occupants and their antecedents, and was conversant as well with the dark deeds and legends attached to certain trees, hills, and berry bushes along our route. I have learned much from these stage drivers. They are a hardy, mainly honest breed of men, who often inherit their vocation from father and grandfather. Certain family names are notable amongst them, such as Caney, Foss, Annable, Savory, Tozzer.

Today's driver was a Moses Savory, and he declared that of his five sons one at least would be a stage driver after him, he was bound. "But not Tom," he added. "His boots are mired i' the furrows. Well, he shall have the farm, or his share of it, one day."

I told him Tom and I were of a mind in that respect, that I had had enough of conjuring and staging; that a fine piece of bottom land, with a stand of sugar maples and enough apple trees for the family cider were what I yearned for. "And four or five little sons of my own," added I, "with a rosy-cheeked lass or two."

"Would that content you then?" asks he, turning wide his eyes upon me. "A man who be used to town life and the like!"

"I thrive but poorly in such places," says I. "For health

and peace of mind, there is more to hold to, in the land. A man wants a piece of his country, he hankers for a home."

He cracked his whip. "I married at nineteen," says he. "And I was on the road then. My Doll and I agree well enough. But I wouldn't trade my wagon for your farm. Lord, the sights I see. I know this country's innards."

"But as a traveller upon its surface," says I. "Your Tom will have a small stake in our Beulah Land, to leave his mark upon, for his sons and his sons' sons."

He spat neatly between the rumps of the rear pair of horses. "You be a worse stick-in-the-mud than Tom," he grumbled. "Farmer! With your magic and books and all! Well, Sir, I hope you may have your bit of the country, and the five sons, too. You'll need a wife, Mr. Medley."

I said nothing.

"Tom's not such a stump at that," he went on. "He'll content himself nowise with my acres over Durham—he's heard tell of some pretty country out in the Ohio territory. That's where he talks of homesteading. Says he wants to beat the speculators to it. Best you do the same, Mr. Medley, the land grows poorer and dearer every year."

For a little I pondered his words in silence. Socrates tired of trotting in the shadow of the wagon and discovered his wishes to me by concluding horses are to be barked at. For the sake of peace, we allowed him up. Thereafter he sat at my right and snuffed the smells of winter, his torn ear fluttering like a banner in the wind.

So went we merrily on, the driver springing the team, until, on a rough stretch of road, over goes our wagon in a smash of splintered wood, tangled harness, and plunging horses, luggage and passengers spilling about the roadway.

We were all (but Socrates) bruised and shaken. I skinned my hands and tore my stockings, besides having the wind clean knocked out of me. The driver fared better, for he fell atop of me. (He later thanked me for the involuntary service I had done him, saying he wished always for such a *solid, substantial* citizen to ride with; a jest not entirely to my mind.)

Three of the passengers in a lamentable temper began to swear at Savory. Then up rose our matron (who had commenced so timidly) like a battlestained Hippolyta from the dust, and so roundly rated them, we all stood in amaze.

"Foul-mouths!" she cries. ". . . Stand there profaning the very air when you should be on your knees before the kind Providence that spared all our lives? Hold your wicked, ungrateful tongues, *Sirs,* and help unharness the horses. Bestir yourselves!" For the horses were plunging and kicking in their traces, and Savory struggling at their heads could scarce hold them. So stupified were these fellows by her fierceness, they obeyed without a murmur, and so was she avenged for the treatment she had received at boarding.

Savory declared he knew a house of entertainment three miles farther on. "If 'twere but a wheel we could have it on again in a trice," he says. "But that unlucky overturn has cracked the axletree. If you gentlemen will but to see to the other horses, I'll unhitch General Putnam there and ride to the inn for help."

I noted that he was much shaken, and offered to ride in his stead.

"Be you a horseman, Mr. Medley?" asks he doubtfully. "No saddle—and the General's blood is up."

"Tut, man, I'm liker to fall off a bed," says I, eyeing the bounteous back of General Putnam. So he led out the General and gave me a leg up. Once I had the beast gripped betwixt my knees I put him to a lope. He went off nobly. Socrates raced grimly behind. I took pleasure in this unexpected canter under the bare, arched trees; e'en though as I went I made acquaintance with a number of bruises and strains suffered in the overturn and searched out for me by the General.

Soon, there stood the inn, all grown o'er with blackened ivy, a small dark house with a deep garrison overhang, set well back from the road. The place must have stood since the first settlement of the region. Indeed, I found the fireplaces in the public rooms uncommon small and plainly meant for peat.

I was in a sorry plight, plastered with mud and wet snow; my stockings torn, the knee bands of my breeches burst. After I sent the hostler back up the road with a wagon, I went to the taproom to refresh myself. The landlord, a tall, grey man, handsome but for a wall eye, served me grog.

"You were lucky to escape without broken arms or necks amongst you," he says with great cheerfulness; and regaled me in vivid detail with accounts of divers injuries suffered by travellers in runaways, overturns, &c. All the crippled (as it seemed) were personally known to him; likewise their physicians, whose gloomy prognoses he reeled off in a sepulchral voice. "I am sorry for your mishap," says he then. "Truly sorry, though it be good fortune to me to have you in my house. Company's scarce. —We're too nigh the Port, Sir, that's where the trouble lies. Most goes on to the Port, so our business is not so brisk as one could wish. 'Tis a shame, too; for there's no house in Newbury can touch us for oysters, Sir. Oysters. Those that try 'em here are never satisfied after, with any other man's. You and your friends must dine here, for Savory will never have the wagon fit for travel before five—so you will yourselves be the judges. Scalloped oysters, before the roast, Sir; and perhaps a good feather bed in my chambers tonight, for I think it unwise for any man of you (or the lady) to travel before tomorrow. The jolting of a stage is the worst thing for the kind of shock your systems have suffered today. Jolting and motion —taken too soon after, they can bring on a secondary—"

But here came on the rest of the company in the wagon. I hastened out to get my portmanteau and to help the lady down. A sorry looking lot, indeed; some in worse disarray than myself, and all mudstained. We gentlemen trooped together into the taproom; whilst our Amazon lady, relapsed into feebleness, was borne off by the landlady and maids for repairs.

As we sat listening glumly to the boniface discourse upon broken bones and oysters, Savory came in to confirm that the stage would scarce be mended before dark. "If you wish to go on then, gentlemen," he says, "we shall. But if your business in Old Newbury be not of an urgent nature, I advise you to stop here tonight. We could scarce reach the Port before midnight; and, I can bear witness, there are no better oysters anywhere than here."

Sore and weary as we were, we needed little persuasion. Three of our party were assigned to one chamber; two more of us, with the driver, to another. The lady won a private bedchamber. Into the kitchen bustled our host to alert them we would be seven for dinner; and we all mounted to our chambers to wash and put on clean raiment. I asked for a tub of hot water, as soon as might be, feeling I must have a winter bath before dining. Afterward I unpacked and inspected my tools of magic for possible damage. (One of my juggling rods is snapped in two.)

We dined with our host and hostess on baked oysters and saddle of roast lamb. —I can bear witness. Those oysters were the plumpest, savoriest, most piquant little fellows— my mouth waters again as I write. After dinner I stepped to the kitchen to inquire of the cook just how those oysters were seasoned. With marjoram, she told me, and dulse; with cider for simmering. A strange concoction to hear! I told her, she was twice the magician that I was, which left her all smiling.

Rest, the fires, and dinner seemed somewhat to mellow my fellow travellers, and we agreed well enough together. But I chose to retire early, leaving them in the tap-room. I mounted to my chamber, but scarce was I within when comes a knock—and here was Mr. Savory. He looked very queer at me and swallowed twice before he spoke.

"Mr. Medley," he whispered. Then again, "Mr. Medley . . ."

"What is it?" says I.

He looked behind him. "I wondered, would you oblige me, Sir—I should like to change beds with you tonight."

The man had taken a misliking to his bedfellows, was my thought; or worse, had learned somewhat about their habits or condition not to his taste.

"Mr. Savory," says I, "I would most willingly oblige you, for it matters little to me where I sleep; only, I needs must know your reason. What, does one of them snore? Or smell? Or snuffle? What's to be my fate this night, if I agree?"

"No, Sir," he says, shaking his head. "I know naught to any man's discredit—they may snore like musketry or sleep as peacefully as any babe. I know naught of them."

"Then, why?" I asked him.

He swallowed again. "To be honest with you, 'tis the room. I do not sleep well in their front chamber."

"You have bedded there before?" I says. The man truly looked paler than when he entered.

"Ay, that have I," he says with a grim ghost of a smile. "And an unchancy place I found it." He paused. "The house is, as you see, an old one. Potter's family acquired it late. The room is known as The Indian Chamber. 'Tis said to be haunted by an Indian, Sir—not a waking ghost, but one that haunts sleepers in their dreams. —Now, Sir, I have been frank with you. I consider you a man of sense and education—not likely to be frightened by country tales. 'Tis why I approached you, rather than one of the others. —I do not believe in it, myself," he added lamely. "But however it is, I sleep but poorly there."

I was amused. "But how if the ghost should disturb my own slumbers?" says I.

"O," cries he with much simplicity. "A ghost would scarce meddle with a magician." This, from a man who claims to have learned wisdom through travel! I was much inclined to laugh; but I saw he was something abashed at discovering his fears to me at all, so I kept my face grave.

"Very well," says I. "You may sleep here in my place. —But nothing of this to my bed-mates, or I may have to endure their night starts as well."

He swore he would keep mum, and that the landlord never spoke of it to strangers or guests. But amongst neighbor families the story of the Indian Chamber was well known, sworn to by many.

"Well, we shall see what my dreams may be," says I cheerfully. "I hope for fairer visions than you predict." My words came sprightly enough; but my heart ached of a sudden, at the thought of Portsmouth and the Treasure therein, and of the miles between us marking our separate destinies.

Is it possible I can have been wounded so grievously by darts of that lame boy Cupid in so brief a time? I must labor to put her from my mind and heart, as I doubt not can be done when good sense and will are brought to bear. I must not waste my days of full manhood hankering after a vanished vision to the neglect of my present fortunes. The farmer-to-be must have a wife; and should seek one within his reach, suited to the rural sphere.

God bless her, then—though I ne'er again look upon her fresh young face.

December 18, 1793

As strange as may be, my experience of last night.

I was disturbed in my slumbers, not by ghostly Indians but by Socrates. About two in the morning he indicated his urgent desire to go out to the yard by springing up upon me as I lay asleep and walking up and down my length. As by good fortune I lay on the outside of the bed, he was able to rouse me without disturbing my two bedmates. I awoke to find him on my chest, staring into my face more grimly than any departed brave's spirit—the glow of the embers just sufficient to show him to me.

Seeing me awake, he sprang to the floor (with a strong kick behind to my ribs) and trotted to the closed chamber door. I needs must light the candle, throw on my dressing gown, and conduct him downstairs.

With as little noise as might be, I unbarred the front door, and out he goes into the dark. Knowing he would consult his own convenience in returning, I went to the kitchen to wait in warmth. The room was nearly dark, but cozy still from the banked fire. I was groping my way toward the hearth when I beheld (with a start) the shape of one crouched close by the ashes—an Indian, wrapped in his blanket and communing with the fiery coals.

I stopped dead in my tracks; so strangely apposite his presence seemed, as he were but lately descended from the

Indian Chamber. But reason promptly returning, I greeted him and sat me down by the hearth, extending my feet and hands toward the warmth.

He stirred at my coming; lifted his face, broken with a thousand wrinkles, from the folds of blanket and looked at me, with eyes as dead and black as midnight waters. Seeing I met his stare, he returned his indifferent gaze to the coals.

His blanket, once patterned red and black, was faded with wear and weather. One battered osprey feather drooped in his rusty black hair. Noting he had cooked a supper of corn in the gridiron left hanging for such purpose by the fire, I took him to be one of the wandering breed common throughout New England, their comings and goings regulated by movements of season or of stars; who enter taverns and farmhouse kitchens at their pleasure, accepting food, a corner for sleeping, as a king might accept tribute from a race of conquered aliens. Seldom will they stay at any house for more than one night. At times they will houseclean or fetch wood for their keep, but most make but sorry servants; and will go when they will go.

I could not tell his tribe. When, by way of experiment, I tried him with a few words of Nipmuck, he looked long at me but said nothing. No telling, did he comprehend one syllable of that tongue.

Soon I heard Socrates commence to snuffle and scratch at the front door, so I bade the visitor goodnight in English (I got no answer) and went my way.

My feet had turned to ice, so I allowed Socrates his imperious will, which was to lie across my insteps at the foot of the bed. My bed-companions did not stir. A wind was come up and the whole ancient house a-stir with creaks, knocks, and whispers. Especially I could hear the inn signboard rattling and squeaking on its arm. By degrees these noises became part of my drowsiness, and at last I slept again. I dreamed no dreams.

We were to breakfast in Old Newbury, but the landlord kindly provided us with tea in the kitchen. 'Twas black night without, our driver having called us at four. The Indian was gone from the hearthstone. I pictured him wandering onward, thinking perhaps on the days when the road beneath his feet was but a narrow foot trail of his people threading endless forests.

"To what tribe of redmen does your Indian guest belong?" I asked as our host joined us.

He looked at me so blank and queer that I hastened to add, "I mean, the old man who sheltered last night by your kitchen fire." I thought he mistook my words for a reference to his chamber ghost.

His wall eye seemed desirous of ignoring my question, but the other leaped in agitation. "Sir," says he slowly, "I know not what you mean."

"I mean," says I, "the old Indian in the faded blanket of black and red. He cooked his maize here by your kitchen fire. He wore a thousand years of wrinkles in his face—and one osprey feather, like his blanket much the worse for wear. —Did you not know know he was in here early?" For he wore a look of stupid bewilderment, in which something like terror mingled.

"No, Sir! Not I," he managed at last to say.

"Why, then," says I, "he must have come and gone through the window. His sort will often make free so. You need not alarm yourself—he was a most peaceable guest, even if uninvited." I grew nettled at his look of fear; judging him to be one of the breed that hates the very sight of an Indian—as if today were a hundred years back and the tribes up with tomahawk and torch, instead of adrift, a broken remnant demanding every right man's pity. My own Indian blood helped fire my resentment.

He made no answer. With the same strange face, he hastened to the parlor and bent to the window, as if to scan the sky for weather signs. After, he went off nor showed himself again.

I was much put out by what I considered his churlish behavior; surprised, as well, for the man had been most civil to us all, with every sign of good breeding.

But Savory, with significant winks, signalled me to pay this apparent rudeness no heed. "Judge not, Mr. Medley," he intoned. "—Have you observed the signboard of the house, outside?"

I said I had not, nor wished to; and, I fear, consigned both signboard and its owner to the D—l.

"Lord, Mr. Medley, you are quick to rise," he cries. "Do but take one look at the thing as you pass under it." And he gave general notice to depart.

My portmanteau stood in the hallway. In the rush to get seated in the wagon I was near forgetting the driver's admonition. But it happened, as I passed out the front door, that a strong gust of wind struck, that strove to snatch the door out of my hand. The same gust caught the sign overhead and set it madly creaking.

I looked up. The sign was of much-weathered pine, splintered at points along the frame. Once varnished, the dried coating had cracked into a network of fine, cobwebby lines. The faded figure of an Indian, one hand raised, met my eye; a blurred feather for ornament and a blanket cast about his shoulders of black and red; the colors so darkened and weathered I could scarce make them out. The face was worn and flaked away.

Savory went by me in a hurry and nudged me in the ribs.

"Ah, Mr. Medley," he whispered, scarce pausing as he spoke. "If you had looked upon it at the hour of two this morning! I wager you would have found him gone from his place!" And he gestured upwards toward the image.

Lord, what sad nonsense is this I write! Old wives' tales, superstition filled the very air of that inn—to say nothing of the heads of host and driver. A sorry example of how such starts and scares can infect the brains of reasonable men and reduce them again to childishness. But *my* powers of rationality shall not languish. I shall call coincidence by its true name, nor harken to the dark suggestions of legend. I record the incident simply for amusement's sake; a striking example indeed, of the appositeness of chance.

Nothing more.

Yet may a message lie in it, for me.

December 21, 1793

Good crowds, here at Newburyport. Even the stuffed sea-cow (with the unlikely billing of Atlantean Sea Maid) and the lady dwarf exhibiting at a house down at the harbor have not hurt me. But I think I shall not stop here long. There comes a hankering kind of sadness on my mind, sprung from the chances of my latter days, that moves me to pay a visit to my mother.

I shall go, as I think, to pass the New Year with her at the Chebacco farm. I should be glad to see Aunt Deb as well, but I misdoubt she will be back from the latest of those autumn tramps by which she has always marked the turning of the year; sometimes selling birch brooms as she goes. 'Twill be the end of January with its muddy thaw brings her again to Chebacco.

December 26, 1793

Fallen behind in this journal, having had no leisure these two days past.

Arrived here at my mother's place on the 24th, not many hours ahead of a northeast storm that rages overhead even as I write. I am in the loft chamber, and it is almighty cold . . . almost too cold for my hand to grip my pen. The wind buffets the eaves and chimneys of the house as it would tear them asunder. The farm and surrounding marsh are blotted out. The driven snow stays but against the north side of house, barn, and fence, where it drifts high. A fine powder sifts through the roof upon me as I sit, and scarce melts upon the cold skin of my hand.

This day I gave to cutting and stacking wood. My mother has let the pile to dwindle, since Sam left her. She says she needs not a man to do the work. Yet will she be fifty-eight years old in March. I must stay till I have filled the shed with wood sufficient for the winter remaining. I must mend the roof and fences and clean the stalls.

My mother is become the most unreasonable of women. The older she grows, the less she will allow me to do for her. She and Aunt Deb will hire on men for the harvest, but she will not take a worker out of season for her greater ease and comfort. Her neighbor Jack Tilley, says she, with his three sons give her help with the sheep-shearing, and for the rest she can do, she can do. Indeed, she shows prodigious strength and hardihood. When I arrived here, she had but just finished slaughtering the pig and, bedecked with his blood, was scalding him in the kettle by the barn. At every return I make here, I am filled anew with the strongest sentiments of respect and affection for her—mingled withal with a kind of rage. The demands such work makes upon her are excessive for one of her years; yet am I powerless as a babe to restrain her from it.

Betimes I regret that I bought this farm for her after the War. The sale price of my veteran's grant I might better have spent to provide her with a domicile in town—but on a farm she would be.

Indeed, she talks of the place and her daily round of labor with infinite relish, seeming not to mind that she is alone for a good part of the year. 'Tis true, the neighbors are kind. Mrs. Tilley and her daughter spent this morning with my mother in the shed, where they made soap. (I worked mightily at my wood-chopping to remove myself from the mess and smells of collected grease and lye.)

Aunt Deb, as Mother says, went off in mid-September, as is her custom. She thinks not to see her before February at the earliest, but declares she is never late for the lambing and sugaring.

As for sister Josie, she wrote last in July from Wilmington, Delaware. She is no longer with the Husseys, it appears, but enjoys life as cook to a family called Rammer.

Socrates is not happy here. He and the house dogs—Jack, Plum, and Toby—have reached a treaty of peace that lasts whilst Socrates trespasses not upon certain sacred grounds—Plum's corner where his straw lies, or Jack's post by the fire. As for the cats, Kitty-Bell in their first brief encounter has taught him caution. I think he cannot believe these two, with their immovable bulk and contemptuous gaze, are truly cats.

I improve our leisure after supper by instructing him in the juggling art. He now can snatch a spinning plate from the stick, and I have hopes he will soon be able to bear it a-spinning, the stick in his mouth. I must fashion a wooden cross-piece, so he may hold the stick erect.

My mother is much diverted by him. At first, she was inclined to laugh at me for acquiring him; but now she says he is clever, and cleverness wins always her respect. She takes great pride in her son's dexterity—she will have me display my skills each evening after supper. Indeed, I find her somewhat too impressed by my magic—last night she sat nodding and smiling at my sleight-of-hand and then remarked in tones of great pride that she knew I was *passed of the devil.*

"What mean you?" says I.

"You be passed of the devil, Josh, *sartin,*" she says, as if paying me the highest of compliments.

"I declare," says I with a snort, "if you think your only son has sold his soul to the devil, you take it calmly indeed!" (For there she sat smiling and nodding as pleased as may be.) "'Tis no black spell enables me to perform what you see, but work! Years and years of hard work. Come, Mother, you have seen me at practice yourself, often enough."

Whilst my mother's lack of learning and the limited company she sees have made her prey to these country superstitions; yet did it seem hard I should so coolly be consigned to the Evil One.

Seeing my face, she laid her hand temperately upon my knee, as she was used to do when I was but a little lad and growing angry.

". . . Naught against ye, then, Josh," says she as one that soothes. "A good lad and a good son you be. —'Twas Josie did it."

"Indeed!" says I. "And how did Sister Josie barter me to Satan without my knowledge or consent? It scarce seems a valid transaction under United States law."

The ironic vein is lost upon my mother. Her serenity and

goodness make me see the absurdity of ruffling at her. Knowing her pride in me, why should I cavil or complain because she thinks me *passed of the devil?*

"I mind when it happened," she says, leaning forward to poke up the fire. The flare sharpened the hollows under her high cheekbones. At such moments my mother's Indian blood leaps out from the black shades and boldly takes command of her beauty. (A beauty she is still, I swear, but for her missing teeth.) "She was bid to mind ye," says she. "Ye were but a babe, Josh, of eighteen months, but some young fry about the place teased her to go off a-playing in the fields."

"—Did they belong to the place, then?" I murmured with affected indifference. My probing brought to her lips a faint smile; as if she said, *Ah, Josh, you shall not catch me out thus!*

"She wanted to go," my mother continues, "but what to do with baby Josh? A sow was there in her pen, giving suck to a litter. So what does my fine Josie do but into the pen with ye and put ye to sucking alongside the little pigs?"

"Josie was ever one for the nearest way," says I.

My mother nodded. "—So off goes she to play in the fields," she says, "and I knowing naught of it."

"Where were you then?" says I.

"At the house," says she, looking me in the eye.

"Nearby," says I.

"Nearby," she concedes. "—So that when you commenced to scream I heard. I ran. There ye were in the mud, Josh, and that old sow grunting and rooting ye about with her wicked old snout—"

"Doubtless she was within her rights," I says, "I having both trespassed and stolen nourishment."

"I snatched ye up," my mother says, "and Josie got the

switch for't. But 'twas that day it happened."

"Come, Mother," says I, "your reasons?"

"Ye got passed when that sow suckled ye," says she. "Search Scripture, Josh. Every Christian man knows, the devil is in the swine."

"Well, well," says I, with something of a sigh. "An' I strive each day of my life for righteousness, I may yet give him the slip, in the end."

"So ye do strive," says she, looking at me. "But as for all ye long for, with something too much of fierceness." She smiled, showing where she has lately lost two more teeth. "I mind when ye were little . . . when I took the two of ye to meeting. Josie would walk demure as a fine lady by my side. But for Josh—he were always darting ahead or running to climb each big rock he spied. If I took ye by the hand ye'd dance before me and fair pull my arm from my shoulder. Ye could never wait a moment with patience."

A log fell with a snap and hiss, and the dogs opened each one eye.

"Yet life beats patience into a man, often with a cudgel," says I then. "You read me right. I am, I own, something impetuous and overquick by nature. Still, have I practised patience these many years."

She looked at me and away, quick as winking.

"For I am thirty-seven," I continued, "yet I know no more of who I am or who my father is—than does Socrates, there, of his."

After a pause: "I judge, there be a trifle hound in him," she says.

"I have spent money and time I could ill afford," I persisted, "riding over half these New England States seeking out this man's estate and that, like a mad land broker—all in search of that knocker you know of. Since I was of an age to wonder—was I no more than seven?—when the mystery of my father began to tease and trouble—"

"Nay, ye were scarce so old," she countered swiftly. "But six ye were, when first ye told me of the knocker ye remembered. When ye first asked, 'Mar, Mar, was that house my Par's house?' "

"And waited something over thirty-one years for a reply," I said drily. "Though indeed, your silence on that point suffices for an answer."

"Ye show yourself a true Jack-stick-to-it," she says. "And think me hard, don't ye, for telling naught?"

"Indeed," I says gently. "For you are doubly mum. You will not name my father. Nor will you tell me why."

"No," says she, very soft, but firm. Yet I thought her voice did quaver as she spoke, gazing into the fire.

"One thing needs no telling," I said then. "—That you keep silent for love of me and for my good, as you think it. 'Tis the one thing you ever have denied me. I berate you not, nor wheedle. Hold-fast's a good dog. Someday, no doubt, I shall find him out without your help and so find myself."

"If ye do, you may thank him, then," says she shortly. "The grudge you bear him has taken you far." Silence fell betwixt us.

"There is another matter upon my heart," I said at length; and felt my face commence to burn. For that I am no eager young swain of twenty, but a portly thirty-seven, with early rheumatics in my fingers.

"I know it," says she. "Shall I name it? 'Tis a lady-love."

"In G—d's name, then!" I cried pettishly. "Is it I or you who are *passed*, as you call it? Or am I so green-melancholy, so hangdog, the world may read me like a broadside?"

"'Tis time you were wedded," she says. "—But not such a one as Polly."

"Poor Poll," says I, and fell to musing.

"The rum was her weakness," says my mother.

"Ay," I said. "Yet did life upon the road not amend it. Never again will I ask any woman to go the road with me."

"Well—who be she?" my mother demands, something impatient. "Have ye asked her?"

"You go too fast," says I. "There is no one."

"I don't believe ye," says she.

"No one," I repeated. "O, 'tis true, I have thought much, of late, of giving up this showman's life. 'Twould like me well to marry and be plain Farmer Medley. But as for the lady—there was but one lass I did fancy for the space of ten days, and that lately. But I saw plain her affections were already engaged, and so I came away. And that is all the matter."

"You did not ask her, then?" my mother cries.

"She is not my sort—she loves her cousin. I would have heard *No* for my pains," says I.

"And that ye could not abide. Ye'd lose a treasure for lack of a bold word and bed your pride the rest of your barren nights," cries my mother in despair.

"Tut, Madam, I shall find another," says I. "Nor need I look far to find out one more suitable. This was but a girl—a Miss of seventeen, full of giggles and whimsy and young vanities; town-bred and moneyed, too, as I think. A creature made for minuets and girlish prattle and nutmeg in a silver box!" I sprang to my feet and paced before the fire. "Would such an one, think you, wed a fatherless man of mixed blood to play at farmering? Or—if should she so consent, being giddy enough for any folly that had no evil in't—could I content her, or she me? Would not my pride tear me for having wed one of my father's race? Would we not live out our days in mutual misery and recrimination?"

"But can ye forget her, then?" demands my mother.

"—I know not." 'Twas a confession hardly wrung from my lips.

My mother said no more. After a time I rose, bade her good night and mounted to this cold chamber. She is asleep. The surf roars on the outer beach. The farmers hereabouts have good fertilizer in the kelp and other weed left by the tides. What should I best use for compost, in Ohio?

December 31, 1793

Now is Christmas passed and the New Year upon us. This good Congregational household held no Papistical feast after meeting; although we noted, whilst at the Tilleys', greenery hung about the house and special dishes of plum pudding, &c. in preparation. They had broiled eels besides, arranged upon the platter in the shape of a wreath! A curious sight. The Tilleys favor the King's church and will drive to Ipswich to attend services there.

My mother seeks to draw my notice favorably to Phoebe Tilley. She is a good-natured lass, and not ill-favored; the more apt to favor my suit, perhaps, for having reached the advanced age of twenty-four without marrying. She was, indeed, betrothed to one Daniel Salop of Wenham; but the young man took sick and died of the pox in last year's epidemic, having gone up to Boston against the advice of all his friends.

Her mother and mine together work to make the match, with as much subtlety between them as is found in a raw radish. My mother forever is sending me to Tilley's for this or that, and when her invention runs dry, the gate soon is heard to creak, and I know I shall see Mrs. Tilley bustling in, with Phoebe shamefaced in her wake.

'Tis conceivable, Phoebe and I might agree well enough if left alone to guide ourselves; but embarrassment at this maneuvering of mothers renders the girl vexed and tongue-tied. Whilst I, at thirty-seven, would think shame to be steered into marriage by two plotting old women. Worse, my mother's boasting of my earnings—which she contrives to offer as a kind of compensation for our color!—sets my pride to bristling. I think I must depart altogether from this place, if only for the girl's sake.

January 6, 1794

This morning, dark early, the dogs commenced barking. Presently I heard the gate to creak.

Lord, Mrs. Tilley! was my first thought. But as I came more awake I knew better. Socrates' voice soared in a frenzy, but the other dogs subsided, helping me to guess who was below. When I hurried down, she was building up the fire: Aunt Deb, wrapped in her blanket and shod in man's boots. She wore too, my mother's three dogs, who were clambering up her legs in their joy. Kitty-Bell was already sprung to her shoulder. Socrates was having hysterics under the table.

Her dark face flashed bright when she spied me, and she clasped me in her two great arms. I had forgot how massive she is—she towers a head and a half again over me—and that familiar smell about her, of wet wool, woodsmoke, and tobacco.

"I scarce knew ye, Josh," she says, holding me off with something of a critical eye. "Ye're grown as fat in the middle as old Governor Adams," says she.

"And you, Auntie," says I, "are sure ten feet higher than when last we met."

"Is that yours, then?" she says with a deep laugh, pointing under the table. ". . . Wondered where Joanna had found such a thing. —Come, pig-dog," and she snapped her fingers.

Socrates was scarce mollified by the gesture. I needs must seize him by the scruff and haul, his braced feet disputing each inch of the way.

"His name is Socrates," says I, picking him up. "A spit-dog that broke his indentures and ran off with Josh Medley to learn the trade of conjuring. Like myself, he has seen worse days and hopes for better. —Socrates, pay your duties to my Aunt. Come, Sir, cease to growl, or I shall put you out in the snow.—One would think he knew your forebears once fancied his in a stew."

My mother was down now, surprised at seeing my aunt in advance of her usual time. The other dogs still danced welcomes, and I took Socrates up with me whilst I dressed. He was calmer; but now and again would remember his first shock, eye the trapdoor sidewise and mutter.

We three were merry at breakfast. Neither my mother nor I asked aught of the places Aunt Deb had been. We know these be matters she will not speak of. Once or twice she has been seen by one who knew us, who later reported having seen her. One neighbor at New Hampshire on business found her sleeping by the kitchen fire in the Durham tavern where he lodged; and once a logger, homeward bound, whom we met in a Salem street, hailed her in surprise—addressing her as Teppamoy and wondering aloud to find her in that town when he last had seen her far up in the Province of Maine. Though but a lad at the time, I clearly recall the angry frown that darkened her face, at being thus accosted from out her secret life of wandering. She made him no reply, but walked on, proud as any queen. Dressed in her yellow gown and bonnet for the day in Salem, she must have looked far different from the Teppamoy he remembered.

My aunt's unlooked-for return allows me to take my leave of this place (and of the Tilleys). By Wednesday at the latest, I go on to Gloucester. The wood is in, the fences mended. I can, with a mind at peace, leave my mother in Aunt Deb's capable hands.

January 7, 1794

Much diverted by a happening of last night. Accompanied Aunt Deb when she walked out to gather somewhat; an herb that she dispenses to sundry neighbors with eye ailments. The snow was no hindrance. As she predicted, the spot where grows the herb was blown almost bare, and last year's dried plants ready to hand beneath. She loves to make mystery as to the ingredients of her specifics; and maintains her reserve even with me, her grand-nephew.

I have little curiosity in the affair, indeed. I went with her because the high white moon and sparkling snow enticed me to walk. Socrates felt the same. He pushed his face into the snow, snuffling, came up hoared to the eyebrows, and barked to us over his shoulder.

'Twas the full moon brought Aunt Deb out, for the leaves she sought must be gathered under its light. We walked to the village pound next the graveyard, and she commenced to burrow at one corner under the snow and dead leaves. Presently she was putting things into her bag.

Socrates joined her in scratching; but meeting no scent of woodchuck or rabbit, wandered with me 'mongst the headstones beyond the wall.

I was spelling o'er the epitaphs when up comes Aunt Deb in a tear.

"Someone comes," says she. "I'll not have them learn my spot, Josh, 'tis the only one in Chebacco where it grows." And down she draws me behind the headstone nighest us, holding Socrates' muzzle firm with her other hand.

It needed not the sight of the walkers to judge they came from the tavern. Indeed, they were very drunk; speaking and laughing loud. As down they come, Aunt Deb chuckles under her breath.

"Zeb Converse," she breathes in my ear, "and his rogue cousin, Sam Perkins."

We waited upon their passing. But one of them paused at the gate of the graveyard and 'gan to rattle a stick, with deafening racket, across its iron bars.

"Arise, ye dead," he bawls. "Arise, ye dead, the day of judgment is at hand!" Whilst his companion guffaws at the impiety.

Without warning, up rears my aunt from behind her gravestone, looking ten feet tall in the moonlight.

"Yes, Lord!" she croaks. "Yes, Lord, I'm a-coming!"

Dead silence from the road—then the thud of desperate running feet. My aunt leans against the stone in a paroxysm of her silent laughter.

"Auntie," says I with mock severity, "you will have turned two heads snow-white this night—their friends will scarce know them again."

"Ay," she says. "I'll have peace for my gathering from now on, Josh. The tavern bully-boys will take the long way home from this night, if they two tell this tale tomorrow."

Still shaking with mirth, back she goes to the pound for another quarter hour, and then we three walked home together across the marsh. 'Twas a world of white silence, like strolling upon the face of the moon itself.

January 8, 1794

Arrived at this Gloucester inn around the hour of four, after an early start from Chebacco. After breakfast, I bade my mother farewell and set out with Aunt Deb in the old pung. The air was bitter, with naught but a dull orange bar in the pewter sky to show where the sun rose. We saw black tidal creeks winding through a waste of white; a few gulls wheeling where the drumlin called Hog Island swells like a hoary bubble from the marsh. The mountain Agamenticus in Maine Province pricked up from the sea.

Till we crossed to 'Squam on the ferry, we met few sleighs or folk on foot. At the tavern by the landing Aunt Deb oated the horses and we dined with the host and his large family. Some young bachelors of the village were also of our company.

After, Aunt Deb recrossed the bay to the West Parish; and I hired a sleigh to bring me here to the harbor.

Along Middle Street we passed a number of fine houses facing the shipping, with long, white gardens running from their doors down to Front Street. In spring and summer they must make a handsome show.

Once settled, I sallied forth to a barber's nearby for shave and trim. From the barber (a garrulous fellow with gold rings in his ears) I understand my audience here should prove a mixed bag: pinkie fishermen, sailors from the merchantmen (that forest of masts visible from my window) and a goodly number of the propertied well-to-do; for

Gloucester before the War was a flourishing port. During the fighting and since, it has somewhat suffered; yet I feel I should do well here.

I am sorry that I could not manage, whilst at Chebacco, a journey to Rowley to see Will and to make the acquaintance of his wife and little ones. The contemplation of Will's happiness at his own hearthside would pleasure me; tho' I fear 'twould also rouse sentiments of an exquisitely painful sort.

January 9, 1794

Last night, Socrates' first public appearance in the role of Juggling Dog. For skill, he is in some respects my superior. If I scale a plate the length of the room he races ahead of my throw and leaps to seize it in his jaws—a feat by which he fairly nicks me! But I was in some fears as to how he would conduct himself before a noisy audience.

I spent much effort upon his appearance for the occasion. I gave him a thorough brushing (which he loves), but his tatterdemalion coat looked not one whit the sleeker. So next I thought to develop his quality of hobbledehoy to advantage. I folded a paper ruff, like a clown's, for him to wear about his neck, and laughed aloud to see him.

But the last laugh was his. Whilst getting myself ready, I imprudently left him to his own devices. When next I looked, the ruff trailed torn and limp along the floor and he was treading heavily upon it; eyeing me carelessly the while. He is an insolent rogue! I despair of ever leading him into more righteous ways.

The inn parlor was full to overflowing. 'Tis most gratifying—more and more I find my name known throughout New England. Imperceptibly but surely, my fame has grown over the ten years since the War; so that now to blow my own horn on handbills and posters is scarce needful. The name Joshua Medley, Conjuror, suffices to fill a house.

The tremendous cheering that greeted me in the parlor here (ere I had done more than bow) went to my head like strong wine. At such times, feeling the sympathies of the audience as a kind of mysterious energy, I am carried beyond myself. Last night for the space of an hour I forgot my doubts, my weariness, my rheumatics. I forgot the farm in Ohio, forgot (even) Miss Reade and my sore heart. I sang, talked, juggled, and conjured like one inspired. Every turn went without a hitch. My magic birds, to loud applause, made their invisible flight to clock and chimney-piece; the nest of locked boxes, yielding at last the vanished dollar, brought murmurs of mystification; and when, the pack of cards having been tossed (by a volunteer in the front row) into the air, I caught and showed the chosen card upon the point of my *magic sword,* the crowd not only clapped and cheered but stamped their feet upon the floor like thunder.

My success moved me to chance Socrates' introduction to the public.

"Ladies and gentlemen," says I. "Tonight for the first time I shall introduce a fellow-artist to assist me in demonstrating for your edification a rare art: the art of making gravity a servant to dexterity. The name of this *virtuoso* is Socrates, for he is the philosopher of the canine world. Let us hope he finds no cup of hemlock among us tonight." And I whistled Socrates from the bar.

At the sight of the canine philosopher a laugh went up. Twice more I must whistle him before gaining his attention; the presence of so many noisy strangers moved him to trot about on his short legs and to pant like a walking bellows. With my hands on my hips and a look of mock indignation, I took full advantage of the audience's diversion before bringing him to order.

"Let us see," says I, "if our philosopher will favor us with a demonstration of his skill." I showed him the plates, and he yawned. (A born clown, that villain!) He did condescend to catch six plates in swift succession as I scaled them, and won prolonged applause.

I brought forward my table with the clamped poles, and after spinning one, three, five, then seven plates at one time, ended by spinning three, with two sticks upon my two forefingers and one upon my nose; whilst Socrates held his two spinning plates balanced upon the cross-bar gripped in his jaws. The turn succeeded finely, so I thought to finish with Socrates' race across the room to snatch the plate from the air. I moved the spectators back, leaving an alley between two forests of legs for the beast to travel. The crowd was almost pressed to death, but bore it with great good nature. So much had Socrates won them, they suffered willingly for his convenience.

I showed him the plate, which he panted at; and then, taking great care to scale it straight down the open lane, I let it fly. Socrates gave it one glance and sat down. The plate crashed to the floor and skidded with a *whang* to the opposite wall—whilst he gazed about the crowd and panted his dog grin.

'Tis a fit meditation for a philosopher—how this final failure pleased the crowd far more than all our hardly learned skills that went before. Socrates was cheered to the echo. Indeed, so much was he the favorite, I foresee the day when Josh Medley will be relegated to scaling plates and picking up the Master's gear!

January 11, 1794

Our crowds continue. Many turned away tonight. Socrates' fame has spread throughout Cape Ann. No longer do I fret, wondering will he do my bidding. Popular when he does, he is still more the favorite when he does not. Whilst I make of my mock anger a warm conspiracy amongst us all, the audience is mine.

Betimes I wonder does the noise of his fame reach as far as Portsmouth? She would laugh and be glad, as I think, to hear of his success; for she liked the rascal well. Indeed, somewhat she might rejoice for his master's sake. I wish she might know, that same master asks Heaven's protection for her each night, upon his knees.

January 14, 1794

A merry surprise, today. Here is come Will Poole with his good wife and all their brood.

Along with many another idler, I was observing the arrival of the stage—one of the chiefest entertainments in this, as in every town—when up behind it rattles a carryall drawn by a sorrel mare. I spied Will at the reins, his whole family with him. Scarce was he down and taking the first of the children from his wife's hands, when I reached them.

"Will, you rogue!" I cried.

"Josh!" says he, with the lightning smile. "Here be honor. We are all come on holiday to see the great conjuror. But I scarce thought to be met at the very door of the tavern by the Mighty Medley himself. —Betty, my dear—" and he presented me to his lady, a smiling red-haired little person, something distracted; with one eye for me and one for her children. She was of such low stature, I could look down at the top of her bonnet; and as for Will, she scarce stood as high as his breastbone. She is something plain, Mistress Poole, but with a face full of goodness and good-nature that make its plainness pleasant to look upon; much as a field that is a poor thing in the natural way can, under good husbandry, blossom and rejoice as a rose.

Their children, as needs must be with two such parents, are full of sweetness. They have not, as I think, been much from home, and display profound wonder at this *brave new world,* their awe subduing their natural spirits.

With round gaze, they bowed and curtsied to Mr. Medley, Papa's friend. The little lad Timothy (scarce four) made his bow as directed, then wrapped himself in his mother's skirts and hid from me. Their eldest, Ann, who is nine, looks much like Will: his eyes, hair, and quiet smile, even to the large teeth. Will Junior, seven, is reddish and freckled like his mother. Hetty, who is five and a half, resembles neither parent. Rotund and imperious, she puts me most in mind of Vice President Adams.

The tavern is near full, but beds were found for all the Pooles, and we supped with our host and hostess and a table of near thirty people. After, all gathered in the parlor to watch Mr. Medley.

I made much of Will's little ones and brought them forward to assist me, which pleased their mother, as I think. They themselves showed eyes like stars. Little Timothy, at the flight of the *invisible bird,* cried out, "Mar, I didn't see it fly," which brought mirth from the audience. Even stern-faced Hetty melted at Socrates' tricks.

When I finished they came seeking me, hand in hand, to thank me (no doubt at their mother's prompting) and to bid me goodnight. Socrates got the lion's share of their attentions. As they trailed up the stair, I commended Will for their good behavior, which I was mightily struck by. "One might think they dined at a public house every week," says I, "so decent and silent at supper, so mannerly and good—your children are prodigies of nature, Will!"

"They had best be good, and they know it," he says, smiling. "Their mother and I have sworn, if they do not behave, never again to take them anywhere in the public eye."

We each took a pipe by the taproom fire, and Will told me how my fame had reached Rowley and made the children wild to come and see. They had heard Will speak of me (as a fellow-soldier-at-arms) and knew we had lately met at Portsmouth.

"They gave us no peace," Will says. "We needs must go to Gloucester and see Par's friend, the famous Mr. Medley—and his dog. Court is out of session, so we came."

"I scarce thought," says I, "when we parted at Portsmouth, that we would so soon meet again." I handed him the tongs, with a coal, for his pipe. "When did you pass again through that town?"

"After ten days at Pownalborough," he says with a grimace. "I lost my case—the finding was for the plaintiff, with stiff damages."

I feared he would be off into the law, which was not to my mind.

"What news in Portsmouth?" I said. "'Twas a lively place, I thought. Come, tell me all you heard, of deaths, marriages, jiltings, and the rest of the tittle-tattle."

He laughed. "I did not guess you to be such a gossip, Josh. —Having stayed but the one night and spoken to not one soul that I can now recall, I am scarce a repository of Portsmouth news."

"I attended an Assembly ball before I came away," I said; "and made the acquaintance of a Miss Reade, with her aunt

Mistress Atwell. A lively minx—the niece, I mean—I believe she was shortly to be wed to her cousin. I wondered if the marriage had taken place."

"I know not," says Will. "I do not move in such circles, as you. —Wait, then! What was the cousin's name?"

"Mr. James Emery," says I; making minute adjustments to my pipe and then testing the draw.

"Had he been lately in Europe?" says Will then.

"Indeed. And returned not at all improved in his manners," says I.

"Then they are wed. There was some chatter of him at table 'twixt the hostess and one of the local bachelors," Will says. "The talk was mainly of his debts and of the dowry. —The one not sufficient for the other, or so it was generally agreed, with headshaking and tongue-clicking. An extravagant young blade, I fear. Your minx should have done better than her cousin. —By Heaven, she would have done better to take you, Josh!"

Then his laughter faded. He grew exceeding grave. "I have a tactless tongue," he says. "—And you, with your Portsmouth tittle-tattle . . . ! Why did you not tell me straight out what ailed you with the place?"

"A man may admit to himself he is a fool," says I, "without wishing to acknowledge the fact to his friends. —Glad I am to know the thing is done. She has wed him. Now can I perhaps put her image from me."

"Well," says he with an anxious laugh, "Betty, did she know, would be cross. I told her of your wish to marry and turn farmer. She has a list drawn up of at least two dozen maids and an assortment of widows at Rowley and Topsfield—you were to come to us and make your choice."

"I beg of you, say naught of this matter," I said with something of quickness. "I thank her for her diligence in my behalf; but I cannot visit Rowley now—and I would be glad to have this night's confession remain betwixt us two."

"Agreed," says he. "I am sorry, Josh. I fear you will not lightly shake off this hurt."

"I will since I must, and there be an end to it," I burst out, something testy as I fear. But Will takes no offence at me.

"I wish you might come to us in any case," says he. "We shall have the ladies away, if you prefer."

"Be sure," says I, "I would come with pleasure if I could. But from this place I go to Boston, in hopes the stir I make here will have preceded me. Strike the hot iron, Will! With or without a wife, I must have that farm. More and more my days seem spent, as Socrates' once, upon a turnspit wheel."

"Yet you do well," says he with a sigh. "I wager you earn in a year near three times the sums I manage to scrape together at the law." And on he went a while lamenting the superfluity of lawyers and how the important cases all fell to a few of name and reputation; leaving him and his obscurer brethren to deal with petty quarrels over strayed livestock and land boundaries. "They get the ten and fifteen dollar fees," says he, "whilst we must content ourselves with five dollars for a jury argument—two dollars for a contrivance.—The very largest litigation of my career was the defence of one Consider Gault of Boston last July. A suit was brought against him for fraud . . . the matter being one close to a private lottery, with the prize a huge sea turtle. That case made some little noise, and my defence won him an acquittal. Yet my career seems no forwarder for it."

"What!" I cried. "One of those pernicious knaves, was he? They care not that private lotteries are forbid by law

—they entice folk to dream of wealth for no effort, ease without labor. E'en the scandalous multiplying of public lotteries is a great evil."

Will smiled at my vehemence. "The public lotteries have accomplished much good, admit it you must," says he. "They have endowed Harvard, built bridges, highways—"

"I care not," I said, refreshing my pipe. "On such matters I hold with our late departed Governor Hancock. He spoke always against lotteries."

"Indeed. Yet is he known to have bought a ticket or two," Will says with a grin.

I told him to spare me his law-court gossip.

"At any rate," Will says, "you are too harsh on my client Gault. The man was palpably innocent of fraud. —Mind you, Josh, how the Maryland companies, the Pennsylvania men and the Virginians would rail at us New Englanders for slick and grasping Yankees, hard to bargain and quick to deal?"

"Ay, I mind their way," I says. " 'Twas snobbery and a great slander, that I had more than once to correct."

"New England had no doughtier champion," he agreed with something of a secret smile. "Well, this man Gault is a type of that slander, if you please—a most shrewd money-nosing fellow. Yet do I believe him honest, or I should have no dealings with him."

Feeling something of disturbment within me, I asked him what dealings he meant. Will is both quick and diligent; but deficient in worldly wisdom. His goodness of heart is too prone to credit another man's claims to virtue. Knowing more than Will of mankind, I expect something less of them.

"What dealings?" I repeated. "Something in the law way?"

He shook his head. "Show me the money in that! I might ride circuit for fifty years and leave my family beggared at the end. No, the fellow is a ship chandler by trade, but also something of a philosopher, something of a scientist—a most ingenious mechanic—in a smaller way he has almost the range of talents of Doctor Franklin."

"And what dealings have you with this paragon?" I repeated.

"Few and small," Will says, smiling. "So look not so fierce. His gratitude for the acquittal has not stopped with my fee. Twice he has allowed me to invest toward the expenses of a—not a lottery, no, but a legal enough relative of the same—that turned a pretty profit for us both."

I told him, I turned a fishy eye on all these fellows who offer, out of the goodness of their hearts, to make my fortune. "Let them prove themselves by making their own first. Whilst your Mr. Consider Gault remains a ship chandler, I remain a skeptic."

"You were not always so suspicious," Will says. "Not in Virginia when we were mustered out. The rest of us made haste to head north and homeward, but what of Josh Medley? Off he goes to seek a post as Magician's Assistant advertised for in the paper—though he knows naught of the magician, or if he will ever see a penny of pay."

"—Poor old Bayly," says I, "I meant but to talk to him at the first. 'Twas pity made me take the job."

"And he an Englishman," Will retorted slyly.

"Would you have me wage war upon a harmless showman," says I, "one ill in mind and body, ruined, deserted by his wife, deprived of his stock in magic; without so much as a suit of clothes other than that upon his back? And he dealt fairly with me. From the beginning, he laid forth the poorness of his prospects. But I was promised a share of the receipts, and he spared no pains in teaching me his arts."

"What befell him, at the last?" Will asked me.

"I know not," says I. "I fear the man has been carried off by sickness. I last heard from him four years back. He was then in Charleston and ill once more. My letters, with offers of help, met with silence."

Will, as I think, was pleased at having turned the talk from his Mr. Gault. But when we rose to retire, he again broached the subject.

"Josh, a word of caution," says he. "Say naught to Betty of Gault or my affairs with him. I shall tell her when things are more in motion. But . . . I must choose my time and method." He paused. "She thinks I am not always overwise in money matters, and I keep from her the full knowledge of just how poor we are."

"Take care you do not prove her in the right of it," I warned him. And so ended our talk.

January 16, 1794

The Dream, last night. Arrived late here at Boston, after dinner at the Anchor in Lynn; crossing by the new bridge where the Medford-Charlestown ferry ran but lately. The span is outlined with a prodigious number of lamps, mighty pretty to see stretched all before us.

I put up here at the Bunch of Grapes in Mackerel Lane —a hostelry hallowed by its associations with the Sons of Liberty. The house is full. We slept last night three to a bed, in a room with four beds. Today the crowd in the public rooms makes the way almost impassable, for a double auction is being held: of books in the parlor and jackasses in the street. The beasts fill the neighborhood with their music, but the book sale draws the greater crowd. But for the lamentable want of space in my trunk, I would buy a volume or two. I heard Pollok's *Course of Time* going very cheap.

Walked out to view the Mall. There is little sign now of the burning and looting by enemy troops during that long-ago siege. Traces of breastworks and kitchen holes dug by the King's troops still pock the Common. The town looks prosperous enough, although I hear (as in every seaport I visit) nothing but talk of the depressed state of the shipping trade. They say that old Sam Adams the Lieutenant Governor is sure to be elected to the Governor's seat that already he fills *pro tem.*

As I walk the streets, a thousand cherished and glorious associations arise in my mind; so that I tread the stones with reverence.

January 20, 1794

Spent an unprofitable afternoon at a tavern nearby that is said to be much frequented by visiting merchant nabobs from Portsmouth. I own myself a fool for going there. I could scarce break in upon the talk of schooners, &c., to demand, *Know ye aught of Mistress Emery? How does she do?*

I begin to see a spiritual danger in my failure to remove her from my mind. Knowing her as good as lost to me when I left Portsmouth, I should never have indulged the habit of making her, in fancy, mine. Now she is wedded, such thoughts are forbid by Heaven as sinful. Already 'tis not easy to cry, "Hold, enough!" and turn my errant thoughts to other matters. God help me as I strive toward righteousness! On the coming sabbath I must attend meeting nor absent myself from the second session, my lazy and worldly custom of late. I sorely feel the need of edification.

January 23, 1794

Examined with much pleasure my advertisement in the newspaper. I also have had printed new broadsides and posters that very much tickle my fancy. In especial, I preen myself upon the first line, an ingenious play upon my own name.

A MEDLEY OF DIVERSIONS

Mr. Medley
The Conjuror and Ventriloquist
Respectfully informs the Ladies and Gentlemen of
__________ and vicinity that his exhibition will
take place at
On Evening
And hopes by his exertions to please, to receive
the patronage of a liberal and enlightened
public.
Mr. Medley will present
his

PHILOSOPHICAL PAPER

The Coffin of Mahomet
Or a playing card turned into a Live Bird
and many other pleasing magical

DECEPTIONS

Mr. Medley will display his powerful but laborious
powers of

VENTRILOQUISM

Mr. Medley's *Learned Dog* SOCRATES will assist him
in his display of his noted agility and skill
in defiance of

THE LAWS OF GRAVITATION

Tickets Fifty Cents—or three for
a Dollar
if purchased before 4 o'clock on
the day of performance.

Children half price—to be had
at the place of performance.

Performance to commence at seven o'clock.

I regard this announcement with complacency. 'Tis in good taste, yet should it whet the appetites for the marvelous of all who read it.

January 25, 1794

A very great crowd, last night. Receipts amounted to one hundred eight dollars. If such throngs continue, I may soon with security give serious thought to that farm.

One disagreeable incident marred last night's performance. (The same thing, as I recall, occurred near seven years ago at Tarleton's in the Cohos Valley.) Some mannerless dolt, having acquired a smattering of knowledge, sets himself up as a know-all to whom a magician's mysteries are transparent as glass. He sees (as he thinks) through every artifice and proclaims the fact loudly to the world.

I know of nothing more damaging to a performer than to have such a fool under his nose. He seems always to plant himself in the front rank and is gifted—perhaps to make amends for his lack of brains—with a prodigious loud voice. The man at Tarleton's was quite a midget, but with the lungs of a bull moose. This wretch of last night was a long, lean creature with a pompadour of greasy hair. He affected a foppish air, but it sat awkwardly upon him—he was most hideously poxed.

Not a turn could I perform without his loud asides.

"It is under his coat. —Note the right sleeve. —There is a false bottom to the box, observe now." A few times he hit the nail right; more often, he was wrong. But right or wrong, his guesses bade fair to ruin my act. I no longer led the audience or held their faith. A few, indeed, cried, "Be still! Let Mr. Medley talk!" But these were scattered voices amongst the crowd. I could feel wrath gathering within me like a thunderstorm, a volcano, a holocaust.

"The gentleman is knowledgeable, as it appears, about the conjuror's art," says I with heavy irony. "Perhaps he will favor us with a demonstration of his skill. Doubtless he can with no trouble make the coin to vanish and the bird to fly."

But my enemy was not quite the fool he looked. "No indeed, Mr. Conjuror," he bawls. "Go on with your flummery, nor take my comments amiss. A doctor need not contract the disease to know the cure."

This raised a laugh. I saw I could not dispose of this fellow as I had my tormentor at Tarleton's, by inducing him to bungle a pass or two. He was plainly revelling in his own cleverness, laughing immoderately and, by his glances, inviting the audience to join him.

I assumed a careless, almost wearied manner. "A doubter indeed," says I. "Then perhaps you will come forward to guard against cheating on my next demonstration. With a watchdog like you, the audience need fear no vulgar artifice."

Suspicious, he would again have refused to come; but my partisans in the crowd set up a clamor. "What do you fear? You understand all, you say—go on!" &c. So at length he came forward, sneering.

I placed upon the table a handful of various coins.

"I will stand five paces from the table," says I, "my back turned. You, Sir, will select a coin from the table. Look hard at the images, front and reverse, and hold it clenched within your hand whilst you mentally visualize its two faces. Then return it to the table—promptly, if you please, for these coins must buy my breakfast tomorrow."

I swung on my heel and walked away. "Select a coin," I cried. "Examine carefully both faces of it . . . Now! Close it in your fist and evoke its image in your mind. Do you see it? . . . Turn the mental coin over, so the reverse side is visible . . . Look upon it. —Now, Sir, return the coin to its fellows upon the table. Push it well in amongst them, if you please—I need no clue to find the coin you chose. It will itself confide to me the secret." Back I swung to the table and quickly began to lift each coin in turn to my ear.

I had risked all on the chance my enemy was unacquainted with the trick's simple secret. Had he been as knowledgeable as he made out he could easily have discountenanced Mr. Medley by handling *several* coins before selecting one. Then I would not have found one coin noticeably warmer (from the heat of his hand) than its neighbors.

'Twas the third coin I picked up; so, unlike the first two, that had held their peace, the third began at once to speak. Wishing for a voice small but clear, I took air a-plenty into my lungs and pushed back my tongue, sending most of the sound through my nose. At the same time I cocked my head as if hearkening and rolled my eyes toward the coin at my ear; thus moving the audience to watch the coin, not the magician.

I am the one! cries the coin. A hush falls over the crowd.

"Are you indeed?" says I. "But are you certain?"

Certain. I was held by a stranger's hand and fixed by a stranger's eye into his mind. But have no fear—I have returned. Your breakfast is safe.

Amid a laugh of surprise and delight from the crowd, I turned smiling to my heckler, holding the coin aloft. He snorted.

"Simple enough," says he in a loud voice. "The fellow peeked round. I saw him do it."

At this bare-faced lie, the crowd's allegiance, already wavering, swung to me. Some cried "Shame!" or hissed. I stilled them with a gesture.

"A doubter indeed," says I again. "But I wager we will yet convince the gentleman. —Sir, you shall blindfold me. Let the blindfold be of your own choosing, I shall submit to it. And then you shall again select a coin."

The fellow, not content with handkerchief or apron, insisted upon draping his greatcoat upon me, so that my head was completely lost in its folds. He pleased me by the pains he took to arrange it; for he allowed ample time for the talking coin to become again as cool as the others.

"Come," says I. "Choose now. You have made certain I shall see naught." I waited a moment, before asking, "And have you chosen?"

"Yes!" he responded. But the audience began to protest. "No, he has not! He wishes to play upon you, Conjuror! —Take a coin! Take a coin!"

I had at last won them to me. For I have no doubt the rogue had invited their complicity in his scheme by winks and smiles; but they would have none of him.

"If no coin is taken," I said when the clamor subsided, "then all coins will remain silent when questioned." This made the crowd clamor the louder, for a coin to be chosen —they were anxious to hear more coin talk. So once more my enemy handled a coin at my direction, and once more

I found it by its warmth. This time 'twas the second I tested, and as it spoke (in a voice slightly deeper than the first) my heckler seized his coat from my hand and turned back into the crowd.

I would have let him go without a word, whilst quietly savoring my triumph; but as he went he flung back over his shoulder that I was a "conniving son of a b—!" So once more I lifted the coin to my ear.

"And how call you this stranger that took you up?" I ask.

He, thinking I may yet fail (for that I cannot have his name) pauses and looks back. Loud and clear, the coin gives out a jackass bray. The crowd hoots and cheers.

January 29, 1794

Business continues amazing good. I must strive to take no more than an honest pleasure in my success; for I know, as does Heaven, the fierceness of Pride in me—the weakness of Vanity. Yet is there a joy finer than mere triumph a performer can feel when sensible of the happiness he brings his audience—a warm kinship with these, his countrymen that approaches (if I be not overbold) that charity whereof writes the Apostle Paul. Loving my audience, I rejoice that they rejoice.

No, 'tis when I encounter opposition that my pride-pot boils over. 'Tis with shamed contrition that I read over, but a moment ago, my entry for January 25th, with its fierce references to *mine enemy.* So far am I still, from bearing affronts with philosophy. Doubtless the fellow wished no harm, but to shine in the eyes of his friends. 'Tis vain to expect the fools of this world to take thought for the one they injure by their folly and boasting; though it may be the injured man's reputation and livelihood they threaten so insensately by their knavish bluster and ill-bred

. . . Lord, lord—even as I write, my resentment arises afresh. So much for wise reflection upon the event! 'Tis sad that, conscious as I am of my faults, I fail so signally to amend them. —The loss of a certain Treasure of Portsmouth could well be the chastisement of Heaven depriving me of a happiness I have not proved worthy to enjoy.

Yet would Providence, to discipline me, consign her to one still more unworthy? To a spendthrift dissolute puppy who will break her heart and render her destitute?

So off again is Ranter Medley. Farewell, journal, for this night—your self-examination proves a futile exercise. I shall to bed.

January 31, 1794

Today a fresh southeast wind bringing rain something heavy and the smells of the harbour. The rain commenced as snow early, and the public ways are a sea of grey slush, wherein every step leaves a boot-shaped well of dark water. The ladies are in a sorry pass, their fouled skirts flapping about their ankles. Even the horses are bespattered to their hocks.

I sallied early forth to take the air. Socrates, wise dog, refused to accompany me, preferring the dry stable. The hanging quadrants and sextants over the shops glistened with wet, and the multifarious *Hebes, Phoebes,* and *Mary Anns* thrust themselves forward and stared with wooden surprise out the windows of the ship carvers at those foolhardy persons braving the weather. I was like to be soaked through to my skin; so returned to the tavern and the taproom fire, thinking a pipe there more agreeable than strolling about Boston.

I found awaiting me a visitor most unexpected—who rose as I entered the taproom.

"Mr. Medley," he says. "My name is Gault, Sir. Mr. Consider Gault. Perhaps Mr. Poole has mentioned me. He is our common friend. —Might I have a word with you at your convenience?"

I stopped short in surprise. Here was a tall, gangling awkward fellow of forty-five or so, narrow of shoulder and short-waisted, with immense long shanks, a lantern jaw, and an eye something enthusiastical. An odd fish; yet was there something engaging about his countenance—a kind of brightening surprise at all he looked at, like to a man ever emerging from out a dark box.

"You know me, it seems," says I.

"All of Boston knows you, Mr. Medley," says he very civilly, "or soon will, Sir. Indeed, I was present at your performance on Tuesday last and was both edified and diverted. —'Tis a raw day, Sir, one of our famous or infamous east winds that plague a man's bones. Will you take a glass of mimbo with me to warm you, whilst I acquaint you with a matter close to my heart? One that may, if you please, turn a pretty profit for all concerned."

I told him I had little interest in any such profitable matters. Content with the livelihood my own profession brought me, I preferred to stick to it. "Mr. Poole indeed told me of you, Mr. Gault," says I, "and of how he defended you against charges of fraud." This was something abrupt; but I thought it best to deal plainly with the man.

He peered doubtfully at me. "Then he told you also that I was found innocent of all such charges," he said. He spoke as if wounded by my manner, and I repented me.

"I beg your pardon, Mr. Gault," I says to him. " 'Twould be wrong of me to cast aspersions, knowing naught to your discredit, upon such flimsy basis as a lawsuit. Many an honest man has been sued, ay, and lost their suits, too, half of 'em. I meant but to warn you. —I like not speculation, Sir. I can ill afford to invest in dreams and contraptions. Because you have seen the crowds come to watch me, you think I must have a ready store of cash to invest. I assure you, that is nothing of the case. My expenses, travelling as I do, are high. I must take all my meals, as well as bed, at taverns, at unconscionable prices. My breakfast of this morning cost me close to fifty cents; and 'twas but a trifle of rump steak, fish, one egg, with cakes and coffee. With all the good will in the world toward original inventions and their devisers, I cannot be their patron. You should seek some propertied person of independent means to aid you. I am but a journeyman like yourself. As for Mr. Poole, who is poor and has a family to support—his true friends would ever urge him to husband his paltry law fees, not gamble them in lotteries and moonshine."

"You are warm, Mr. Medley," Gault says. Perhaps I had that sound, though I had intended to speak civilly. He showed no answering warmth indeed, but examined me curiously and with a certain relish, as if holding under a magnifying glass a choice specimen of human choler. "You have said enough, Sir, to show me how futile the endeavor to interest you in my *dreams and contraptions.* A fine, telling phrase, that; indeed, it has a grand American ring to it, your *dreams and contraptions.* I would like it well as a signboard to swing above my door. —Will you take a glass with me, Sir, on the strength of it?"

Something about the man disarmed me. "Very well," says I. "I shall take one with pleasure, Mr. Gault, and thank you heartily."

The taproom was crowded, but we contrived to snare a

brace of seats in the chimney corner where we could be famously snug. Whilst the landlord was stirring the loaf sugar into our rum and making pleasant music in the glass tumblers with his toddy stick, I proposed a pipe apiece. Mr. Gault assenting eagerly, we each selected a pipe from the drawer, and I passed him a live coal in the tongs. As we puffed our pipes to drawing, the landlord brought the mims, and Mr. Gault raised his glass to me.

"To our better acquaintance, Mr. Medley," says he.

Maintaining a prudent reserve, I bowed in response and we both sipped away.

Mr. Gault smacked his lips. "Ah," says he, "the landlord here knows his business. They serve a grand flipdog at this place—have you sampled it? They use a fine strong beer."

"I fancy cider rather than beer, for flip—*bottle,* we name it where I come from," says I. "Rum and cider makes a superior drink, Sir, with molasses, not sugar, for sweetener; or, best of all, dried pumpkin."

"Do you prefer it so?" he asks in surprise. "Well, doubtless the house would mix it to your taste. The loggerhead is kept always hot in the ashes, as you see, and they will stir you up a generous great tumbler of foam and bubble. —I am no toper, Sir, but I confess my bones need warming in this weather. As you see, I have but little fat on me to shield them from the east wind." He took a generous sip from his tumbler, clasping it in his two hands as if the heat was indeed grateful to his fingers.

"I myself suffer somewhat from that ailment," says I. "Stiffening fingers are no small matter to a juggler."

"Sir, Sir," cries he, "try thistleroot. 'Tis a sovereign remedy, I would use no other. 'Twill make your joints supple with but two or three judicious applications. I regret I have not my ointment in my pocket, you should try it at once."

I raised my hand to quiet him. "I am not troubled that way just at present," I lied. The man seemed ready to leap to his feet and rush home for the box. "'Tis our harsh New England climate that is the cause of our miseries, Mr. Gault."

"Ay, indeed," he sighed. "That, and the privation of the War. I declare to you, Mr. Medley, I got so cold then, I have not—I take my oath on it—felt rightly warm since."

To this I could only nod agreement; minding me of the hard winter of '77. "What was your regiment?" I asked.

"First Massachusetts Militia, at the start of it," says he. "In '78, when my time was out, I came home and signed on a privateer, the *Defence,* out of Salem. But she was taken, Sir; taken after taking three prizes of her own, by the frigate *Cumberland.* I ended prisoner on the *Jersey.*"

On hearing this, I examined him afresh. "That hellship!" cried I. "Why, how long were you prisoner on board of her?"

He sucked at his pipe. "Seven months, two weeks, four days, six hours," says he wryly. "You will note I paid strict heed to the time."

"I marvel at you," I says. "Yours must be a great and stubborn tenacity of life, to have survived so long 'neath those decks. The history of the *Jersey* is infamous. She is an atrocious barbarous blot on the name of the navy and nation that spawned her—"

"Indeed," he says, quietly sipping his mimbo. "We were looked upon, not as enemies in an honorable war but as mere pirates. Yet even pirates, as I think, have some claim on the humanity of their jailors." He smiled a little. "'Twas a battle of wills, at bottom. We were to go over to them or die. They made plain and enforced the choice every day.

Whilst we were as determined as they. Most had to die. A few of us managed to live in their despite."

"'Tis a sad tale, but a proud one in our country's history," said I. "'Tis claimed, but one man of all her prisoners agreed to fight for them."

"Ay," says he quietly. "And we, too, were harsh in our own way. I mind the day they rowed the wretch ashore—every man of us not too weak to make a noise jeered after him the whole of the way."

For some minutes we sat in silence, watching in the fire the brief flare of old memories.

"Mr. Poole and I served together in the 8th Massachusetts," says I. "And after, in the Light Infantry Corps under Lafayette."

"Ay, so he has told me more than once," he says heartily. "And now we be all free men, citizens of a republic—and General Washington leading us still."

"May it be to march down the years to glory," says I, lifting my glass. And we drained our glasses.

"Now, Sir," he says with greater business and leaned forward with his hands on his knees. "We must put aside the bond of our service to America. If you think better of me than you did, that is all very well; but let not kindness for a fellow veteran soften you. —'Ware, Mr. Medley! For I might have turned the talk to the War for that very purpose, might I not? So take a moment, Sir, before I speak of business. Stiffen your spine, which has relaxed there in your seat, and jut your chin at me as before. I will speak the freer for it."

This was indeed the oddest fellow that ever I met. I knew not—nor know at this moment—whether to admire his candour or to call it subtle artifice meant to disarm me.

Either Will is right as to the fellow's slyness or he is wrong, all wrong, in his judgment, and mistakes the man's ingenuousness for policy.

"Have no fear, Mr. Gault," says I. "My plans are, to marry and buy me two hundred acres or so of good farmland; retire from conjuring and grow old in peace and security with my children about me. Judge, then, whether I am likely to risk my savings—hardly won, Sir, hardly won—on any chancy venture."

"But you are just the man I want," he cries with enthusiasm. "A hard head and a strong sense of the value of money. Your hanging back, Sir, recommends you highly. I am not myself a good man of business—I own it to you, freely. Long ago the shop would have failed up were it not for my wife. Mrs. Gault, Sir—she knows more than most men about the hardware of a ship—no man can beat her down. E'en now, with business in the port so slow, she gets our living from it. She has her heart in the business, that's where it is; whereas I have no heart for't and never have. 'Twas my father's and came down to me; but from boyhood I showed myself a sorry failure in that line. *Dreams and contraptions, dreams and contraptions* are my meat and drink."

"And what new inventions have you contrived?" I asked him.

He shook his head in sorrow. "I could show you many a fine thing on paper," says he. "A submarine ship of better design than Mr. Bushnell's *Turtle;* mine would not have failed to blow up the British *Wasp* there in New York harbor. I have built a small model that walks the bottom of a tub as pretty as may be, but to make one the size to carry a man is beyond my purse. I have written to Secretary Knox about my design—but as yet have had no answer. Then there is my Compass Impervious, enclosed so as to be free of all attractions to incidental iron without the case. My tinderbox, my—"

"—And you wish to sponsor a licensed lottery to put these projects in motion," I said at a venture.

"No, Sir, not a lottery," says he. The enthusiastical light rekindled in his eye, and he grew much agitated in his manner. "Something altogether novel in this part of the country, yet a proven crowd-pleaser. A feat that will at once sell tickets and advance scientific and philosophical knowledge in America—perhaps pioneer the future transportation of this country, open the wilderness, extend the frontier, and make her invincible in war, even against the armed might of England or France."

"Lord, lord," I cried. "And what is this paragon of devices?"

Thrusting his coattails to the sides, he shifted his seat toward me.

"A *balloon,*" he whispers, all in a tremble of eagerness. "A balloon ascension, the first in New England; a balloon of the Gault design, one that can be navigated into the wind. 'Twill be a prodigy, Sir, a prodigy. You have read of the ascension, January last, at which General Washington attended?" He waited not for a reply. "'Twas an amazing success. And this, Sir, was accomplished by a Frenchman! The French are all very well in their way; but I count it a thing almost shameful that we allowed the first aerial ascent in America to be captained by any but a citizen of our Republic. And done for the President, too! But that cannot be mended now—we must see to it, we do not abandon the skies to them altogether. —I have a design, Mr. Medley, of which I hope—the first navigated aerial flight, and it can be ours, Sir!"

The man spoke with such passion that his voice gradually rose to a near roar. Beads of sweat stood upon his face. I confess I grew alarmed for his reason.

"Mr. Gault, Mr. Gault," I cried, "pray compose yourself, Sir. You need not make all Boston to know your plans."

To this note of caution he responded with a suspicious glance about the room.

"You are right, Sir," he whispered. Leaning back in his seat, he produced a large handkerchief from his pocket and slowly mopped his brow. "I grow too warm," he says then. "My apologies. The subject is one that never fails to fire me with scientific and patriotic fervor. But mum's the word. You are i' the right of it—the greatest circumspection is called for, or some other may anticipate us."

"Gently, Mr. Gault," says I. "You go too fast, with your plurals. 'Tis not *us*, nor is it like to be." Yet, I confess, the novelty of the scheme tickled my curiosity. I have, of course, read of such ascensions, but I know little of balloons or the principles of their operation. Gault's concept of a balloon capable of sailing into the wind seems to me against every law of nature; the more I think on it now in sober reflection, the more I fear the man may be naught but a half-mad enthusiastical quack. Yet he held me with his talk. Indeed, he seems knowledgeable in the ways of such contrivances. If such a flight could safely be made, there is no doubt it would draw vast crowds.

Gault was quick to point out the advantage of attaching a well-known name (mine) to the business; he was full of startling fancies, placing me in the suspended basket juggling colored balls as the balloon rose above the earth.

"Mr. Gault," I cried. "There may be one chance in a million that you might persuade me, against all judgment, to invest in your enterprise; but as to making the ascent—Sir, the sun and stars shall fall first. Say no more, Sir."

He looked crestfallen. "'Twould have made an almighty grand spectacle," he says.

"Ay. And so would the breaking of my neck," says I.

"Well, well," says he, "if you so mislike the scheme, we can let that pass. But a balloon ascent is safer, Sir, than a stagecoach."

I said I had read of flights abroad that had proved the reverse of safe for the unlucky aerialists.

"Bunglers!" he cried. "Indeed, there were but de Rogier and Romaine killed. Others had some trouble, but were not seriously injured. If the balloonist knows what he is about, there can be no danger."

"What thinks Mr. Poole of your scheme?" I asked.

"He inclines strongly toward it," says he quickly. "But the initial expenses would be considerable—considerable. Neither Mr. Poole nor I have the capital necessary for the enterprise."

"And so Mr. Medley is thought of," says I. "I'll wager, Mr. Gault, the suggestion that I participate in this mad idea was none of Will Poole's making."

"No more it was!" he cried with a strange kind of triumph in his voice. "But I knew you two were well acquainted; the thought of you came naturally to mind. 'Twould be a grand combining of novelty with the notable, Mr. Medley, to have you allied to the ascension."

"And these formidable expenses," says I. "You have made some estimate?"

"Ay, Sir, that have I—in a general way. First of all, there would be the balloon itself. We would need a very large quantity of light, strong silk. We would have to hire stitchers to sew it to my specifications, with special stitching, the strongest thread, and reinforcement at the seams. We would need much silk rope—light but strong—and a wicker basket specially woven to hold a man. A large fire basket of thin metal, and all these must be constructed to order. Then my sail and rudder—I would make those myself, but I needs must have lengths of bamboo for the stepped mast and the cross-spar. We would need three or four boys as helpers on the day of the ascent, but it may be we could find a number who would work for the honor of the thing. Then we would have the advertising, the printing of tickets, the renting of an enclosed field or tavern yard large enough for our balloon and the paying spectators—you would be more knowledgeable than I as to the costs of such matters. (I hope we can have invitations printed upon playing cards. I must own, I have always fancied the look of a playing-card invitation.) —As to the total cost, I think it could be safely done under four thousand dollars—but that is a rough estimate. The chief expense will be the balloon. I will not skimp on that, Sir. Nothing but the best for the balloon." He jumped suddenly to his feet. "Mr. Medley, give me no answer now," he cries. The agitation of his face and hands returned. "I will take none, Sir, I will take none. Do but sleep upon the matter, think on it for some days first. I will be content, Sir, to have you give it your judicious consideration."

"I cannot have you go off with false hopes," says I. "My answer is final. Although I own I have enjoyed this talk with you, Sir—I cannot invest in your balloon."

"Take a few days, wait but a few days," he cries, backing off from me in a kind of desperate dance. "I will not hear it from you today, Sir, upon my word; but I shall on Wednesday. If, on Wednesday next, you send me word your answer is No, you shall not see me again, I promise you. Wait till Wednesday then, I beg, and think, think, think on it meanwhile. Good day, Sir, good day." And he danced himself backwards out of the room.

The more I reflect upon this fellow—his ideas, his conduct, his character; the more am I at a loss what to make of him.

Indeed, I know not what to make of myself. Mr. Consider Gault has unearthed a vein unsuspected in my own nature. *Know Thyself,* says the sage; I thought I was, on the whole. pretty well acquainted with Josh Medley—we have long been intimates. What, then, am I to do with this new element, this reckless folly in my composition, apparently dormant for these thirty-seven years? I quite long to adventure into the unknown with Gault and his balloon.

Needless to say, common sense sternly puts down the mad itch whene'er it arises. I have not labored these many years to throw my savings into *hot air.* Still less to end my career by smashing all my bones.

Were I fool enough to make such an ascent, she would surely hear of it. Would she be at all stirred by the feat, I wonder? If one were to believe all her chatter, she is a lass of mettle, ready to admire, where the ~~heroic~~

Enough! Culpable, idiotic, *besotted!!!*

To bed, to bed.

February 4, 1794

The dream last night—bringing, as always, great peace. Yet 'twas a disturbment to me, minding me how I have neglected my search for the serpent knocker. The very extent of possibilities here dampens my ardor. In a country neighborhood there will not be found more than one or two large seats where such doors are likely. But about Boston, to the north, south, and west, dozens of elegant seats will be found. I must needs be an army of conjurors to view them all, exhausting my poor purse and all the local horses. Oh, my mother—to what teazing frets of mind you sentence your son by your silence.

But I shall not give up. A day's ride will profit my health—from want of exercise my digestion is grown sluggish. Tomorrow I shall try my luck out Dedham or Quincy way.

If my father still lives—should he know of my questing—he would be certain that only designing greed could spur such a dogged search. Could he credit a longing fierce as greed to repudiate him? My pride craves to be offered the world, that I might cast it back at his feet. No doubt I shall be made to account, one day, for the hours I squander in vain imaginings wherein I heap coals of fire upon my father's head. 'Tis far more likely, as common sense tells me, I would be denied admittance as beggar, imposter, &c., and sent off with a flea in my ear—an idea so galling as to make me shrink. Yet in spite of this, the worm continues to gnaw and I to search.

February 5, 1794

The crowds continue. Last night, the large parlor was crammed to the last inch, and a horde of would-be spectators surged back from the door, e'en to the street outside. I had to go amongst them, assuring them of a second performance, would they but wait in patience. This did the trick; I finished near exhausted at midnight, after Socrates refused altogether to perform on the second round.

The *take* was worth our labors—totalling the satisfactory sum of eighty-one dollars. (As usual, Socrates' reluctance before our second crowd won him more plaudits than all his juggling skill displayed for the first.) Our fame is being noised about throughout Boston and beyond. Many that clamored for admittance pleaded they had come from as far off as Framingham, Lincoln, and Sudbury. I bid fair to be a rich man; something I scarce dreamed of, when first I sought out Mr. Baylor in Alexandria eleven years agone. I shall soon be in a way to indulge in gold-serpent knockers for myself.

Yesterday's expedition through some pretty country toward the South Shore produced a clear head and hearty appetite. I saw many a handsome house, e'en one knocker of silver in the likeness of a fox's head—but came no nearer to my goal. What is maddening to my mind—at any mile I might be within holloaing distance of the very place and yet ride past all unknowing. I used once to inquire for the serpent knocker of farmers in the fields I passed and of wayfarers upon the road—doubtless acquiring in the way the name of eccentricity astride its hobbyhorse—but folk are singularly unobserving of door knockers. Mostly I have given o'er putting the question. It got me no forwarder, and left behind me a trail of comment I was loath to set astir.

Despite my failure, the day was a pleasure to me; the air brisk and keen from the northwest, the skies full of great overblown clouds (like balloons, indeed) that made an endless shift of sun and shadow. There was to be seen so much brightness and ripple I could almost believe, despite the calendar, I rode along the marge of spring. My heart felt light as a lad's. Indeed, I cared little for my purpose, but moved in a blessed tranquility of soul. Under some benign influence of Heaven's fair earth, for the first time in my life I was able to breathe a heartfelt prayer for my unknown father; to feel forgiveness in my thoughts of him. I was able to bless that young beauty of Portsmouth, without the anguished craving to possess her.

Such moments are vouchsafed a man all too rarely; a spur

and reminder of the detachment we are told to strive for, a heart free of, and rejoicing in, the things of this earth. 'Tis already passed from me; but I must be grateful for such a gift, be it but for an hour's space.

February 7, 1794

A letter come from Will at Falmouth. So he is again off on his law circuit. He writes, says he, to tell me how famous I am grown. Where'er he goes, he hears talk of Medley the Conjuror. (That this is a friendly exaggeration I be certain; but some stir must there be, for Will so to puff it to me. To have made at last a name—most gratifying indeed.)

Whilst in Portsmouth (the letter goes on) I tried to amend my former failure as a gossip. Knowing your concerns, I became the most sociable creature going, and fell into talk with all and sundry. You would have *bravoed* to see me. I was the rattle of the place.

—Sweet, quiet Will, a *rattle!*

So I have learned somewhat. Alas, you read too well the character of a certain Mr. E—. I own, I thought 'twas jealousy made you severe upon him. But you are proven a true judge of human folly. I heard the fellow's debts proved too much for his wife's fortune. Indeed, he has run off to Barbados to escape his creditors; in such haste, as the tale goes, his wife scarce knew him gone. Now he writes demanding that she join him in exile. They say she is in train to go to him, like a dutiful wife, and puts a brave face upon it—but all declare it a sad case for a young bride, as indeed I think it.

I fear I may cause you some distress of mind by telling you of this. 'Tis my hope that the news may prove the lancet that eases the pain. You must begin to look about for another, and without delay, for your peace of mind. —Little Hetty has declared she herself means to marry you, but since the match would mean for you ten more years of bacheloring it, I fear it will not answer. She is most decided, and says she will have no other. "For," she declares, "he is a lovely man. He can dance with his nose on fire." 'Twill be a sad day at our house when you do take a wife.

So, so. I have no heart to write more. To bed.

February 15, 1794

Man is a hapless creature, after all, upon this earth; all his vaunted powers as nothing in the face of Loss. This have I tried and proven more than once.

This day I was met in the Lane by a small lass in a sore way of crying; who called out my name and seized my coat in her little hand. She had hung about the door waiting for me; and, *O, Sir, look! Could I not make it to be alive again?* Wrapped tenderly within her apron was a dead canary.

I was stricken by her simplicity. Having marvelled at such wonders as her childish eyes found in my sleight-of-hand, she thought on me as a kind of miracle worker who could, an' he would, make all well again. There was in her utter trust an innocent blasphemy that made me shudder.

Most tenderly, I spoke to her; explaining how far my poor gifts at conjuring fell short of what she asked.

My words brought forth a fresh burst of tears. *Then my bird's dead! Charlie's dead!* My heart welled with pity. How can one speak to Six Years of the bending of man's stubborn will to the Divine purpose? All I could find to do was to palm a coin, fumble in her hair with a "What have we here?" and proffer the coin to purchase another bird.

Child-like, she made pause at the bright money. But then she shook her head mournfully. She wanted no other bird

—she wanted only Charlie. Off she went a-weeping, the dead bird cradled in her apron.

Poor little maid! Perhaps till this day her heart has known naught but joys. *My bird is dead.* Be it youthful dreams, or first love; be it the sense of infinite possibility contained in one land, one idea; we all, soon or late, must utter that same cry.

February 24, 1794

Have a mind to add engraving to my broadsides, as a touch of elegance. I wonder what the cost of such may be. Last night I attended a public performance of certain tragic scenes from Shakespeare's plays, performed as *moral dialogues* by a company of actors from Newport. I found them affecting, particularly the sad fate of Desdemona, who falls victim to the base passion of jealousy in the breast of her husband Othello.

But to my point. I was mightily struck by their bills posted outside the hall; engraved illustrations, done, as I thought, with great spirit. Indeed, the reality onstage fell considerably short of the playbills' promise. The passers-by avidly examined these lively scenes, convincing me they were a whet to ticket-buying. If the cost be not too high, I am of a mind to try them. I must consider what designs would best represent *A Medley To Please.*

February 26, 1794

My man for engraving would seem to be one Josiah Moulton, who keeps a shop by the Long Wharf. He will, I am told, come less dear than any other. I shall walk to his place of business this afternoon, with some rough sketches I have made. No artist, I! He will doubtless laugh at my efforts. But if he likes not my conceptions, I shall present him with a ticket to tomorrow's performance, that he may be inspired with his own.

And I had best take Socrates with me. No man would believe such a dog shape as I sketched exists, unless the beast confirm it in the flesh.

February 28, 1794

Too agitated, last night, to write or sleep.

The knocker, the gold, the green-eyed serpent knocker, is found. Found in the dusty back room of an engraver's shop. O mysterious Providence! Had I not gone to the moral dialogues—had I not been struck by that company's broadsides—had I not been directed to J. Moulton's—had I not found him out and been asked to wait, as he was expected—had I not wearied of sitting amid the clutter and smell of printer's ink and poked my nose into the back room of the place—. Beyond credence, the chain of coincidence that led me thither, to view in portrait the man who is like to prove my father.

'Twas a strange meeting. He on his painted canvas, behind the door with one ray of thin sunlight slanted 'twixt us, so that I viewed him first through a drifting haze of dust motes. All about, hanging, standing, or stacked in piles, were other portraits in oils—like a family gathering, men and women alike with wasp waists and long noses.

I had not known Mr. Moulton to be a painter; nor could I deem him a success at this second calling. Such a crowd of worthies, rejected for honorable prominence over the subjects' mantels and stuffed into a storeroom, pointed to a multitude of dissatisfied customers.

I was more amused than interested. Indeed, I gave the

painting behind the door but a glance. It showed me a man (long-nosed and wasp-waisted) in a red coat, a profusion of laces, and a feathertop wig. Behind him a painted window framed a square mansion off amid stiff trees. The whole betrayed the journeyman engraver's hand. The pupil of the man's eye and the carving of the mansion's portico were equally prominent. I was turning away when my eye was caught by the door of the house and its knocker.

The indescribable rush of sensations I felt made me tremble—to breathe suddenly like a man running. I staggered back, then crouched to view the knocker; scarce able to credit mine own eyes. But there was no mistake. Golden, ornately twisted—complete e'en to the minute speck of emerald paint marking the serpent's eye. I lifted the unframed canvas and carried it to the window for a better look.

The house spoke not to me; I had no memory of it. With a painful, ravening curiosity I turned my attention to the subject in the foreground. He stood with one hand resting on the hilt of a ceremonial sword, two small, keen, blue eyes looking a challenge. What might be the connection 'twixt him and the house beyond his drawing-room window, I could not begin to guess. He might be my father; he might be some complete stranger.

I sought in his features some resemblance to my own. The eyes were not like; but not so unlike, either, in set and shape. His nose was the same nose found in every portrait in the place; clearly Mr. Moulton could paint no other. The mouth was well shapen, but thin; unlike mine, which is something rounded and full in the lower lip. As for his figure—not even when eighteen could I boast such a trim, small middle. Another of the artist's standard niceties, that was plain, and more suited to his female subjects than to the male.

At length, and reluctantly, I returned the painting to its corner and went to sit again on the bench in the main shop, where Socrates lay curled beneath. But I had fallen into such a flurry of spirits I could not remain still. 'Twas not warm in that place; yet did I feel I must stifle without more air. I jumped up, Socrates following, and went outside.

There upon the wharf I furiously paced; before me, the cold harbor and masts of vessels black on the sky. Socrates sniffed amongst the hogsheads and found a fishhead for rubbing in. (I paid him no mind, so tonight have had to wash him under the pump.) At last returns the engraver Mr. Moulton; a squat, swarthy man, spectacles astride his nose, and with his own grizzled hair in a bagged queue.

I watched to see would he prove my man. When he turned into the shop, with a glance at me, I followed hard upon, introduced myself, and produced my sketches.

He listened to my explanation, his eye upon the sketches; and when I had finished, "Sir," says he, "Mr. Medley—these be but pen scratchings. What can I make of them? Nothing, Sir—Though the dog is shaped, for a fact, like to a canoe, you have that done rightly."

I then produced a ticket to the *Medley*, but to my surprise he shook his head.

"Can't be done," says he firmly. "I go nowhere out upon the town without Mrs. Moulton."

Reluctantly, I added a ticket for his lady. But still he appeared dissatisfied.

"Can't be done, Sir," he repeated. "Though it be in the way of business. What sort of father would I be, say you, and Mrs. Moulton what sort of mother, to go gallivanting off to a magic show and leave six children to pine at home? For the eldest is but nine."

Refusing to take this hint after further tickets, I inquired, did he not have some neighbor to look after their wants for one evening?

"Nay, Sir," says he, "I meant not I should leave them alone. Their grandmother—my wife's mother—resides with us. But when they hear that a magic show's afoot—"

"Need they be told?" I asked him.

He drew himself up stiffly. "Yes, Sir! If asked—and be assured, they will ask and ask—I will give my children an honest answer. 'Twill set off a merry noise in the house, to be sure—they will all cry to go. It does seem an unnatural thing for parents to go out to an entertainment and the children to bide at home. They get little enough of such pleasure, Mr. Medley, with business the way it is. 'Tis all I can do to fill their mouths, without treating them to magic shows."

I felt disgust at this shameless beggary; but in my hurry to get on to the portrait I would not haggle with the wretch.

"Here are six half-price tickets," says I, pulling them from my pocket. "Here is also a ticket for your worthy mother-in-law, whom I'm certain you cannot allow to stay alone at home. —Now, Sir, to another matter—" and again I found my breathing short and labored— "I have taken a fancy to one of your portraits. The red-coated gentleman behind the door yonder. What is its price?"

"Mr. Medley, those paintings are not meant for public sale," says he. "As you observed, they are not framed for display. I keep them only as a reminder of my youth, Sir—an itinerant artist was I then, roaming from farm to farm all over these New England States—colonies, then, Sir, only colonies. Six years I spent painting our rural squires and their ladies, before I retired here and set up as printer and engraver. I am a fair engraver; but I never was much of a hand at portraiture, to be frank."

"Ah," I incautiously observed, "you had trouble with noses."

"No, Sir!" cries he; in surprise and some displeasure. "Noses were never a problem. Why, I could slap on a nose as quick as winking. Hands came hard to me; and ears. I cannot tell you why. —But my rejected works were few. I would paint fifteen or twenty portraits a week, and those you see in back yonder are all I did not sell, in six years' journeying. I have no thought of selling them."

"Well," says I, "it matters little. 'Twas but a whim that made me fancy it. The gentleman has the look of a—an uncle of mine. Who is he?"

"That, Sir," he cries, "is Sir William Buckland—King's Collector before the war. A very pretty gentleman, as you can see. 'Tis a good likeness, one of my best, indeed; but, Sir, he would have none of it. 'Twas but to please his wife that he sat at all. I thought to delight him with the view of his own house through the window—'tis exactly like, as even he had to own. But still he would grumble. He complained 'twas not in nature for a man to see his house out through the window of that same house."

"No more it is," says I, in a voice strange to me. He was too full of his grievance to mark my agitation.

"Not possible, I own it," he says quickly. "But a pretty conceit of my own, I thought, so handily to represent the man with the mansion, a monument to his substance in the social community."

"—It was his country seat?" says I. "Pray, where located? I think I may have passed it in my travels."

But I had been too eager. The man's face changed, his eye flashed an inquisitive gleam. "You are keen, Sir, for this picture," says he, without replying to my query. "Doubtless you have private reasons for your interest. Indeed, if it so resembles your uncle you shall have it. I will sell it to you (and a frame into the bargain). The price we will not haggle over. 'Tis thirty-five dollars, and the frame but three dollars more."

The grasping affrontery! Not content with wheedling eight extra tickets from me, he would fleece me further for a daub we both knew to be worth no more than a few dollars.

I expressed my opinion of his great bargain by screwing my face into a whistle. "That is too steep for my purse," says I. "You put considerable value, Sir, on a portrait rejected by the subject himself."

At this he took a high tone. "Did I ask you to buy it, Sir?" cries he. "I thought but to oblige one with whom I am to be in a way of business. You may please yourself, buy or not; but I hold to my price."

"I cannot afford it," says I. "Sir William must bide. — Where was't you said the house stood?"

"I did not say," he muttered defiantly. "I do not recall. This was a sitting that took place over twenty-five years agone, Sir." He eyed me with a sharp malice of curiosity. "—'Tis an odd thing, too, that *your* uncle should so resemble Sir William," he adds with an evil smile.

At this, I lost my temper more thoroughly than I have fall'n to for many a month. I scolded, fumed, and roared till Mr. Moulton shrank back from me and turned pale. In the midst of my raging, in bustles the lady of the house all in amaze—tall, dark, rather a handsome woman but for a chin chopped off something sudden. At sight of her, my anger cooled. I cut off my words and bowed, abashed.

She looked from me to her husband and back again to me. "Is aught amiss, Mr. Moulton?" she cries.

"—Madam," says I. "I have stopped in to engage your husband's services and to present a set of complimentary tickets to my performance at the *Grapes.* I am Mr. Medley the conjuror—"

Here Moulton broke in. "Take your pasteboards," he cries. "We want none of them, nor of you, Sir. I do no business with one who abuses me as you have. You have an ungovernable temper—"

He was in his turn interrupted by Mrs. Moulton's smartly snatching the tickets from his hand. As he gaped at her, she bestowed them in her apron and turned smoothly to me.

"We are heartily obliged, Mr. Medley," says she. "—Don't you be a fool, Mr. M. —Greatly obliged for your thoughtful consideration. The children will be that pleased—*I said, don't you be a fool, Mr. M.!* —You will see how prettily they will thank you for the tickets. —Annie! Dick! Jethro! . . . Come and thank the kind gentleman. We be all a-going to his magic show, what say you to that?"

A horde of little boys and girls poured into the room and commenced a kind of solemn ceremony of joy, circling me and their mother and leaping straight-legged into the air, like jointless jumping-jacks. In the midst of all this to-do, Moulton and I met each other's gaze sheepishly. The play was taken utterly out of our hands, and Mistress Moulton, with her small army, was in command.

"I'll bring my designs for your approval in a day or two," says he lamely.

"I am obliged to you," says I. And so things stand, for the present.

I sadly bungled my dealings with the engraver; but having found out so much it should not be hard to learn Sir William's present whereabouts—be he in America, in England, or in the grave.

But here is a thing passing strange. With an end in sight to the mystery that has tormented me since childhood; now that my dogged search is at last to be rewarded—instead of triumph, eagerness, even the old anger which so spurred me on—I am conscious of melancholy; of a strong misliking to proceeding further. O, Man, strange are thy contradictions.

Socrates, too, is melancholy. No doubt he misses the rich, fat odor of rotten fish that I have scrubbed from his freckled hair. Fluffed to a caterpillar's fuzziness, he seeks to wear off his bath by grinding himself headfirst along the carpet.

March 4, 1794

The Moultons in attendance this night, complete with mother-in-law and all the children. The latter twice performed their jumping-bean dance—the solemnest form of childish glee that ever I saw. I would have favored the little ones with some particular attentions—have them choose a card, &c.—but that I feared their father would promptly demand salaries for all of them.

He is come today with his designs. I selected one that shows me dancing, juggling, and breathing fire all in one moment; whilst Socrates (rather over-sized and wolf-like) assists. ('Tis to be regarded as a neat compendium of my talents, rather than a literal representation—I would be hard put to manage all that at once.)

Two other designs I rejected as smacking of the supernatural. Ever have I striven to avoid the least suggestion of necromancy, insisting that I am a demonstrator of "natural" magic, of scientific phenomena; not a sorcerer. 'Tis an approach calculated to appease those in authority, ecclesiastical, &c., who might look askance upon entertainments with too much of the Devil in 'em. Indeed, the idea raises my own hackles. As I strive to be a Christian, I eschew any pretence to powers mere man can ne'er possess, unless by the connivance of Beelzebub.

March 5, 1794

I must get a hold on myself. The unsettling effect of my late discovery bore bitter fruits for me, last night. Not only did I miss two plates in my juggling turn, but in attempting to cover my mistake I brought the whole airy structure crashing down. One plate on its way to the floor bounced off my head.

The laugh this mishap raised at my expense lost me my audience. Strive as I might, I could not recapture them, not even with the gems of *spontaneous* wit that I keep ready for such emergencies. My remarks fell as flat as the plates, and my face burned with a confusion I have scarce felt since my apprentice days with Mr. Baylor. It needs but a few such sorry performances to lose me all the good repute I have toiled for years to build. *Is this the Great Medley, this fumbling bungler*? The word will spread like the pox to ruin me.

I see my fault plain—too much excitement, heat of blood, and want of total concentration of my mental powers. To amend it may be no easy matter.

The Buckland place lies in Hopkinton. This have I learned through inquiries here in Boston; also, that Sir William still resides there!!! He did return to England at the commencement of the late hostilities; but his Hopkinton estate was spared confiscation because his American-born wife, her relatives, and a number of slaves remained in residence. Some years back he returned to this country, his lady being then in her last illness. Now he resides at the place in somewhat straitened circumstances.

Ignoble, my pleasure at finding him a King's man and Tory, that I may hold against him one grudge the more.

It must be on to Hopkinton, and that right soon; for my peace of mind and the mending of my juggling! So one point of my whole life draws nigh at last. But look you, Josh Medley, where be vanished all your old eagerness? Avaunt, all vapors, mopes and ditherings! By this day week I shall go, and an end to 't.

March 9, 1794

I lift my pen with a heart so full I scarce can find words for this entry.

But to tell all in order . . . Down to the wharf I went this morning, to Gault's ship chandlery. I thought it seemly to bring him my *No* in person. He took my answer well, though 'twas plain he had hoped on me to the end. E'en now he attempted to win me to second thoughts; he took out a sheaf of careful drawings, of balloon and gondola shapes all cross-hatched with lines, to show me. I had to put them away with a firm hand.

"I am exceeding sorry, Mr. Gault," says I. "'Tis a waste of your time."

"Ah, well, I feared it would be so," says he; putting the papers down with tenderness. "Had you shown interest, Mr. Medley, my first duty would be to tell you this: I now estimate the costs to be much greater than first I thought."

This, from a man in hopes of luring investors!

I left his shop with a regret that surprises me. Had I but three times my present savings, that aery globe of his would take shape to fly or to fail; but 'tis well I kept my head. I shall write to Will and admonish him to keep his.

There was a vessel in, unloading, and I strolled down to view her. The *Prudence B.* was emblazoned upon her bow. In the shadow of her bowsprit a-hang above the wharf, a handful of passengers were huddled upon trunks and boxes, awaiting a barrow man to take their gear to an inn.

What first drew my eye to her, I know not. Her face was hid beneath the hood of her black cloak where she sat upon a trunk. But something in the look of her made my blood to burn. I walked past the group as if idly strolling, and glanced aside. Our eyes met.

Then 'twas *Mr. Medley! Mistress Emery!* and she gave me her little gloved hand.

She looked thinner and paler than at Portsmouth. The fresh high color that drew my notice at the very first was absent, despite the raw airs from the sea. I thought it likely she was not recovered from motion sickness suffered on her voyage.

"Welcome—welcome home again to America," says I, at a loss like any schoolboy.

"Thank you, Sir," says she. "Thus far, I have met with poorer welcome than yours. The man with my other trunk was to set it down at some lodging close by and then come back. But he has been so long gone . . . !" She looked about her in a lost way. "Can rooms be so scarce in Boston? —I was about to seek the aid of Captain Doehr," she adds, nodding up at the ship. "But that I cannot just see how to come at him."

"If I can do any service," I began, and then—"Does not Mr. Emery travel with you? I must offer belated felicitations upon your marriage."

She gave me a look as if I had threatened her, frightened; incredulous.

"My husband is dead these five weeks," says she in a quavering voice. "He died at Bridgetown, of a fever." Too late to mend my blunder, I noted the black of her gown beneath her cloak.

I stammered some condolence, scarce coherent as I fear, whilst she looked out at the harbor and bit her lip. Confusion overwhelmed me at my own reaction—e'en now I blush to recall it. Just at the first, the very first, 'twas a surge of joy at finding I might hope again toward her. May the just Judge pardon my selfishness nor hold me accountable for that one moment's springing of instinctive gladness. Indeed, indeed I rejoice not at the fate of the poor young man her husband; still less at the sorrows of one whom I yearn to shield from every trouble. My heart aches for her.

She had nursed him, she said, then fallen gravely ill of the same malady (a putrid fever); recovering only just in time to attend him to his grave.

"They were kind to me at Bridgetown," says she. "Indeed, I made fast friends there—they wished me to remain with them." She looked about her. "But I had seen there happiness too brief and sorrow too great. I yearned for America; for home and my aunt. Even the raw March airs, Mr. Medley, are as welcome to me as old friends."

"But turn chill upon you, as old friends should never do," says I, seeing her shiver. "You, who have had your blood attuned to a tropic climate! New recovered from illness! We must get you within doors at once. You must have tea, hot, weak tea, and a cordial without delay. —

Confound the unconscionable villain of a barrow rogue who abandoned you here to freeze! He shall have plain words with his fee!" Excusing myself, I ran back to the chandlery and in no time had Gault's eldest, a lad of thirteen, set upon the precious trunk, against the barrow man's return. He was to direct the fellow to the *Grapes* with it. "And he is to fetch back her other luggage after," I said. "He shall be paid, tell him, when all this is done, and done with dispatch. We have had enough of his oozing about town at a snail's speed. As for his failing to get the lady at once into shelter, he shall hear from me on that score as well."

I turned to her. "The *Lamb* is nearer," says I, "but much frequented by mechanics of the North End and so something noisy. Can you bear to walk a few streets over to my tavern? 'Tis uphill; but the wind will be at your back."

"I shall relish a walk, Mr. Medley," says she. "How very kind you are!"

"You once told me with a look, that I might be your friend," says I. "I have not forgot that favor, and will hold you to it."

"Have a care!" she cries with a haggard laugh. "I am so tired out, so forlorn, I am like to take you very much at your word. —I used to think Aunt too fussy, too worrying. I often longed to be free of her constant concern, though I knew it stemmed from love. Now I am in a mood to be dosed, cossetted, O, all hemmed about with care and fussing. You may play aunt and uncle and father to me, Mr. Medley, and welcome."

Was ever such a lass? I am scarce eager for any of the roles assigned me. Was she subtly putting me in my place?

Upon reflection, I think not. Such devices are foreign to her nature. And she took my arm most gratefully. We left

Gault's boy atop her trunk like a half-grown chick on its coop.

I told her Mistress Lobdell of the *Grapes* was a good, genteel sort of person. "She will, if I know her, make free to scold you for not taking proper care of yourself. She will lay down a strict regimen and insist you abide by it. But she will prove a nurse both wise and kind. And Lobdell's table is rightly famous."

"I will stay but tonight," she says. "If a place may be had on the Portsmouth coach, I will start tomorrow for home. —A sorry return," she added, with something like a dry sob. Despite her brave words, she looked unfit to travel farther, and so I told her.

"You must rest," says I. "You can write to your aunt. If she come not herself she will find one who will. Or if she will commission me to see you safe to Portsmouth, I will undertake the charge with pleasure—when you are fit to travel."

Nothing more she said for some little way. Then, with studied cheerfulness, she asked me how Socrates did.

I assured her he was flourishing and in mighty good conceit with himself. And so we talked of trifles until the *Grapes* was reached, whereupon I put her into the capable hands of Mistress Lobdell. I said she should have a chamber to herself because of her weakened condition and her sore need of rest. Mistress Lobdell agreed.

"Poor lass! She shall have my daughter's own bed," says she, "and Sally shall bed with me." She hustled Mistress Emery upstairs, with a promise (or command) of tea to be drunk; and I sat down in the tap room to await the tardy barrow man.

When he came, off I sent him again to fetch the luggage (left by him at the *Lamb*) but was so bemused by what had befallen I forgot to lecture him. 'Twas with a most chastened spirit that I pondered the mutability of human affairs.

What straits Mistress Emery may now be in, by reason of her husband's debts! But to ask would be an impropriety. So here I sit writing and stewing in the worst disturbment of spirits imaginable. Heaven only knows what my performance tonight is like to be. —I should perhaps plead an indisposition and let Socrates go on alone. (The rascal is near independent enough to manage it.) His master is quite unmanned by joy, love, compassion competing all within his breast.

March 10, 1794

It seems I have turned all the kitchen here into a hostile fortress arrayed against me. My hostess informs me in no uncertain terms, that I am not to trespass there again—all because I endeavored to instruct the lady and her helpers in the proper way to nourish one in Mistress Emery's precarious state of health. I even offered to oversee the nice preparation of two or three specifics of my aunt's, of virtue well proven by me in my youth; volunteering to fetch from Faneuil Market the requisite ingredients, herbal &c., myself. But alas, for good will! All I have accomplished is to give the ladies a distaste for seeing so much as my face in the sacred frame of the kitchen doorway. I was told to stop away; that they knew their business; they needed no fussing, bullying or carping in order to do their duty by their guests, &c., &c., &c.

Well, well. It seems I have offended where I meant but to help. I retreated indeed to the tap-room, but found disapproval e'en there. For falling (in my agitation of mind) into an absent way of juggling, I commenced passing four of Mistress Lobdell's china cups under and over my crossed legs, whilst watching the fire. She spied me through the door, and like a veritable tigress snatched them from me; with a grim quirk at the corners of her mouth.

"Mr. Medley!" she cries. "You would drive a saint distracted. —The child is looked after. She will soon mend. As for you, I wish with all my heart you would take your dog to walk or go to bed!"

Rather, I hung about in vain hopes Mistress Emery might venture downstairs. She stays in her chamber and is, I hear, much exhausted.

I hung about Socrates' neck a short note conveying my good wishes for her recovery; then slipped the maid Agnes a coin to take him into Mistress Emery's room. He was gone for fifteen minutes; and the maid assures me the patient smiled at his entrance and again upon reading my note. News that will make Master Socrates a busy courier henceforth.

One thing is certain. Till Mistress Emery is safe and well at home with her aunt, there can be no thought of my leaving here. That business at Hopkinton must be shoveled under, so to speak, by dearer concerns.

March 11, 1794

Mistress Atwell is to come to Boston.

She came downstairs today for the first time (Mistress Emery, I mean) and breakfasted with the family. She thanks me for my attentions and says she does better; but to me she looks not so. The tired ghost of her former spirits shows itself at rare intervals, faint and wistful; a sight to break the heart of any that knew her five months ago. She creeps from table to chair with cheerless mien and climbs the stair as it were a high mountain. Her sorrow, so fresh and sore, impedes her recovery, as I think. Indeed, as she sat by the parlor fire (about three o'clock) I surprised the tears dropping through the fingers that hid her face.

I asked, might I do aught for her; whereupon she blew her nose with more vigor than elegance.

"No, I thank you," says she. "I am not fit yet for company, Mr. Medley. If I speak frankly, it is with one's friends one can make so free. I hope I shall not offend if I say I would liefer be alone. As yet I cannot much converse or feign cheerfulness where I feel it not." She smiled sadly. "It distresses me to see you standing about, looking helpless and hangdog for my sake. I assure you, I shall turn to you at once in any need. Meanwhile, 'twould please me better not to see you tied to this parlor."

I bowed (with, I fear, something of stiffness) and was for departing when a thought struck me. I turned.

"Would you have Socrates the Philosopher to keep you company?" I asked. "Better than his master he can make himself agreeable to ladies. I am used to being solitary; yet oft I find the rogue's presence a positive comfort."

With a look of compunction she thanked me. But the ungallant Socrates did not mean to be left. Thinking me about to go a-walking, he was at the door before me. Instead of departing with dignity, I must wriggle like an eel through to the hall, with the door nearly to. He got his snout into the crack, was caught in the pinch, and yelped.

"O, poor Socrates!" Mistress Emery cries, running to his rescue. Seizing the uncivil wretch by the collar, I dragged him, with considerable Confounding, back to her feet; and bade her hold him till I made good my escape.

Was ever a dog so indifferent to his good fortune? The

last I saw, she was upon her knees on the sanded floor, her arms about his neck (and laughing!) whilst he—O! the wretch, the idiot—scrambled still to get free.

March 14, 1794

I have plunged in over my head. I fear I have marred all by too much impetuosity. God grant I may be wrong!

'Twas Mistress Lobdell set me off. After breakfast she took me aside and told me she thought Mistress Emery penniless.

"I have not mentioned money in her hearing," says she. "The poor thing herself brought up the matter—she showed such confusion, Mr. Medley! She begged me not to think ill of her; that her aunt when she came would settle her account, and until that time she must crave my indulgence. —Indeed, Sir, I think she denies herself many a small comfort here. When last I asked if she would take some tea, she would not; yet I thought she looked longingly the while."

This conversation sent me blundering off after Mistress Emery. I should have thought twice. Since I am not kin to her and but of short acquaintance, we two are delicately situated. But my mind had room for no thought but that she should, she must, have her tea.

I found her in the parlor, and with something of abruptness I began to chide her for foregoing what would help to make her well. "You need deprive yourself of nothing here," says I. "Mistress Lobdell feels great good will toward you and is in no fear for her money. She will trust till your aunt arrives; indeed, she knows me only too happy to make good on any debts you may incur under her roof."

'Twas the first time I have seen her angry. Her eyes

brightened with resentment and something of her old high color returned to her face. "Indeed, Sir!" she cries. "I cannot think what I have done that gives you to think you may presume so far. You overstep all bounds, Sir—offering to pay my bill! My bill here, my money or lack of it—the tea I choose not to drink—are none of your concerns. You take advantage of friendship, to speak so—mean advantage of my solitary condition. I had thought you a better friend. I had thought Mistress Lobdell more worthy of confidence. If I had known she was such a gossip—that she would babble to the world what was spoken for her ear alone—I should never have—O dear Heaven—!" She covered her face with her hands and burst out a-weeping. "O why does not my aunt come!" she cries.

I stood listening to her with my jaw fallen; feeling my face turn from red to pale and back again to red. Such agitation, such confusion of mind, I have ne'er felt in my life. Self-doubt, mingled with hurt and anger at her taking so high an offer of good intent; self-reproach at having so distressed her, and my pride firing up at the rebuff. (My sole comfort is there was no one about to overhear us.)

I had to take two turns across the room and back before I could speak. "Madame," says I then, "with you I seem fated to get upon the wrong foot. If I have overstepped, through my concern for your welfare, I ask your pardon. Since you misdoubt of my respect—since you find my friendship wanting—the best proof I can make of them now is to trouble you no more. My good offices serve but to set your teeth on edge. —What *friendship* may mean to young ladies, I confess myself ignorant. I would never accuse a friend, on such grounds, of *meanness.* But I am a poor, ignorant conjuror—a mulatto bastard. Such refinements are beyond me."

I started out of the room, but turned again at the door. Still she wept, not looking at me.

"I would pack and leave this place," says I, "that you might be oppressed no longer by the presence of such a *mean hangdog* fellow. But I am engaged to play here for three nights more. Though you must endure my being in the house, rest assured, I shall not force my presence upon you. Doubtless we can avoid meeting, but for meals, until your aunt is come."

All of this was spoken with overmuch bitterness. Calmer now, I deprecate the self-pity I displayed. But in excuse I spoke in great heat, sore and smarting from her harsh speech.

To avoid her, I needs must stay in my chamber or spend the daytime hours wandering about town. Socrates would like well to go a-walking, but I can take no pleasure in 't. Indeed, so fiery is my mood, I am moved to attempt for tonight a novelty I have not used for over a year—namely, The Man Salamander, the art of fire-eating. (The requisite alum and tow I have in my luggage.)

I must cease to brood. I must make allowance for the lady's feeble health and sickly state of mind. Though she does me great injustice—indeed, was ever a man so rated, so stuck all over like a porcupine with sharp words, and for what? Is't a crime to do a kindness? There is, I think, but little kindness in the lady and still less friendship.

And so I begin to rage all afresh. And is this, Josh Medley, your *great love*? O Lord, mend my pride, my unforgiving temper. I am stiff-necked, 'tis certain.

But she has treated me as badly as may be!

(Midnight, the start of) March 15, 1794

D—l take the burning tow and the black mood that led me to it! My mouth is so sore and blistered, I cannot eat. Yet it went well.

To show my fiery breath to best advantage, I extinguished all candles but one. My audience gave a kind of low moan, of awe and anticipation. I have oft noted the same: when the conjuror darkens the room, a new note is struck in the murmurs of those watching.

More important, the dim light masks much of what I must do by way of preparation, so that the illusion of suddenness and mystery be not lost. Working rapidly behind the door, I coated tongue and mouth with alum and powdered sugar, laying over that as thick a coating of soap as might be. In a dish I set afire a small ball of tow, and next coated the palms of my hands well with alum. My feet I had earlier prepared in the same manner; so all was now in readiness. The waiting in darkness had held the audience in suspense. Pulling off my boots, I strode back amongst them, barefoot.

Portly as I am, 'tis harder for me than for some to impress by appearance alone. Not to let them linger on a man of my figure walking barefoot (which might stir their risibilities to the ruin of my act) I moved at once to the fireplace, where the poker glowed red. Plucking it forth, I brandished it aloft not by the handle but by the end red-hot from the flames.

A gasp and moan rewarded me, and stifled shrieks from the ladies. Then came a sudden clap of applause like thunder. Pausing for them to savor the feat to the full, I next laid the poker down upon the hearthstone and with my bare feet danced a hornpipe upon it.

"I am like to most folk, in this—I prefer my food piping hot," says I then. Lifting the poker I licked the glowing tip with my tongue. Again a chorus of gasps, shrieks and moans. I smile, as one enraptured. "Delicious!" I exclaim. "It has a flavor most . . . piquant. It carries a tang, I promise you." A titter of nervous laughter answered me.

"But the shape of this poker mispleases me," I went on. "I have a great cart horse—a giant beast, indeed—in need of shoeing. Is there not a shoe for him here?" I seated myself, braced one bare foot against the glowing iron and, with a sudden thrust of my leg, bent it to a U-shape. More gasps.

I examine the bent iron critically. "Confound the thing, it is too small," says I. Straightening it quickly with my hands, I hurled it back into the fireplace with a crash. "My apologies, ladies and gentlemen," I say. "But mine is a fiery nature—most fiery, as you shall see." 'Twas time for the final wonder of the evening.

Quickly I stepped behind the door to my dish of tow, now burnt almost entire. Wrapping a layer of fresh tow about the first, I thrust the whole into my mouth and approached the audience, breathing sparks and flame from my mouth.

Brightly and eerily they glowed in the semi-darkness. Now the shrieks were many; I heard to my sorrow some child in the crowd commence to wail. About the open space I pranced, careful to breathe in only through my nose and feeling no great discomfort through my shield of alum and soap. As I neared the hearth once more, an angle of the hallway met my gaze. A few patrons unable to squeeze into the parlor were craning there. Behind them, in the shadow of the stairwell, stood a slender, black-gowned female form.

The sight came near being my ruin. Forgetting the perilous supper in my mouth, I caught my breath. Had I breathed in more deeply I should have seared my lungs and doubtless perished. As it was, small flames licked the back of my mouth and my throat, forcing me to give out a prodigious burst of fire to the tune of a howl of agony.

The crowd was startled, uncertain. Summoning all my fortitude I bowed, raising my arms to show all was achieved and the unearthly cry part of my climax. Then, I hastened from the applause to nurse my damaged mouth in privacy.

I shall have no sleep tonight. Nor may I take more than liquid nourishment for some days to come. My tongue is forever seeking out and nudging the pretty array of pesky little blisters—here is *disorder in the members* with a vengeance, I cannot force it to desist.

What, what am I to make of her coming to watch the Man Salamander? Scarce seemly for one so recently widowed to attend a public show; but, as earlier observed, she is a lass who will go her own way. Then it must have been her wish to see me perform. Why, forsooth? Curiosity alone? If so, I have paid dearly for't. (The skin of my mouth hangs in festoons, or so it feels to my exploring, aching tongue.) But I can scarce blame her for that fool's trick of taking in air through my mouth.

The receipts for tonight are my sole comfort. One hundred eighteen dollars!!! Since I must lie the whole night awake, I shall strive to meditate upon this sum; to make easier, by somewhat, the long misery.

March 16, 1794

Mistress Emery's aunt is come. They depart for Portsmouth on Friday next. She has thanked me very civilly for my care for her niece.

I can speak but little, my mouth pains me so. When I assay a few words it is mumblingly and slow, like to a man with no teeth in his head. My engagement here must close two days sooner than planned.

Nor can I think of journeying to Hopkinton. I have no wish for a confrontation, needing an interpreter to translate my mumblings. So here I stop in my chamber; subsisting upon honey and bread milk-sopped. God grant this affliction mend soon, or I shall run mad.

March 21, 1794

At breakfast comes Mistress Emery up to me and prettily offers her condolences upon my injured mouth. 'Twas the first time I assayed solid food in public—the smell of ham and eggs, creamed salt fish and biscuit, was too much for me to bear. But I made painful work of 't. The company feigned to notice naught; and talked assiduously to one another whene'er I made one of my more extraordinary faces.

Breakfast done, I was in retreat when I heard the rustle of skirt, and she caught up with me upon the stair.

"Mr. Medley—" she says in a rush, "I must beg you to hear me for a moment, although I know you are in pain and not inclined to company. —Indeed," and she rolled her eyes, blushing, "I fear mine would be now the last society that you would choose."

I made a short sound that I left her to interpret as she would.

"I know you to be a proud man," says she, her eyes upon the stair. "I hope you can understand how it was my own pride in its hurt and shame made me speak harshly to my friend."

"Mistress Emery—" I began; so impetuously as to pain my mouth and bring the water to my eyes.

"I was barbarously harsh," says she, still looking at the stair. "And after such kindness as was shown me . . ." She looked straight into my eyes. "There is worse shame, I have learned, than dependence upon the loyalty of friends and the charity of strangers. Indeed, Mr. Medley, I can scarce look you in the face; but I would ask your pardon for my conduct."

As I started to speak, she lifted her hand to stop me and then held it out in a boyish gesture. "Do not trouble yourself to answer," says she. "If you will but have the generosity to take my hand on it, I shall know I am forgiven."

All my resentment melted in a moment. I took her hand with such fervor that she winced. With a laugh almost merry, she feigned to stagger down a step or two.

"That is forgiveness with something too much of vigor in it, Sir," she cries. "But indeed, indeed, I am grateful to you."

She slipped from me down the stair and into the small parlor to her aunt. I followed as if drawn by a string; bowing to the dame, who greeted me with more complaisance than ever she showed me in Portsmouth.

"So you are to depart this week Friday?" I said, lifting my coattails and taking great care with my tongue.

"Indeed, if my niece's affairs can be attended to by then," the old lady says. "We must see a lawyer here in Boston. —Do you know of a reputable lawyer, Mr. Medley, whose services come not too dear?"

I told her I had done no legal business in Boston.

"Aunt prefers not to parade my poverty in Portsmouth," says Mistress Emery. "The lawyers there are one and all friends or the fathers or brothers of friends. But I tell her there is no hiding the fact we are beggared."

"Are matters indeed so fallen for you?" says I.

Mistress Atwell's countenance seemed to shrink and tighten. "The death of my niece's husband, so sudden and untimely, left his affairs in disarray," says she.

"He left monstrous debts," says Mistress Emery. "—Nay, Aunt, Mr. Medley is my friend—to him I shall make no secret of my situation." She turned to me, her lower lip a-flutter in piteous fashion. "Poor fellow, he had been merry and heedless—he acquired them almost unawares. 'Twas a heavy burden on a young man of limited income; but he swore to me, many's the time, he would find the way to face down all his creditors at the last."

'Twas plain she put firm faith in those promises. May young Emery have received no less loving judgment on high!

"I am acquainted with but one lawyer, and that not in a business way," says I. "He is my friend. For diligence and honesty—ay, and discretion, Will Poole is staunch. But he is in Rowley, not Boston. If it is your wish I should write to him—"

"Is it your friend of the War, the old veteran you had reunion with at Portsmouth?" she cried.

I told her emphatically he was none so old. Will is two years younger than myself! Again I offered to inquire, could he come up to Boston.

Mistress Atwell seemed disinclined to wait so long. "We are at a disgraceful expense at this place," says she. "Indeed, there are many doors that would be open in Boston to welcome us; only then our affairs would be no more private."

But Mistress Emery wished me to write, and her wishes (as is their wont) prevailed. I went at once to the taproom desk and inscribed a line to Will; our host assuring me that he would himself put it into the hands of the post rider.

Thinking the ladies might have had their fill of my company for a while, I took Socrates a-walking along the docks. I thought to look again at the ship that had brought Mistress Emery from Barbados (and to picture her on board with her second husband, the renowned and esteemed and wealthy conjuror); but that vessel had departed for ports unknown. Failed in my fond conceit, I walked on, shoving Socrates ahead of me with the side of my foot. (He was nosing another dead fish with intense interest and making obeisances, the preliminary to rolling upon it.) As we approached Gault's ship chandlery, I was amazed to see emerge, like an echo to my wish, Will Poole himself.

Looking almost clerical in his sober black and white, he came down in haste when he espyed me and we clapped each other on the shoulder. I told him of my letter and explained the affair. Upon hearing of his prospective client he smiled; his eyes searching my face.

"So the lady is a widow; and so soon," says he. "Be you her suitor, Josh?"

"Nay, not now—if ever, I know not," says I. "I can be her friend. I trespass no farther into her grief, poor lass. Can you help her, Will?"

"I am due home the 26th," says he. "But I can send word business detains me until the 1st. Longer than that I cannot stay."

"Was it with Gault, the business that brought you down?" I asked, wagging my head toward the shop.

He took my arm. "Save your lecture," says he; looking, however, more than a little shamefaced. "I am into the balloon business, Josh, be it for a high flight or a smash.—He told me you had refused him."

"Ay, that did I," says I. "The man flies too high for me. I think him honest; but surely this scheme of his is too steep for your two purses together?"

"He is seeking other backers," Will says.

"Then may he find none!" says I. "Or you both may lose your shirts in this venture . . . I grant you, I should like to see the sight—a man, soaring higher than those gulls. 'Twould be a crowd-pleaser, if successful. But if 'tis too chancy a thing for me, I wonder at you, Will. You with your family—your way still to make."

"The law leads nowhere," says he. "In such straits, who would not risk the little he has on the chance of a windfall?" But he looked uneasy. Will is no gambler. He must be desperate indeed to throw his all into Gault's dreamery.

He stays with Gault; but came back with me to the inn, and is presently engaged with the ladies. (His modesty and transparent goodness won them at once; albeit they were something amazed by the apparent rapidity of his arrival from Rowley! He needs must have come by balloon, indeed.)

March 28, 1794

I write in haste, for the inn is full this night. I have acquired two bedmates (lawyers from Bedford come up for the Court Session) and they beg me to put out my candle.

I ride out to Hopkinton on Friday next. My mouth,

though tender still, is better. I must eat gently of the softer foods, but can speak freely.

Emery's affairs must be in a sorry tangle. The ladies have been closeted with Will for the better part of two days. He goes forth each morning early to consult the law books of a colleague for certain statutes. Then back and to it again with the ladies. I am but in the way now; and too long have I delayed the reckoning with my father. (???)

I have decided against the vanity of a handsome hired chaise to make the journey. I will, however, insist upon a fine horse, cost what it may. Further, I have bought new riding boots, which cost me as dear as a chaise. I am ashamed of those boots. They stand in the corner now, reproaching my conscience with their saucy, glossy smartness.

I shall make the journey a working one, with stops at Howe's in Sudbury and perhaps Buckminster's in Framingham. There will be little time to apprize the populace of their inestimable good fortune in having me amongst 'em; but keeping busy will be physic for my nerves. I am full of quivers and disturbments.

Will knows of my plans. I believe she knows naught, other than the fact of my departure. Doubtless they will be gone off to Portsmouth before Friday. When, if ever, I shall see her again is as God wills.

Will knows how I feel, but not all I feel. He tonight shook his head to me, over the lady's debts. " 'Tis great pity," says he. "Mistress Emery is poor. And, Josh, should she marry again, bringing such debts to her new husband, she will make him poor."

"No, Sir!" says I, and I was high with him. "She would make any man rich."

"Why, this is the impetuosity of youth," says he with a

troubled smile. "You were ever a headlong being, Josh. The lady is indeed lovely; but you must keep your head. Marriage can be an enterprise more perilous than sending a balloon aloft."

March 29, 1794

She came to me this day, looking tired and troubled.

"You leave us tomorrow," says she. "Mr. Poole has told us so."

"Since I can be of no more service to you," says I.

"Then we must bid you farewell," says she. "I had hoped I might ask you to take me up to view the town from Beacon Hill. My aunt cannot walk so far."

"I will take you today with pleasure," says I. "But will not that climb tire you?"

She said no, she was pining to walk out. "Mr. Poole is most kind, but never, never could I abide the law, were I a man. It makes my head to buzz."

"You were to go a-soldiering, as I recall," says I. "When would you like to walk?"

She appointed three o'clock, and we parted till that hour.

I donned my blue broadcloth coat and the plum-colored smallclothes of plush, which made me a fine dog indeed. 'Twas the first time I have had her upon my arm since meeting her upon the quay. The air and exercise brought a faint flush to her cheek.

"Mr. Poole let drop a word . . ." says she. "He told us naught indeed, but I guess at the purpose of your journey. Have you found out your father, Mr. Medley?"

"Indeed. I think I have," says I, and thereupon up and told her all the tale of the knocker and Sir William's portrait. She heard me with keen excitement in her look.

"So you ride out to face him down and throw his name and wealth in his teeth!" cries she. "It has a fine noble American air of independence, your plan."

I told her I could scarce throw in any man's teeth what had never been proffered to my hand. "That I fiercely long to parade my independence," says I, "and that of my mother, I do not deny. But a kind of distasting comes over me at moments. I fear it ill becomes a Christian to seek such wrathful satisfactions. What think you, Mistress Emery?"

She walked steadily on, her gaze upon the roadway. (Boston has few foot ways.) "I think you must go," she says at length. "You will ever regret it, else. But go not as into battle, Mr. Medley. Your father must be an old man. However much he has sinned against you, 'twould be meet to part in amity."

"Perhaps—if he will it so," says I doubtfully.

We climbed the wooden stairs that scale the lower slope of the hill. Then must we find footholes where others had mounted before us. I went before, giving her my hand at the steepest parts. Arrived at the top, we sat down upon one of the benches beneath the Bulfinch monument. I pointed out the sights: Dorchester Neck, the marshy flats of the back bay, and the North Meeting House of sacred fame to every citizen—but I fear she saw but little. Her eyes were screwed shut again, and she peered along my pointing arm as a man might squint down a gun barrel. She is still girl enough to cosset her vanity. Those spectacles, the existence of which I believe in as firmly as if they were perched upon her nose, remained invisible. She *oh*'d and *ah*'d indeed; but I might have pointed out the pieman's barrow below us in Spring Lane, calling it the Governor's coach, and she would have pronounced it handsome.

I indicated Charlestown Neck with its bloody hill across

the water. "You have, I know, heard much of that engagement," I said.

"Ah, yes!" she cries, eagerly, myopically gazing. "How our men were driven to retreat only when they had no more musket balls. Brave Prescott—poor, gallant Doctor Warren!"

"Ay," says I. "But another tale comes to my mind concerning that hill."

"What is it?" she cries.

"The account of one Captain Aaron Smith of Shrewsbury," I told her. "I made his acquaintance one night at the tavern, long after. He was at the redoubt in that battle. He took part in the final retreat. —Mark you, when first he told me this he was unaware I was not wholly a white man like himself. —He had sought refuge behind a fence—the fire so hot he scarce could get off a shot, the British advancing rapidly on three sides—when he spies a fellow-soldier lying with a bloody leg in the grass nigh him—Caesar Bason, one of a number of Negro fighters at the hill that day. He had taken a ball in the thigh. Smith was struggling to reload. 'Here, Captain, quick!' says Bason, 'Take this piece of mine and give me yours to load.' So they fought for some minutes, Bason to load and Smith to fire. But then comes a ball and shatters Smith's musket into bits.

" ''Tis too hot for us here,' says he to Bason. He hoists him onto his back and sets off for Charlestown Neck."

"Oh, good," she breathes; her eyes wide.

"But Bason was a big man," I continued. "Above six feet, Smith said—whilst he himself was of a smallish build. With Bason on his back he could make but a poor show of running. The British came ever nearer. Then did Bason beg him to save himself and to leave him—said his wound was mortal. Smith had exhausted his strength but could not bear to abandon him. He lowered Bason to earth, shouting for help to others running by. But with the shattering din upon the hill—cannon, rifles, muskets—he could not make himself heard. Here came the British on the run, now very near.

" 'Go on, Captain, go,' cries Bason. So Smith at last 'gins running, in a rage at his own helplessness, and he hears the other call after, 'Next time you fight—give 'em one for Caesar.'

"When he spoke to me of the failure of his strength," I ended, "the water stood in his eyes."

Out over the marshes a straggle of geese wavered low and headed north with distant cryings. I could find no further words to tell her why the story so moved me. She said naught; but I believe she understood. After a minute we strolled again, for the southeast wind was shrewd. I thought she shivered and asked, was she cold? She shook her head.

"'Tis the future makes me tremble," says she. "I fear after all I am a sad coward, Mr. Medley. —You would not have wished me to march in your army. I look ahead and am frightened by the length of days. 'Twas not so with me, once. No day but seemed too short, for seeing and doing. But now . . ." Her voice tailed off. "—Now, my prospect is all of the grey hue of that ocean. Unvarious and lonely."

"'Tis natural you should feel so," I told her. "But Heaven sends peace after sorrow. You will be glad again, one day. Life is not over for you that are so young and beautiful. You will marry again."

She colored at my words and ducked her head. "I cannot think it," she says at last. "You are very kind; but there be few men who would take beggary with beauty and think it a good bargain. Is that not a sailing ship yonder coming into harbor?"

"'Tis a sheet drying on that near shed roof," says I. "—Mistress Emery, I can show you one man who would clasp tight such a bargain and count it a pearl of great price. An individual no farther from you than now I stand."

She plucked her hand from my arm and stared, half doubting, half affrighted as it seemed. I was in for 't then, and told all my love at once, making a sorry hash of it and stumbling over every second word. As I blundered on, my voice grew harsh and despairing, for her face—stricken and still, with incredulous eyes—was small encouragement to me. Indeed, ere I ended I fear I spoke like one aggrieved; as if my love were an injury she had wrought upon me.

"In God's name, tell me plain if there be hope for me," I finished. "I have bungled and babbled enough to mar my suit twenty times over. —I have spoken untimely, too, and shocked you. I meant not to do it—but 'tis out, 'tis done. So soon after your husband's death—but to me 'tis as if I have stifled with my unspoken longing for half a lifetime."

She began to stammer that I did her honor—

"Nay," I said, "You need say naught. I read my fate in your face. Belike I am too old—too fat—too *black*, to aspire to such happiness, and only your great kindness has borne with me so far."

Turning, I walked away, my hands clasped hard behind me. At my feet lay the wide prospect, but I saw none of it. My eyes were misted o'er, and I felt stifled by the turmoil in my soul. As I hung my head, there were those d—d plush smallclothes and new buckles I had donned with such proud and hopeful spirits half an hour agone. Now it seemed but a clown's trick to have arrayed myself so, and the clothes I took such pride in, a clown's livery.

Socrates dawdled at my heels, and she came, stooped, and fondled him.

"Look you, Socrates," says she, "what an honest man is your master. He offers to wed me, and presents me in the same breath with all the reasons why I should not."

"Nay," says I, spinning fiercely round. She was still stooped, and I could not see her face. "If those be your reasons, I scorn them." (I spoke perforce to the top of her bonnet.) "I am a citizen of a free republic. I have served my country honorably in her struggle for liberty. I have made my own way to the top of my profession and have hardly earned what wealth I have. As for my Negro and Indian forebears, I glory in them. No man may call me his inferior."

"Nor woman, either," she murmured. She rose, her face suffused from stooping. "I trust you do not accuse me of holding such matters against you," says she. "Did I do so, I were unworthy of a second glance. Indeed, Mr. Medley, there is no one whose friendship I esteem more than yours—no man has more of my respect and admiration. —Excepting only General Washington, of course." (I was too troubled to smile at this ingenuous exception.) "But, Sir, I cannot marry you."

"Because you cannot love me?" I cried. (I fear 'twas in wild and piteous fashion.) "You cannot bid me hope at all—that a later time—?"

There were tears in her eyes now. She shook her head. "I cannot think I will ever again wish to marry," says she. "My heart lies in Barbados. This has been the first great grief of my life, for I was too young to weep when my parents were taken from me. My elders all tell me I am mistaken, that happiness is not at an end for me. Perhaps they are right. Perhaps one day I might love again, might wish to marry . . ." She looked desolately at me. "I must pray God I be spared such a misfortune," she says flatly. "Encumbered as I am with debt, I would bring ruin to my new husband for a dowry."

In my agitation I began to babble dollars and cents, my assets and savings. "I have at present $22,000 safely banked," says I, "a considerable fortune. I meant to retire from conjuring and buy a farm. But I could continue on the road for five—nay, ten years longer, could you but bid me hope. I fear not your debts—I am yours, and all I have is yours, if only you will have me."

She shook her head. "You would be left with nothing. I would not do my friend such an injury." Suddenly she took my arm. "I am tired," says she faintly. "I would go back to the *Grapes.*"

"I have distressed you," says I.

She brushed at her eyes. "It mislikes me to make my friend unhappy," she says.

We walked back down the steps in silence; she thinking her own thoughts, the nature of which I could not guess. My own mind was a-whirl and my heart sore. I did not wish to converse. But note, how stubborn a thing is hope! More and more one fact leaped forward to demand my full attention. *She had not said she could never love me.* 'Twas like a flame that licks feebly up from beneath cold ashes.

"Mistress Emery," I said, and I sounded hoarse as a crow. "I have said overmuch already. Permit me one question more—and if your answer be No, no further word shall I ever speak on a subject painful to us both. You have my solemn promise on that."

After some hesitation, "Speak, then," says she.

"Were you debt-free," says I. "Were the thought of wedding another no longer intolerable to you. Might you then look with favor upon Josh Medley? Or would any or all of the reasons I have named—named, mark you! to repudiate—make my suit fatally repugnant to you?"

A freight wagon rattled past us and we needs must flatten ourselves against the door we were passing. She waited until the racket of wheels was something diminished; smoothing her skirt with one hand.

"I like not these, 'An' this were that, an' what is, were otherwise,' " she said at length. "Of what profit is it, Mr. Medley, to speculate thus?"

"Poor consolation, indeed. Yet, since it be all I am like to have, I would grasp it eagerly," says I. "And bless you for it."

"Then take it, in God's name," says she, starting off down the street.

A disagreeable doubt struck me. I hurried after. "You say it not from pity, as I hope," says I, something stiff. "I will brook no man's pity."

She smiled somewhat. "And I am no man, Sir," says she. "I would not dare pity you. You look too fierce on me, for that."

Now I confess this wounded me. I think I have behaved toward her (excepting on one or two trifling occasions) as soft as any cooing pigeon. I bowed acknowledgment of her good word—if good word it be! "Thank you," says I. "I must rest content with that. —Though even from my father I think I may expect a warmer word than yours."

She spread her hands. "What would you have?" cries she. "I have told you, 'tis possible I might come to love you—that at least I see naught to hinder—if all were arranged as it never can be. Do not go on so, worrying me for more, or I shall take back the word I gave you. I think you are plaguey hard to please."

"And yet, you please me in all things," says I very low.

Her face softened. "Truly, Mr. Medley," she says, "yours would be a steadfast, loving heart. Any woman of discernment must find you loveable." And she looked on me so sadly, so kindly, my heart throbbed.

We said no more on that walk. At the corner of State Street and Mackerel Lane Socrates began a fight with a piebald tyke of the butcher's there, and in the melee my poor plush smallclothes and white stockings were sadly dirtied. So ended our walk, with Mistress Emery making much of Socrates as I bore him in my arms to lock him up; and he wrenching himself round and growling curses over my shoulder in a fever to finish his battle with Piebald.

March 31, 1794

At Howe's in Sudbury, where there is much company. I share a bed with a Mr. Jones, a draper en route to Albany, and a Mr. Josiah Pease, a peddler of tinware. Four others take the chamber floor upon straw pallets; for every room in the place is full. So I shall have an audience after supper. I carry only the cards and the Philosophical Paper in my saddlebags, but the cook has given me leave to borrow a string of her red onions from the beams for my juggling turn.

I am delighted with my mount (and a pretty penny his hire is costing me). He is something hard-gaited, but handsome in appearance: dappled grey, the rosettes clearly marked, and with dark stockings. His name is Royal Duke, so I travel with rank. He bore me merrily today through

Waltham, Weston, and Wayland. The day proved fine, with little wind. The countryside is greening, and the maples brandish crimson fists at every hand. In the small kitchen garden here I saw crocuses, purple and white, basking in the warmth from the brick wall.

From farm after farm as I rode I breathed the smell of wet, new-ploughed earth and furrows freshly dunged. In Wayland the lowlands are in flood from the Sudbury. At one bridge, as I came through, the water lapped the road, and all the green fields cupped pools and fingers of blue; the sky seemed melted down upon the land.

I departed the *Grapes* at daybreak. Mistress Emery was still abed, and I saw her not. I left Socrates in the care of the stableboy Tom, whom I have grossly overpaid to see to his wants. The rogue knew I was off—from the box stall he set up a frantic barking sufficient to rouse every soul within a circle of half a mile.

Before turning my horse's head toward Hopkinton, I rode down to Gault's. This, because of a secret resolution to which I came during the dark morning hours. In short, I have settled in my mind that I shall go in for all I am worth with Gault and Will on the balloon scheme.

When I try to trace the roots of this decision, the steps run somewhat as follows:

1. She might yet be brought to love me.
2. But she has debts she feels prohibit her remarrying.
3. Ah, but I have considerable saved.
4. Yes, but her debts are equal at least to your wealth.
5. I would wed her all the same.
6. But she will not wed you, to your ruin.
7. Then must I speedily make more money—enough to overcome all her scruples.

This, or something near it, seems the way my thoughts have led. Mad, no doubt, against all prudence and common sense; but much to the liking of some reckless strain in me that all this while has nagged me with balloons. Who knows? Great prizes ere this have been won against great odds. 'Twould not be the first venture I have shared in, where success was won against long odds. (Independence Forever!) Still, 'tis best I parade my fortune to my father now, ere Gault's affair can beggar me.

'Twas with something of sheepishness I broached my desires to Gault and Will—such a turnabout, and I feared Will would guess at my motives. Luckily they were both up and breakfasting with Madame Gault and the family. (I took a slice of pumpkin bread.)

Mistress Gault made me welcome, but in her face I saw tightness and a darkening at the word *balloon*, that bespoke hours of domestic strife. Indeed, she spoke to the fire, the crossbeam, and the cat upon the settle, declaring moon-madness to be not only chronic but catching; since one benighted man could infect other men of apparent sense and substance, and make them run as mad as himself, &c., &c.

Will and I were embarrassed by her talking so before us, their guests. But Gault was not a whit put out. My coming had set him up; his eye glowed; and all his wife's rating and prating to the cat, the fire, the furniture—she made every article in the room her confidant and ally—brought only winks from him, toward us and the children. They of course were agog for their father's balloon, bubbling over their porringers with excitement second only to his.

The poor woman has some excuse for her bad temper. Sole manager of the business (as Gault freely acknowledges), she must feel herself fighting alone against the world for the survival of the family fortunes. I sympathized the more with her when we three speculators, breakfast being cleared, bent our heads over Gault's plans spread out upon the table. 'Twas then that first I learned, he has plunged ahead without waiting to turn up investors; being already in debt to the banks to the tune of thousands of dollars, with his shop on the line as security.

"But now you are in, Mr. Medley, that will all arrange itself," says he. "I had thought we must hobble ourselves to the *Montgolfier* balloon, which is made buoyant by mere hot air and very limited in its capabilities for extended flight. But with your capital at our backs, we can inflate with inflammable air. There will be scarce a limit to the new horizons we may conquer."

His airy assumptions struck me so disagreeably that I myself came near addressing a few words of protest to cat and crossbeam. Will looked tense but said little. Doubtless his own meagre savings are vanished already into silks and silken ropes, &c., &c. So I told Gault I was committed to his scheme, but on certain conditions: that whilst he should have full charge of the construction of our balloon, all financial decisions should be jointly agreed upon by the three of us as a corporation. "Further," says I, "all questions of advertising and promotion shall devolve upon me, subject to your approvals."

He agreed at once to these points. Indeed, the man is so engrossed in his plans for the flight, he brushes away all contingent questions like mere buzzing flies about his ears.

At his urging, I looked over his scale drawings of balloon and rudder device; also his plans for a contrivance to create inflammable air from iron filings. They meant little to my unknowledgeable eye. But I gave good help on the matter of the suspension basket.

He wished one of wicker, he said, for its lightness, but had not found out any basket maker to whom he was willing to entrust his life for the strength of the weaving.

"Seek no further," I said to him. "I have an aunt who will work you up a basket safe to bear a brace of bullocks."

He looked as if griped with sudden cramp. "My respects to your lady aunt—" he begins, shaking his head.

"Tut, man, she is Indian," I cried. "Powerful in her arms as any man and with the Nipmuck weaving skills in her fingers. You cannot do better."

His eyes opened something wide. "I did not know you were of Indian blood, Sir," says he. "That gives a different aspect to our affair."

I became high with him, at this; told him I was not only Indian but African and asked did my lineage taint my money in his eyes, so as to make it unfit for him to touch. Will shook his head at me throughout this impetuous speech.

Our inventor blinked painfully. "You mistake me, Sir," says he. "I intended no such—indeed, I have heard that 'mongst the Randolphs of Virginia—than whom you will agree America boasts no family more genteel and illustrious—one scion positively brags of his dark hair and complexion, his high cheekbones, as proving his descent from the native princess Pocahontas." And he bowed, as though paying me high compliment.

I cared not for his Randolphs, I told him; not even for the remarkable *condescension* of that scion who boasted of such lineage whilst holding hundreds of his fellow men in bondage. I would have continued in this vein; but was brought up short by Gault's suddenly directing his attention, not to my words but to my *ears.* He came close and examined first one, then the other, with intense interest.

"Yes," says he musingly, "you have the black man's ear, Mr. Medley; not the Indian's. The Afric ear is small and neat—smaller than either the Indian's or white man's. I have somewhat studied ears amongst the races—it chagrins me to think I did not deduce your mixed blood from your ears when first we met."

This being examined as a *specimen* filled me with choler. I was on the point of exploding when I caught Will's eye. He was helpless with silent laughter; and at the sight my own funny-bone was tickled. The man's curiosity was avid and artless as any child's.

"Here, then, is the man of science," I cried. "Mr. Gault, you are welcome to inspect my ears, but you may not *collect* them."

"You must pardon me," he returned. "I am something too enthusiastical. I forget my manners. I meant but to say—before you took me up so sharp—if your aunt be of the Nipmuck she shall have the basket commission without further parley."

"Nay, she shall, as I know, do the thing for pure love of me, her nephew," says I. "And we shall save outlay on one item at the least." And so it was arranged, Will should take Gault's specifications to her at Chebacco.

The drover's staircase here at Howe's lies behind the wall at the head of our bed. Feet have pounded it busily all evening. Most inns have some such arrangement to keep those early-risers from disturbing the other guests. Indeed, Howe's does better by them than Pease's at Shrewsbury; where only hand-and-toe holds cut for them up the outside wall enable them (clambering like squirrels to the window) to reach their loft chamber.

That I should miss the bright presence that cast a glow

about the *Grapes* is not to be wondered at. The mere knowledge of her nearness transformed that house, as a good fire warms a chilly chamber. But that I also find myself hankering after Socrates . . . ! To my shame be it told, I miss the dog sorely. What a sad old bachelor must I be, so to crave for the sight of that rogue stretched by the fire.

I stand in need of comfort, this night. Tomorrow—in all probability—I may look for the first time upon the face of the man who fathered me.

Never have I felt so eaten by loneliness.

April 2, 1794

Back at Buckminster's, having come away from Hopkinton at near a gallop. Please God I shall never again set eyes upon the place.

I must set down things in good order. I must write with a steady hand. So.

After rain in the night, yesterday dawned clear; something cold, for April; a north wind tossing the budded branches. About nine I had my horse brought round and rode for Hopkinton. Having made inquiry at the inn, I knew the Buckland place to lie this side the town; halfway up a long hill leading into the Green, I was to watch out on the right for a broad avenue lined with chestnut trees.

Royal Duke, freshly brushed and curried, danced me on my way. My boots glistened like new-peeled horse chestnuts. But so constricted felt my chest I could scarce breathe, and my hands upon the reins were not steady. Thirty-eight years, or near it, to bring me to this day.

About eleven-thirty we reached the chestnut avenue, down which I made the Duke to pick his way, that we might arrive unmuddied at the house. The deep shade cast a chill. On the upper hand, the way was densely wooded. To my left, running to the hollow, I saw plowed fields and on the slope beyond, a young peach orchard. Then came barns and outbuildings and, on the right of the avenue, terraced gardens sloping upward to the house.

My head turned this way and that, looking for the known, the forgotten, the pasture slope of my dream; but naught saw I that spake of early days. E'en the house was familiar only from Moulton's painting. A central walk, shaded by a sycamore and two large elms, ran to the front door.

I tied the Royal Duke to the hitching post and mounted the brick walk, that rose by two wooden steps to each new terrace. My boots spake on those steps with great loudness (it seemed), so quiet lay the place. Yet the fields were new planted; the front walk bordered with snowdrops and yellow crocuses. The portico was quite o'erhung with woodbine.

There, the serpent knocker. Placed so easily to hand—how small must I have been, to stretch for it vainly! Though the green stone eyes sparkled at me finely, the gold of the scales was peeled and broken. Beneath it I spied the hue of lead. The thing felt cold to my perspiring palm.

I knocked twice over before aught stirred behind the door. At length the bolt was shot back, and an elderly lady opened to me. Her cap bespoke Housekeeper, and she had a face of faded fair.

I presented my card and begged a few words with Sir William, were he at home.

Peering in some surprise at this stranger, where doubtless few strangers come, she bade me wait in the hall, whilst she went off to convey my message.

The hallway was pillared with four white fluted columns, and at its inner end was a door with a ponderous granite sill. The walls of the hallway, green patterned, appeared to be tapestry; but when I touched the covering there came a slight sound of paper, and the design moved under my hand. The outer paper was pasted upon cloth and the whole hung loose between molding and panel. The house smelled both musty and damp; as if were needed good fires in the rooms and the windows thrown open to the spring airs.

Very soon, comes the housekeeper, my card still in hand, to say Sir William would have me state my business with him. A kitchen clatter had commenced behind the door with the stone lintel.

"Tell Sir William," says I, "my business with him is of a private and personal nature. Although it closely concerns him it will, I can promise, take but little of his time." She looks doubtingly, but goes.

In a large mirror opposite the stair I catch sight of my image, hollow-eyed and haunted, like to a fine-feathered ghost. Indeed, I am a kind of ghost in that place, and almost wonder to see my shape so solid in the glass.

The clatter in the kitchen ceases, but from the same quarter a female voice strikes up a tuneful humming. So might my mother once have hummed as she went about her work in that place. The air was *Innocent Maid;* and is like to haunt me till the day I die.

Back comes Mistress Housekeeper; to tip me the shortest of curtseys and bid me please to follow her. I pulled at my shirt ruffle as I passed the glass, catching my own eye once more, peering askance as at a stranger.

Through a door behind the stair she ushered me into a study. The walls held bookshelves and ships wood-carven and several busts; a fire of apple wood made the air dry and sweet; and in a high-backed chair close to the fire sat an old man, all pink and white and clean, wearing a claret-colored dressing-gown of silk. He was smoking a pipe.

"Mr. Medley, Sir," says the housekeeper.

He shoots a look at me, very quick and sharp. One of his still shapely legs clad in black silk stockings is thrown over the other; a scarlet slipper dangles from the toe.

He looks down at my card, which he holds, and takes his pipe from his mouth.

"Mr. Medley?" he says civilly. "You will pardon me if I do not get up. In the mornings my natural strength is somewhat debilitated. —You are a conjuror by profession?"

"I am," says I; and stuck.

"Perhaps I can guess the nature of your business with me," he says surprisingly, next. "I myself can have no personal matters to discuss with one who is a total stranger to me. You are the first conjuror I have met, though I have enjoyed a juggling turn now and again; particularly in Europe. There are many skilled artists of sleight-of-hand, of tumbling and of juggling, abroad, Sir, in France, Italy, and Spain. Perhaps you yourself come from Europe? You studied the art there?"

"No, Sir, not I," I say. This talk left me all at sea.

"—No?" says he. "A pity. America is raw in its theatre, as in all else. You might have profited from Italy. Italy's the place for juggling and such games." There was a contradiction in the man 'twixt eye and manner that puzzled. His eye resented my presence in his house, would demand to know my business, yet his tongue rattled on, making it difficult for me to come to the issue.

At length he paused and looked me up and down; still with that superficial complaisance that, more than hauteur or rudeness, put my hardihood to the test.

"Have a seat, Mr. Medley," he said; as if the words cost him pain.

"Thank you, Sir William. I prefer to stand," says I. "My business can be briefly stated. Before I commence—"

"—I can guess it," says he again. "It concerns my grand-nephew, does it not? You are an emissary from this fellow Oliver?"

My manifest bewilderment answered him. His face darkened. "Well, then, Sir," cries he impatiently, "what the D—l *do* you want? What is your *personal* business with me? —I want no juggling turns," he adds with something of a sneer. Whatever trouble his grand-nephew be in with the mysterious Mr. Oliver, once Sir William found he was not placating an ally of that worthy, his anger at his own error turned upon me.

I was glad of it. Rudeness placed upon me none of the restraints his courtesy had imposed.

"Before I state my business," says I, "I must make clear my motives for coming here. If I seem to boast, 'tis from necessity, to convince you of my disinterest. I have done well, Sir, at conjuring. I am what most would call a man of considerable wealth. Retirement in comfort upon my own holdings is within my grasp, though I am but thirty-seven years of age." (No mention I made of balloons.) "The inheritance I shall leave my sons may well exceed what you here enjoy."

He bowed ironically. "You are to be congratulated," says he.

"My bankers can back up my every word," I said. "This being so, I trust you will believe what next I say. I take no interest in aught you have. I would, Sir William, touch not one penny of yours if my very life depended upon it. The idea is so repugnant to me, were I the most indigent of paupers instead of a man of independent means, I would still repudiate it with the utmost scorn; for myself, Sir, and for my mother." I trembled. I had the odd sensation of speaking in a dream, so often having fancied how I would stand before him proclaiming these selfsame words.

He had raised, whilst I spoke, one half of an eyebrow. "Admirable," says he. "'Tis with fervor positively noble that you repudiate that to which you have no possible claim. Rest easy in your mind, Mr. Medley—I shall make no unwelcome offers." He smiled a smile of January chill. "That question being settled—to our mutual satisfaction—will you please to state your business? Am I, perhaps, in train to be presented with a long-lost son?"

"Indeed," said I—and despite my resolve to meet his sarcasm with lofty dignity, I spoke in some confusion—"I have good reason to believe you are my father. I assure you, no more than you, do I derive satisfaction from the fact."

"But something more of interest," says he, "since you are here. I may tell you, had you stated your business plain at the first you had not crossed this threshold. Doubtless I have left a bastard here or there in my younger days. But even if you be such a one—and we have but your assertion, unsupported on that point—I fail to see how your bastardy gives you the right to intrude yourself upon my privacy. Good day, Mr. Medley." And he turned to the fire, as if wearied of the sight of me.

"You are mightily mistaken," says I fiercely then, "if you think I expected or hoped for any more civil or Christian response from you. Had you offered one, I should not have known what to do with it or with the loathing I have felt for you since first I grew old enough to understand my mother's friendless situation. A man may wish to know his father's name, Sir, whilst holding the owner of that name in the utmost scorn." I clapped my hat upon my head. "My mother has never once spoke your name to me," I cried. "It has taken me near forty years to follow up the clue my own dim recollections of this house provided me. Now, to show how little we need or want your protection, I have forced this meeting. Retribution for your base conduct I leave in God's hand—and as you dealt with her who was your slave, so may He deal with you!"

This was scarce a Christian prayer; but I was pouring forth the bottled wrath of years.

He heard me without looking at me; his face showing only a deadly, wearied courtesy; a cold patience. But at the end, I saw his countenance change; he looked faintly surprised.

"May I ask the name of that most estimable and most wronged lady, your mother?" says he with a disdainful flutter of his eyelids from my face to my boots. "If you are *mulatto,* Mr. Medley, you conceal it well."

"I conceal nothing!" I cried. "Your share in my heritage is the sole part of me that I feel shame for. —Mother is of Afric and Nipmuck parentage. She is called Joanna, sometimes Joanna Medley. She bears the brand of the slave on her face. I was here at this house as a young child. I remember it plain—"

"—No doubt you do," he says then. "I mind Joanna. A strapping lass." He smiled sourly. "You need not look so fierce, Mr. Medley. I am not your father."

"You lie," says I.

He closed his eyes. "You may easy make such charges," says he. "For me to resent them as they deserve, two things are lacking—in me, vigor; in you, breeding. Consider then, if it be manly on your part to utter them. —I repeat, I am not your father." He opened his eyes sudden and fiercely blue upon me. "Come, *Mr.* Medley," he cries, glancing at my card. "I begin to think you honest according to your own lights. You deserve no particular consideration from me on that account, or on any other. —Still, I will try to satisfy you. When were you born?"

"In September of the year '57, as my mother tells me," says I.

"Ah," says Sir William. "And know you not that from June of '55 to February '61 I was resident in Lisbon as the Crown's agent in that place? Has not your mother mentioned that? There is, I assure you, abundant documentation attesting to my absence from America. Of my household of slaves, I took only my manservant George and my wife's maid Lena. This, too, is easy proven. (Indeed, if your mother denies it, examine her upon her life in Portugal and the customs of the place. You will soon be convinced that I speak truth.) For five years and eight months I was not absent from my post for more than the space of a few weeks. No secret voyages to America to bed one of my slaves." He paused. "Your white paternity is plain to see; but, Mr. Medley, unless yours was a miraculous gestation of twenty-five months, then your mother has sadly misled you, and you must look elsewhere—to my overseer or among the local farmers—for a father. I have not that *honor.*" He took up a small silver bell next his pipe and rang his housekeeper in and me out; with no further glance at me, after one final examination of my boots (the D—l take them, and him!) at which he chose to make a show of much secret diversion.

I believe him. I must in honesty here record that I credit his word. A man to whom the begetting of bastards is a matter of such indifference would scarce find it worth his while to fabricate that elaborate denial. My mother, indeed, may have a different word, but this is a faint hope in me now.

Why, why has she so misled me? My mother you have been in all else a mother most staunch and true. Why have you so long suffered me—nay, encouraged me—to make this ill-founded notion of high connections the lodestar of my life? To let my pride and anger o'ershadow all my feeble virtues and lead me to yesterday's crowning humiliation? Instead of healing my pride, I have myself so mortally injured it I fear I can never again hold up my head. No wonder that d—nable old man looked with laughter on my boots and my pretensions. To parade one's independent worth to a neglectful father is one thing; to strut it before a stranger is the act of a sinful fool. Fool. *Fool.* O God.

Well, well. Done, done with forever. Will she, when she hears, tell me my true father's name? I have prayed upon my knees for strength to tell her all with gentleness; to accept this heavy chastisement as sent by Heaven for my amendment.

'Twas but an honest error, after all.

Hear, O God, the plea of your servant. For my mouth is in the dust, and I cry to Thee.

April 6, 1794

Today the Perleys and I spread forty-two barrows of good Chebacco salt weed upon the fields. I must sit tonight with my hands in a brew of burr dock boiled in hard cider, for they are mightily blistered. I put them to the labor with a ferocious kind of joy; as if, with my aching back and shoulders, I said *Farewell to resentful ambitions, to cravings for superiority—farewell. Come like the rising tide that steals through-*

out the marshes, O simplicity and peace of mind!

Yet is this but a mood of recoil that will itself pass and be followed by—what? Restless heart, look not for peace in this world. Seek thy peace in Heaven.

My mother met me at the door with glad cryings yesternight. The dogs whipped about our legs as we embraced. This I can swear to—naught did I show in my voice of hurt or of anger, such pains I took.

"Mother, I have been to Hopkinton," I said low. 'Twas my only word, and I kept my arms about her whilst I said it.

I felt her stiffen. —So lean and bowed is her strong body now! She broke away to look into my face, her own stricken still; then turned from me and walked—nay, she came near running—across the yard, into the barn.

I knew not what to make of this, and I followed. In the barn I found my aunt at work, but her I found not, for she had slipped out the back.

My aunt smiled unsurprised, making me welcome without ceasing her labors. There stood the base of our suspension basket, woven of willow saplings to a triple thickness. The upright withes rose near to the height of my armpits in a circle seven feet across (this, exact to Gault's specifications). She knelt weaving a horizontal withe, shaping its resistance to the in-and-out with her powerful hands.

"Lawful heart, Josh, be ye come? How do ye, then?"

"Middling, Auntie, middling," says I. "—You have been swift—have you e'en slept, since my word was brought?"

"In all my varsal life, I have not built a one for flying," says she, disregarding my query. "'Twill house a horse when done. So you will fly next, like the goose? You must have strong medicine in your trunk, to float in a basket, Josh."

"'Tis done by gas," says I. "Fear not, Auntie, I am not hankering after testing this out myself. 'Tis my partner will be the aeronaut."

Still on her knees, she looked slyly round at me. "I think 'twill be you," says she, laughing silently as is her wont. (I know not how the Indian has earned his repute for taciturnity and gravity—my aunt, I swear, has ever found food for laughter in all things; her grand-nephew in especial.) "You. Like the eagle." She sobered then and moved her head toward the orchard. "You went to that place? To Hopkinton?" she says.

"Ay," says I. "To make of myself a fool. Sir William Buckland is not my father."

"What said you to her?" she says quickly, moving her head again toward the orchard.

"Naught—but to name the place I had been. Nor did I speak in anger," says I. "Why will she not speak to me e'en now about my birth? After leading me all my life up Sir William Buckland's garden path, why does she shun me like the plague?" I had begun cool, but now I waxed angry.

My aunt rose from her knees and moved to the window. So massive is she, her shadow like a tree's fell about me, across the floor, out into the barnyard.

"She's likely gone up to the spring house," says she.

"What for?" I ask.

"'Tis a right pretty spot. She has a fancy for it," my aunt says. "Ye can see all the farm stretched out to the dunes. 'Deed, you'll never budge her from this place, Josh—do ye never ask yourself why she's bound so to the farm? Because ye won and gave it to her, no reason else." She turned and looked at me, but I could see naught of her face. "The pride in ye's a dark pride, from hers and mine, but she's turned it all on her son. —Mind ye how she used to put small Josh to his books, when his druthers be out in the furrows or off nutting in the woods?"

"Ay," says I, thinking on Deerfield days.

"Her that could not read!" cries my aunt. "But she read *you*—cross-hatched text that ye be, Josh—because she loved ye. She knew ye'd be staunch to her—that your pride would turn in anger upon your notion of a right Gent father—that you'd push to the top in his despite." She laughed again, soundlessly. "The father you shaped from her hints and your own old memories, and strove against in all you strove for—has been a dreadful pretty game, these thirty years, 'twixt ye and him."

"You knew I was led false," says I. "You might have told me."

"Ay, I might have," cries she. "And where might ye be, I wonder? Grubbing an upland furrow in the hills? Answering the call of the year like your aunt, with brooms to your back? Shaving beards and cutting hair and selling wigs in Little Guinea? Or mayhap in your grave from a rum-rotted liver, like Polly . . . for there be fierce appetites in ye, Josh, it might have took the rum pot to squench, did not your will to rise i' the world crush them down." She left the window and returned to her basket work, after lighting the lantern on the wall nail. It cast a warm circle about us two.

"Well, you and she think poorly of me indeed," I said. Yet I meant it not for complaint.

"Nay, then," says she. "Ye be a good man, Josh, striving to live by the Lord; ever fierce toward the faults of nature in y'erself. A warrior before ye went off to war, and bearing plain in ye the blood of chiefs."

"Well, well," says I with something of a sigh. "You be a pretty pair. I seem fated all my days to be the fool of you women. Can I, think you, set all right with her? Or will she fly from me again?"

"Go and try her," says my aunt. "God bless ye, boy. Go and try her."

I climbed to the upland spring, all my anger ebbed from me. But I felt old. Indeed, does not youth leave a man together with his last illusion?

She was seated on the spring rock, chin in hand, but straightened when I came into view. Beyond stretched the white line of dunes, to the great swelling mound of Hog Island. The harsh saltmarsh is late to show new grass, of a spring. Last year's straw keeps winter on the marshes until May.

I went and stood before her.

"Mother," says I, and I made my voice of the gentlest. "You had no call to fly from me."

"If I'd a-known," she says, rocking to and fro. "If I'd a-known ye'd found out that unlucky gold *sarpint,* I would have told ye then. D'ye believe that? I'd have let ye from making a meeting with that man. I know how dreadful hard that be for ye, Josh."

"I shall survive it," I says.

"What said Sir William to ye, then?" she asked fearfully.

"That he had not the honor to be my father," says I; my words coming dry as Sir William's own.

"He spoke truth. Did ye believe him?" she asks.

"I was perforce convinced," says I. "—Now Aunt Deb has told me somewhat of how it was. You have judged your son something harsh, as I think. —But who knows? 'Tis certain I had enough in me of pride, even as a lad, to make me wayward. Doubtless 'twas shrewd to put it to account and make me drive myself upwards through the world. Only . . ." And here my voice shook, for I was troubled in my mind. ". . . *What doth it profit a man—*"

"I saw how it was with ye," says she. "After that first journey to Brighton market with the stall-fed cattle. Ye were wild to go again—I would have you at your books, but the Nipmuck in you must needs set to wandering."

It made me smile somewhat, to hear her so cast blame upon the Indian in me; to Aunt Deb 'tis my black (and white) parts that be of poor account.

"I am half sick of all this pother about blood and race and lineage," says I. "My faults, like my virtues, are those of human kind and hence my own. *In Adam's fall we sinned all.*"

"I mind when first ye said that verse by my knee," she cries. "And taught me the great A by it, after. —O Josh, Josh, how wondrous good and patient a son have ye ever been!" She began to weep, great hoarse sobs that increased in bitterness when I took her in my arms.

"Enough, Mother, in God's name," says I. "Do you wish to set your stout, middle-aged Josh a-crying too?" I raised her from the stone. "Walk with me," says I. "And I will tell you a tale." And with that, I told her of Portsmouth and of all my love. It served (as I had known it would) to draw her mind away from the past. Whene'er my mother smells a wedding she sayeth amongst the trumpets *Ha! Ha!*

"She sounds a good gent sort of lass," says she when I finished. "But something young, for all her be a weed. I misdoubt she be good enough for ye, Josh."

"I want no better," I says with a sigh. "Could I win her, with a rich piece of new Ohio land to leave my sons, I would die content."

"'Tis not in ye to be *that,*" she countered in a flash. "Be sartin, Josh, for the lass's sake, that 'tis love you feel—not pride again driving you to seize one above you on the world's ladder."

"'Twere liker my pride," I told her, "to fold my arms and demand that she and all the world come to the rung where I stand. Never would I have chosen to love one not of our own—I was in ere I knew."

"Then may you fast win her," says my mother. "Tell her she need not know or see aught of me—that were wise to do."

"The D—l!" I cried. "Why will you talk so? Think you she would take the man and scorn his mother? She is not such a one. Think you I could love one who despised our color? That I would so demean her, you, myself—?"

She hushed me with her hand. "Be still, Josh, rave not so loud," says she. "Say naught, if it mislikes ye."

In silence we walked to the house. A chill air off Ipswich Bay blew the chimney smoke sharp into our faces. Aunt Deb had left the barn to start supper. In the stalls the sorrel mare stamped the floor twice, with a ringing sound.

"Ye did ask and ask me all your days," says my mother, sorrowful. "Mean ye never to ask again?" My father's name, she meant. 'Tis strange, I had quite forgot. A great emptiness, a distaste of fathers and sons (myself most of all) possessed me.

"—Who then?" says I. "Does he live yet?"

"Nay," says she. "He died too soon to look upon his son. You came four months after. —We were right wedded, Josh, though 'twas in Little Guinea by a preacher of my own people—so it may be, he thought but little of't. Yet did he come to see me whene'er his ship called at Boston, and brought me somewhat from the Indies islands—we met secret, whene'er I could find errands from the house."

"'Twas a strange sort of marriage," says I. "But then I was not a yard child—someone's bastard brat."

"He was used to say that when he rose to mate, then he

would buy me," my mother says. "I know not . . . his ship was lost, off Hatteras, with all hands, in May of '57."

"And his name?" I asked after silence.

"Isaac Somes Medley," says she. "And that is every all I can tell ye of him, Josh, except his people kept a farm in Maine Province, nigh to New Harbor."

And so is the *great secret* out at last.

Back in the house, my mother showed me a silhouette portrait, cut out full length, of Isaac Medley. (I cannot yet call the man my father with any sense of its truth.) It shows a stocky figure like to my own, and a short profile with prominent bridge to the nose; the hair in a sailor's queue. They each, my mother tells me with an old tenderness, had such a portrait cut on the day they were wedded. She showed me, too, a piece of *papyrotamia*, a great fad in those days; a paper cut in an ornamental design and embroidered in hair: two hearts, a pair of turtle doves, and the words *God Is Love.* These papers being used most often for lining a shagreen watch case (to keep the watch from joggling), he had given it her to keep till he should own a timepiece; this, shortly before his last voyage.

The pair of them must have exercised great ingenuity to come together so as to have produced Sister Josie and me. Doubtless my mother's condition after the fact was a matter of little concern in the family, except as it represented an increase in property values.

My sister was dark. My own lightness of complexion did arouse some curiosity, as my mother tells me. Lady Buckland's sister may have suspected her own husband in the matter. But the shipwreck was fresh and sore on my mother's heart, and at the first sharp question from her Mistress, she up and told all in a burst of weeping.

The man being dead (and Sir William's brother-in-law

exonerated) her Mistress was most kind, as my mother says; and did not confine her more straitly than before. The household by then was removed altogether to Hopkinton, so that no sailor's roving eye could again be struck by my mother's beauty.

I think I have never felt so sad and tender toward my mother, as when I watched her fold away again with such care her meagre treasures.

Now I look upon my image in the glass as at a stranger. My craving for land, powerful as hunger, is then my own, it seems; my early call to wander mayhap comes from my white father as much as from Hassanamisco blood. Every man is a puzzle.

Will *she* think less of me? Would she show more regard toward one who came of gentle blood, even through bastardy? Surely she is too ardent a republican to hold such old-world notions. Yet I am hard put at times not to rejoice at her straitened circumstances. My fortune may turn the trick for me; if, as I hope, I hazard it but to swell it.

May 7, 1794

Our business goes forward apace. By mid-June Gault hopes to have all in readiness. The silken envelope is sewn (at prodigious cost) in handsome stripes of red, white and blue. My aunt brings the basket up by wagon before the end of the month. Our posters, tickets, promised by the printer in two weeks' time. Upon these last I expended all my powers of description. I hope the public may be staggered by our *Archimedial Phaeton*, our *Vertical Aerial Coach*, that engine of amusement and wonder our *Patent Foederal Balloon!*

To Rowley tomorrow, to bring Will abreast of our doings. He is late returned from the Court at Nantucket and has since been sadly indisposed, unable to eat and with the ground (apparently) still heaving under him as he walks. So much for our New England waters and their effect upon lawyer stomachs!

I shall play two nights at Rowley. Every performance is promotion for the balloon; a chance to whet the appetites of my listeners for further wonders. I should like to set all of New England—nay, the whole of America—to talking of the Medley-Gault-Poole Schooner of the Skies. Soon I must swing north, south, or west to spread the news. My heart draws me northward; but duty commands that I set my face for Newport, Hartford, and the Litchfield Hill towns, where I have not played this year.

'Twill do Socrates good to run beneath stage wagons for a week or two—he is grown uncommon fat. I must note here the welcome I received when first he nosed out my return to the *Grapes.* The landlord tells me that since my departure the beast had inspected every horse and vehicle that arrived at the innyard, e'en in the dead of night. But when I did come, *he would not look at me.* Instead he stood and gazed steadfastly to the northeastward of me, like to a merchant puzzling if a distant sail be one of his or no. The rogue heard me call—indeed, I saw him note me with the tail of his eye. Then he commenced to bark frenziedly at the horses; this, to show how assiduously he attends to my interests, as he sees them!

Anxious as I am to set southern New England talking of balloons, I own I am not keen to leave the enterprise unguarded in Gault's hands. He has no more prudence, no more notion of the nature of a dollar, than the veriest babe. Already he has made repeated expenditures not authorized by the corporate membership, and when he has explained,

"'Twas needful for the balloon," thinks he has satisfied all reasonable objections. His balloon is both dream and gripping passion; a patriotic duty and a toy. Deadlines, costs, are but trifles to him. I doubt not he would take flight alone from a desert waste full as happily as from a village green surrounded by cheering thousands. Such disinterest is admirable and maddening. In short, the fellow's ways fill me with foreboding. I must contrive to show Will how Gault must be watched at every turn.

Attended meeting yesterday and heard a most affecting sermon on grace and the blood of Christ in its redemptive power. Found myself full of grateful feelings toward my mother, who early instructed me in the doctrines and moral precepts of faith. Full of the old Adam as I know myself to be, it has ever been a struggle for me to combat the World and my own faults, so as to strive for righteousness. Doubtless my angel would say his charge is but an indifferent Christian at best; yet though often I falter in the battle through pride or anger, or lusting after worldly things; still, through God's merciful Providence I have ever repented of my backslidings and marched forth to fight anew. God grant that final victory come, as in that cause (to me scarcely less sacred) to which I gave myself when all looked darkest in the land.

May 15, 1794

Left Newburyport last night, after a profitable stay. Socrates refused to catch on the second night. No matter—I make a comedy of it whene'er he balks, and so please the audience with laughter, rather than with legerdemain.

Made use of the *Bonus Genius* to advertise the balloon; to good effect, judging from the number of people who came to me after, requiring me to make the "little man" tell them more.

The trick ran as follows. I showed the finger-sized doll to the audience, and the cloth cape containing the hidden bag for his detachable head.

"Ladies and gentlemen—this lad I call my *Bonus Genius*. Here is his cape." Then I smile and raise a warning finger. "Look now, as steadfast as you will, nevertheless will I cozen you—for therefore am I come." I insert his head through the hole in the cape's center. "Now he is ready to go to any place I choose to send him—to Spain, Italy or where I will, and bring back to me the news. —But he must have somewhat to bear his charges." Whereupon I pull my right hand from under the cape, bringing with it privately the doll's detachable body. Under pretence of feeling for money, I conceal it in my pocket. "There are three crowns for you, now begone." I turn his head about, from beneath the cape. "But he will look about him before he goes." Then, laying my right forefinger on his crown: "Just as I thrust my finger down, he shall vanish." As I thrust down, my left hand conveys the head into the little bag within the cape. Then I turn cape about, saying, "See—here he is gone." Murmurs from the audience.

I allow their wonder to have its full bent. Holding the cape up again, I wait several moments, remarking, "He must be gleaning news of interest indeed, that keeps him so long away." At last I draw the head from the bag and thrust it upwards again through the hole, crying out, "*Hic meieus Genius!*"

A roar of approval as the little head pops up, and much clapping of hands. Here, by my custom, the trick ends. But just of late, I have not whisked *Genius* and cape from sight ere first I inquire of him, "Do you bring news?"

He nods hard.

"Is it from Spain? From Italy?"

A violent shake of the head.

"From whence, then is the most exciting news in the world today?" I hold up a hand to the crowd and bend my head to hearken.

"From Boston!"

At the sound of the thin little tones, as shrill and thread-like as my back voice can produce, a dead hush falls. Ventriloquism, more than any other of the conjuror's arts save fire-eating, smacks to the populace of the uncanny.

"And will you share with us your news?" I say. Then does my *Bonus Genius* announce the coming ascent of the never-before-seen Colossus of the Skies, the Aerial Phaeton, the *Liberty*, to course through the skies of New England bearing her inventor aloft to heights never before reached by man, &c., &c., &c. Place and date could not be announced by the *Genius*, but 'tis no matter for that—the whole of Newport is agog, thanks to the local newspaper's account of my performance. If I can but make equal noise where'er I play, we should draw throngs for the ascent.

Since a balloon ascent is, of its very nature, a public event, and since every man prefers a free spectacle to one requiring to be paid for, we needs must raise a goodly sum by subscription from the public. So far, sales have been e'en brisker than hoped for. Some means we must devise to give those holding tickets the best places for viewing up close.

May 18, 1794

How is it, that all my latter days be tinged so with grey?

Since meeting with Sir William and my mother, I have existed like to one half alive. My performances are listless.

I go about the business of Gault's balloon dutifully but with little heart. That humiliation toward which I raced impetuous and headlong for nigh forty years burns bitter in me. God forbid that Pride, thwarted, should poison life and darken my hopes and days. A dull longing and despair possesses me whene'er I think of Her in Portsmouth. Though she be no more out of reach than ere she has been —I never hoped to impress *her* with Sir William—I cannot think I shall win her. Were it not for Will and my pledged word, I would throw up Gault's business. It can do me no good—'tis more like to prove my ruin.

May 23, 1794

Came on here to Newport from Boston, by way of Roxbury and Dedham, where we oated the horses. Stopped for the night at Wrentham. On to Providence through Patuxet, where there is a fine fall of water and many mills. Next day we journeyed by water to Newport. There were twelve in our company, and the sail took four hours. 'Twas a day of thin sun and haze, and the sea calm; yet was I plaguey sick that night and morning following. My fun at poor Will and his seasickness came back upon me with a vengeance—along with numerous other matters of dinner and breakfast sort. I fear I disgraced my sailor father.

Yet had I naught to eat upon the water that should have distressed me—we did but lay in a trifle of roast beef, biscuit, wine—naught besides, save some cherry rumgamon and a bushel of oysters.

May 26, 1794

Here at Providence, at the *Bull* for this one night. After what took place at the *Gommery,* the landlord and I could not part soon enough, and so I am come on here.

I returned from Newport prepared to stay a week at his inn. Commenced last evening with a turn before dinner. (They dine late at this place, and give the lighter meal at midday.) I gave one of my best performances; having had time to reflect upon and to condemn my desultory efforts of these weeks past. Skill alone will not maintain a reputation for excellence where spirit is wanting. Moreover, to perform with less than my best is sadly to cheat my audience and ill becomes an honest conjuror. Ashamed of my late skulking, I whipped myself and the audience to a frenzy of enthusiasm and ended to cheers for myself, for Socrates, and the *Bonus Genius.*

Then, to be informed I was not welcome, because of my *color,* at the dinner table! There sat the guests, their appetites whetted by my exertions, but this landlord would not seat me amongst them. Not one of that group but piddled and hemmed and looked anywhere but at me, who had so richly entertained them a few scant minutes before. Their faces told of their resolve to hear naught of what passed—to speak not one word in my behalf. How I despise them for their d—d complaisance and complicity with injustice! Upon which they could not even put a brazen front.

Any loud outburst of resentment to *mine host* would have lessened my dignity in mine own eyes. I was, however, fair choked with the violence of my emotions, and sat down with precipitance by the fire to compose myself. The fellow followed; but his offer to allow me my dinner in that corner (a fine condescension!) I quelled with a look. He backed away, declaring he saw not how I should take it so ill; that I must have high and saucy notions to expect to sit at table with present company; &c., &c., &c. I have not met with such a bigoted, villainous, unChristian knave but once in

Tidewater, whilst still Hayley's assistant.

My first thought was to remove self, custom, and drawing power from under his roof as soon as might be. Yet I stirred not. Past me where I sat, the server brought to table a small pig roasted whole, fragrant with brown, fat, crispings, and savory. The landlord returned to the company at table and prepared to carve.

As he plunged the knifeblade in, a frenzied squeal shattered the room. Transfixed, mine host stood clutching his knife and glaring down, like the horrified guests, at the pig upon the platter. Some diners half rose from their seats.

The host cast a haggard glance about the table, but found none to help. So again he commenced to saw at his roast—and produced a new series of squeals, e'en louder than the first.

Several gentlemen actually leaped from their chairs and ran from the room. One I saw through the window setting a spanking pace, as he meant to put a good mile 'twixt him and a pig so bewitched. The landlord had more of mettle or of obstinacy about him. Ashen to the lips, he yet again began furiously to slice, as if by dispatch to reduce the roast pork to the silence proper to its state in life. Squeals followed upon every pressure of the knife. The pig's protests grew successively weaker, but it stubbornly refused to submit in silence.

The landlord's shaking hands at last sent pig and platter skittering off the table. All his guests had fled the board, but for one lady, half-fainting in her chair, supported by her husband.

Taking pity upon them, I ceased my ventriloquism and let the pig rest in peace upon the floor. Marching upstairs, I threw my belongings into my trunk, lifted it to my shoulder, and marched again downstairs with no look to right or left. Pausing only to whistle Socrates from the stable, I shook the dust of the place from my shoes forever.

This inn is small, crowded, and inconvenient. With five to a chamber, I must bed upon the floor. But all this is of no matter. Upon arriving afoot, my trunk upon my back, I plainly put the case to the landlord, presenting him with my name and full antecedents, as well as with an account of my reception at his rival's.

He made a most civil response; declaring I was well known by reputation, and he had heard naught but good reports of me; that he had hankered to entertain one so *notable*, but had no hopes of so doing in light of the modesty of his accommodations.

"As for a man's color," says he, "'tis my creed that I am brother to every man Jack in the need to be washed white in the blood of the Lamb; so that I can ne'er set up as better than my neighbor." A fine, stout, old Congregationalist, this landlord. He laughed heartily at my account of the squealing roast pig. "We have a spring lamb this moment upon the spit," says he. "And I trust you will have no occasion to set the little fellow a-*baaing*. Though indeed, were it not for the peace of mind of my other guests, I would welcome such a curiosity."

'Tis a fault in me that one man's bigotry should disturb my spirits more than another's piety and good will can lift them. In the main, I find men's love of novelty and shows o'ercomes any misliking for the man who provides such entertainment. The slights put upon me have been relatively few and trifling, particularly (to sound a note of cynicism) since fame and wealth have attached themselves to me. Yet do I brood and burn over this late incident more than o'er the daily servitude of thousands of my colored brethren to the South; more than o'er passes required, the walking-sticks forbidden, the other slights and restrictions laid upon free Negroes here in New England; of which I have been mainly free but by daily observation made aware. Who, forsooth, is Joshua Medley, that a wrong done him should produce more bitterness of spirit than a million worse wrongs done to other men? I should look upon today's events as the rod of Heaven chastening my selfishness, my pride.

Yet 'tis not altogether pride in me neither. I dare so to plead. There is in my nature a kind of hopefulness that springs quick to apply the particular to universal principles of virtue and justice. I have been dreaming, that is plain. That I am oft made an exception, in no way amends the rule.

When now I look back upon the early days of our independence—all the hopes that bound our small army and folk together in their great peril—my heart floods with sadness. *My bird is dead.* O America. O my country.

June 1, 1794

At *Sheldon's Tavern* at Litchfield these three nights past. A pretty high town set about a green. On every side are prospects most fair: much goodly farmland and the rolling Litchfield Hills. Already the summer haze hangs upon the summits, fruit blossoms are fallen, the trees are in full young leaf.

I had thought to travel north by easy stages as far as Deerfield. But a letter from Will brought by a post rider demands my return as soon as may be—the balloon is near completed. Also, our friend Consider Gault is taking the bit and running with it, just as I forebode. He is borrowing against future profits to pay for elaborations of his rudder and is not stayed by rebuke. "He will not hearken to me," Will writes.

Well, he shall d—n well hearken to me! I must fulfill tonight's performance here, but tomorrow early, I set forth for Springfield; whence the stage runs to Western, Spencer, Leicester, Worcester, Shrewsbury, Northboro, Marlboro, Sudbury, &c. 'Tis an old tale to me, that route—I could travel it alone with eyes tight shut.

June 2, 1794

Here at West Brookfield. This rising at three o' the clock, to set out in darkness with no breakfast, is most wearing. I fear I shall fall ill from it. But rest I dare not.

Last night I contrived to send a reply to Will, assuring him of my swift return; though he may well see me before the letter. I also spent a fuming and pen-biting hour composing an epistle to Mistress Emery. I made of 't considerable of a bungle, as I fear. Friend Socrates had many a crumpled sheet to pounce after, for in my distraction I missed more than I hit the fire. Yet 'twas an indifferent performance to read over at finish. I did but inquire after her health and that of her aunt; expressed my continued concern for the readjustment of her fortunes; and dropped a word of our present enterprise. I gave no hint of the purpose behind this risking of my all. Will she guess at it, I wonder?

June 3, 1794

Much diverted this morning by a word of the landlord at West Brookfield. One of my fellow travelers started out of the door without paying for his breakfast (an oversight,

I trust). But our host called the omission to his notice with these words, drawled out inordinate slow and dry: *Mister —if you lose your pocketbook between here and Marlboro, remember you didn't take it out here.*

June 5, 1794

Back at the *Grapes.* Arrived last night late, so exhausted I scarce recall getting to bed.

In the hour before dawn, comes the dream to gladden me. 'Tis strange—I had thought to dream it ne'er again, after Hopkinton, where I spied no prospect resembling it. No passage of years, no new planting or natural growth, could disguise that line of hill to my eye.

Am in dire need of the comfort of Old Friend Dream and of all the philosophy I can muster, to deal without loss of temper with friend Gault. The man seems to have no clear idea of what has been spent, nor has he kept records, more than random notes on slips of paper. I fear he has taken out considerable loans for which I must cover him if our matter is to go forward.

I reproved his rashness—I spoke sharply, reminding him of our original agreement. He owned his fault; making excuse only thus far: since absence made me unavailable for consultation, he thought he might venture to keep matters in motion; that unexpected expenses are bound to arise in such a project, &c., &c., &c.

All very well. But whilst he was speaking thus reasonably, that enthusiastical eye of his burned with a look of passion all greedy and gloating upon his design. Unless he be firmly held in check, 'tis plain he will gladly ruin himself, Will, and me for its fruition.

June 14, 1794

Matters are fast in train. Our day for the ascent is set, the site determined. The die of my fortunes is cast.

The morning of June the 21st (weather permitting) is the appointed day. The place, the Rowley Green, to be roped off for ticket-bearers, against the throngs that will watch from a distance. Throngs indeed we hope for—and to the greater firing of the local population, we will manage two notable parades—one bearing the inflated envelope from Will's farm to the Green; the other, with Aunt Deb's basket that will come from Chebacco by wagon along the Ipswich road. Besides these brave sights, we shall have notices in the papers, and my army of lads will plaster the streets with broadsides.

The advance sale of tickets has swelled to a noble high tide; so that my first fears are proven happily ill-founded. Already we stand to profit by several thousand dollars each, and the end is not yet. I trust the fervor of the public will soar still higher when that glorious envelope, swelled with gas, makes its triumphal journey to the Green. Spread limp o'er Will's acres at Rowley, it looks already of an astonishing bigness. I hanker mightily to see it rise, august and beautiful.

Gault has hired six men to assist him in inflating the envelope. This, I can have no quarrel with. He needs many hands for his furnaces throughout the night of the 20th and morning of the 21st. Neither I nor Will can be of assistance there. His several sons are assigned to manage the ropes.

I have twice visited his works, set up in the pasture behind Will's barn. Whilst he lectures me on its workings, I listen with profound knowledgeableness written upon my deceitful countenance. In truth, I follow but little of all he says. He has there a large reverbatory furnace with brick fireplaces at either end, into which he will put his barrels and barrels of iron filings encased in cast-iron tubes. He will brick the whole in, but for one end, keeping the hearths blazing with brushwood (presently stacked ready against the fence). A round water tank is erected over the whole, with the most curious, convoluted system of little tubes coiling downward (like wisteria vines) into the tubing; this to separate the elements of the water so as to send the hydrogen into the lower tank. There it is to be lightened—(I forget how—somewhat to do with carbon and potash)—and sent through the final tubing to the envelope. All this hurrah's nest Gault displayed to me with a pride fit to burst his waistcoat buttons. He has performed prodigious labors indeed; and for up to forty hours prior to the ascension, he and his men must labor incessantly to keep the fires a-blazing, fill the envelope with gas, and transport the inflated balloon to Rowley Green.

June 16, 1794

Audience here greatly diverted when informed by *Bonus Genius* that the news most momentous in the world was from their own town of Rowley. No man within one thousand miles, I swear, but knows of our balloon; yet do they love to hear *Genius* sing its praises. I begin to fear we may have too great a crowd for safety and convenience.

Will, come for my performance, proved a spectre at the feast; applauding an echo to his neighbors, but with the look of one who sees ruin but a mile down the road. 'Tis painful to see Will, whom I have observed steady under circumstances of pain and peril, reduced to gnawing at his fingers. 'Tis plain, he is in mortal fear our balloon will miscarry.

June 20, 1794

Winds light and variable tonight, skies clear but for a mare's tail or two in the southwest quarter. All signs point to good weather. May a favorable Providence see us safely through!

Too restless to stop away, I rode out to watch Gault and his crew. The envelope hangs flaccid as an empty glove from its support; yet (Gault assures me) by tomorrow 'twill hold gas sufficient to lift him off. He and his helpers, hands and faces sootied black, labor like fiends at their furnaces. Indeed, the whole pasture, with the smoke, flames, clangor, and shouting, presents a graphic picture of Hell. On the road, the curious drift about to watch the spectacle. Will discourages any nearer approach by keeping his bull Ticonderoga loose in the front field.

The papers are full of us. Does she read them, I wonder? What are her thoughts if she does? I got back no answer to my letter.

I sometimes hanker to pilot the aerial phaeton myself—a childish vanity. But too, I yearn to know the sensation of flight. To soar in majesty like a cloud upon the wind! But next I picture a wicker floor 'twixt my two feet and boundless space. Then am I well content to leave the glory to Gault. Heaven grant, he get off safely and in good time. I am conscious of perils he regards not, in the heart of a crowd. A murmur of the immense noise we have raised rolls upon my ears with every hour, every rattle of wheels; in the long white cloud of dust that day and night hangs over the roads into town; the chatter as of blackbirds from the growing press of people encamped about the Green. A Great Audience—may it not turn Mob and rend us for failure! Gault, whose impervious ardor I marvel at, tells me (airily and in passing) of two Italian balloonists that were near killed by a crowd—and their Montgolfier destroyed—when it failed to lift and provide the promised spectacle. Whilst I would trust to the superior virtue of my fellow-citizens here in New England, yet do I recall certain occasions when Mob ruled even here. *Former Governor Hutchinson would attest to this.*

The basket, driven by Aunt Deb herself, arrived this evening, accompanied by a cheering crowd. Indeed, my aunt drew the greatest notice for her prodigious size and impressive mien, like to some prodigy of nature carven into granite.

She sleeps tonight at the inn, from preference by the kitchen fire. My mother steadfastly refuses to come up, misliking to present herself in public as my mother. This effacement, that I neither countenance nor desire, comes all from her tenderness for me. How I love and rage at her, for it!

June 26, 1794

I must strive to record every happening from Thursday last. 'Tis something painful, yet, to write; but contrive to I must whilst memory is clear.

Though indeed, I am little likely to forget.

I slept by snatches during the small hours of the 21st, being fretful as a hen in the night of the fox. I was roused by a surging roar and hubbub from the Green without. I had last seen it strewn with sleepers—ticket-holders come a day early to insure themselves a good place, along with the inevitable rascals with no ticket who contrived to pass our rope barriers. As I looked out, the first streaks of the new day—our day of destiny—lay curled like feathers to the east. Some high cloudiness to the west; fading stars, and the piece of a moon.

Many on the Green held lanterns. Their paling lights swung to and fro. I saw what had roused the sleeping multitude—here is come the *Liberty*, looking scarce half full of gas; her bottom silk hanging in flaccid folds. E'en so, she looms immense in the half light, being twice as high as the roof of the inn. She makes a spectacle monstrous, but beautiful withal; like to some swollen minaret sprung up by magic in the street of our New England town.

I made haste to dress and downstairs at a gallop. The slack look of her filled me with the direst alarms. I shouldered my way through the crowd till I was come up to Gault's wagon. He and a dozen men were holding to the sides of the basket or to stout cords that dangled from the net encasing the envelope. Behind followed a second cart, with Gault's precious rudder. The basket, already attached to the netting, was piled with sacks of sand.

By shouting, I contrived to draw Gault's notice to the envelope.

"No, no, no!" he bawls, something impatient. " 'Tis right it should be so—'tis right. There be lift enough there to take off six of my weight—we shall soon see it full when the gas expands aloft. Trust me, Mr. Medley—I know what I'm about."

I followed the wagon to the Green. One of my hirelings (the idiot) demanded my ticket, and I needs must shout to convince him of who I was. No doubt whilst we wrangled a score more of spectators slipped under, free. The sight of the balloon fired the crowd. There was a surging from all the streets and ways, a press of bodies at the center, so that the horses could no longer move.

I clambered into the wagon and waved my arms for silence. Many in the crowd knew who I was; and supposing I was about to perform some prodigy, joined in my call for quiet.

My lungs are good. Addressing them as friends and fellow citizens, I told them the *Liberty* would make its ascent promptly at ten o'clock; that they had near five hours yet to wait, and I hoped they would remain orderly so as to cause no delay. "Mr. Consider Gault, our aeronaut and inventor must attach his wonderful rudder to the balloon," I bawled. "Then you shall witness the very first *navigation* of the heavenly aether! At nine o'clock, one hour prior to his departure for the regions next the zenith, I shall endeavor to entertain you with some sleight of hand and conjuring." I paused. "Till then, I suggest you entertain yourselves with breakfast, as I mean to do myself—and that at once!" To laughter and applause, I leaped down and made my way to the inn. The public rooms were jammed. I am one who thinks well of breakfast but I vow that morning I might have dined on ashes I paid so little heed to what was set before me. Twenty times I rose to look out toward the Green. The balloon was off the wagon now. Gault and his workers were struggling to attach the rudder. A number of sandbags had been removed and an equilibrium found about three feet from the ground. The whole was still secured by ropes on every side.

At half past eight Will and Betty and their children arrived on foot; all decked out in their best but dusty and hot from their long march. So clogged were the roads with wagons and people, they had abandoned their horse and cart at the farm of a friend, and come shank's mare the remaining distance. Will pressed me for news. Did all go in train, was Gault in command of his machine? And did I think the crowds presented a danger? Poor Will. Striving to put on a holiday face, he fooled nobody. Betty was visibly ill-at-ease, and e'en the children fretted without knowing why.

I strove to reassure them. All had so far gone smooth as might be, and the crowd endured the hardships and tedium with singular patience and good humor. I lifted Timothy to my shoulder and marched the family upstairs to my bedchamber where they might view the ascent in comfort. I found the windows filled with spectators, and peremptorily demanded that they make way for the children. Little Hetty kissed me as I set her down. "I wish you were to go up," says she. "You would do it better than Mr. Gault, *I wager.*" This made me to laugh. "So do not I, my dear," says I. O the irony of those words!

I planned to remain at the tavern till it was time to whet the crowd's appetite with a few conjuring turns and a deal of words gaseous in nature, suited to my subject the balloon. But toward quarter after nine comes one from Gault to say he wished a word with me.

Out I ran to the Green. The sun was brighter, and all signs for a hot day with uncertain airs. Those seated without shade were fanning themselves, and a pretty sprinkle of parasols guarded the complexions of the ladies in the crowd.

"There will be delay," Gault says, the minute I reached him. He glanced up but once and then returned to his labors with the rudder. "The clamp is bent somehow, so it gives not free play to tiller or blade. I have sent Jacob to the blacksmith's for a file and a longer knuckle-piece, here."

This was dire news. "In God's name, how long?" I cried.

"I know not," says he, peering at his work. "Can you not keep them happy?"

Filled with foreboding, I clambered into the wagon and stemmed the noise with my lifted hands. A juggling turn was the only show for such a multitude, to end with the paper cone and balls. I dared not use fire in the neighborhood of our inflammable gas. Gault's men had already seen to't that all cooking fires kindled about the place were extinguished.

I juggled till ten; until ten-thirty; and still no sign from Gault. Then comes word that the blacksmith's is locked. He and his family are no doubt at the present moment interested spectators at our show. We debate, Gault and I, whether to call for the blacksmith from the wagon. I fear that to do so will advertise our difficulties and increase the crowd's restlessness. Already our audience shows the first stirrings of impatience; as, in the sea, slow swells and tossings, a change of sound, presage the storm behind.

Will comes white-faced down to ask what is amiss.

"Smile, man, look not so sick on your peril," I hiss at him. Those near us in the crowd are now alert to any rumor and watch our comings and goings, our murmured conferences.

"I must have a blacksmith," Gault cries. He springs into the wagon, waves for silence, and calls out his need at the top of his lungs.

This produces a general groan. The call for the blacksmith is taken up, tossed about, echoed and re-echoed back into the streets beyond the Green. A few fellows adopt the cry in falsetto notes and cockcrowings, at which a ripple of dark laughter scuds across our sea of faces. All innocent as they are of the ways of crowds, my companions note it not;

but I (seasoned mariner of such waters) hear it and tremble.

The sun grows hotter. Close to eleven, there is a ruffle of disturbance on the far side of the Green. 'Tis said a woman has fainted, from the heat and press. By the entrance of the main road into the Green a small party of chanters take up a mournful refrain. *Take her up! Take her up! Take her up!* The chant catches fire at that side and swells to an ominous thunder. Will and I look at each other's desperate faces. Gault tinkers, cursing under his breath.

A new sensation from the other side causes the chant to fade and break up. Here comes the blacksmith like a miracle (we are told he is the blacksmith by a score of cries); a dark burly man in his best suit, with a kerchief tucked under his hat to shade his neck.

When he reaches us, "What's amiss?" says he; whereupon Gault shows his clamp and volubly explains his needs. They confer together. The smith has some trouble understanding and must have the rudder's operation explained in detail. He makes two or three suggestions that Gault impatiently rejects. The thin wailing of several children among the spectators comes to our ears.

I decide to withhold no longer my climactic nose-cone turn. Back I leap into the wagon and perform it to my best, but the crowd is no longer appeased by such trifles. The smattering of applause is drowned by the renewal of that chant, *Take her up! Take her up! Take her up!* Now the whole multitude joins in, beating like hammers upon our brains.

Down I jump and grasp Gault by the shoulder. "No more delay!" I roar at him. "Forget your contrivance and go aloft! They need not a navigated flight to be pleased—but they'll wait no longer."

He flew at once into a furious temper, at me and at Will who supported me. He spoke like the man who saw himself robbed of his birthright, and as for the crowd he minded it no more than a fly. I warned him his balloon might be destroyed by a vengeful mob, our own persons endangered, I reminded him of the fate of those unlucky Italians; all of which but made him more obstinate. High words passed betwixt us, whilst all about the crowd tossed and clamored. 'Twas good fortune, most of what we said was lost in their noise.

I gathered the blacksmith could fix the trouble, but not here and now; that he doubted the requisite piece could be found at his shop but knew of a colleague in Newbury who could supply it. With eyes blazing, Gault cried that he would not take flight without his rudder. "What, Sir! A free flight? What is that to me? 'Tis a toy, a syllabub! That balloon, Sir, flies my country's flag—will I not honor it by a feat ne'er successfully attempted till this day?" &c., &c., &c. "You, Sir, are a mere showman of tricks to delude the vulgar. What do you know of the creed of a man of science? I will not cheapen the *Liberty*. No, not to please you or your mob . . . My noble experiment! An' I cannot perform it in its integrity, I shall not go up at all!"

I could scarce believe my ears.

"You would cheat them of their spectacle?" I cry, swinging my arm toward the crowd. "Do you dare dream of it, prating of your honor the while? Then by G-d, Sir, the conjuror has more of honor than the man of science! Is not their money in your pocket? Have they not waited days and nights to see the flight? Naught they care for your *navigation*, 'tis the balloon ascent they are come for. They shall not be robbed of it, Mr. Gault, by you or any man. I'll not allow it."

"Then let them come back tomorrow," says this madman. "But without my rudder clamped properly in place,

I shall not go UP." I could scarce hear his words, though we roared into each other's faces.

Gault began to climb into the wagon to address the crowd. In a flash I foresaw the balloon wrecked, the three of us beggared, e'en tarred and feathered by the rowdies in the throng—Will before the eyes of his family.

"Stop him!" I roared to Will. Shouldering my way, I got over to the basket and clambered in. It dipped as I swung aboard, and touched the earth. I commenced to heave out sandbags as fast as I could lift them. "Loose the ropes!" I shouted.

A cheer arose from those nearest me. Raggedly it spread and swelled until it seemed to beat upon the zenith. Scores of volunteers leaped to help on the ropes. In the wagon Will was forcibly restraining Gault, both shouting at me as in a dumb show. Not a sound reached my ears.

Now might I wish I had heeded Gault's talk of balloons! I had no notion, how many bags to unload. But seeing new strain in the faces of those upon the ropes, I gambled that the moment had come. With a wave of my hat I signalled them to let go.

At that moment Gault broke from Will and leaped toward me. I could see him cry out, "No!" his face twisted. The floor of the basket thrust suddenly upward against my feet—a lurch threw me down inside the basket. The Inn swung at me. I had a clear sight of the petrified faces of all the little Pooles in their window as I brushed by. Then a stiff jolt against the parlor chimney, and the *Liberty*, as if affrighted, tore aloft like a mad thing, whilst I clutched the creaking sides of the basket with a white grip and closed my eyes. The noise suddenly sank to a buzz, then to nothing. An immense quiet closed me round.

Venturing to open my eyes I saw naught but the pale sky

above me, the towering balloon dark against it. Silence but for the creaking of the ropes that held the basket. Moving slow, like to a man scaling a cliff, I rose to my feet and ventured to peer over the side.

Then 'twas *O God, O God,* and my belly crawled; for I saw the earth had left me and was fast sinking farther off, a widening gulf separating me from my terrestrial home and all my brother men. Like ants, I saw them run—their thread-like cries scarce reached me from that Green that now (as it seemed) I could span with finger and thumb. The rooftops of the town were drawn together in a cluster, the meeting-house spire pricked up no bigger than a (!); and of a sudden the hazy coastline dipped and swung before my gaze, the sea, and the widening curve of the horizon.

Vertigo o'ercame me. Down I plumped again into the basket (closing my eyes not to see 'twixt the withes to the great Nothing under) and prayed aloud. To my shame be it, I was totally unmanned by terror and could scarce lift my head.

But as I lay and trembled, there came a hot splinter of shame into my breast. "What," says I inwardly, "if I face death this day, have I not faced it before and with far better grace?" I sat up. 'Twas done now—done in despite of Consider Gault and his d—d-everlastingly rudder! Were he aloft, he would be steady; I needs must grant him that. I thought I must prove as good a man as he. But why, why, why had I not attended to his lectures? Many a rueful glance I cast at the immense hollow envelope overhead with its many ropes and cords mysteriously dangling to hand. As he had predicted, its sides had filled to a smooth, swelling symmetry. Like the chimney of some gigantic lamp, it stood against the blue. I could perceive no motion, not the slightest breath of wind touched my cheek. The banner hung limp on its halyard. Yet when I ventured to look earthward again, Rowley was vanished and the sea but a strip of haze. The Liberty was riding a light southeast wind. To my eye, 'twas the fields, houses, trees under me that moved. Whilst I hung suspended they drifted endlessly behind. The prospect was ravishing in its beauty: wooded hills, orchards, and planted fields, with here and there a farmhouse, or a pond flashing a bright eye from its dark clump of trees. I was spellbound, gazing. Now and again I spied tiny running figures in a field, or a travelling puff of dust that meant a wagon on a road. If the dust cloud ceased to move and subsided, I felt I had been sighted. Then would I wave my hat; certain, indeed, that my greeting was invisible to those so far below, yet was this tenuous contact with my fellows extraordinary comforting. Once I saw what appeared to be a dark bird of a strange, rounded shape drifting with perfect smoothness over the fields below. 'Twas the shadow of the *Liberty* that skimmed there. How oft have I seen the cloud shadows race across the fields and gone, the sunlight flowing before. Now I was of the clouds and as high as they.

Gault's accursed rudder no longer dangled from the basket. The collision with the chimney had knocked it loose. Indeed, I recollected it, lying small upon the roof, when I took that first appalling look down at the world I was leaving. No matter. I could never have used it. Now I belonged to the *Liberty* and she to the winds.

The balloon still rose. Farmhouses, the woods and ponds grew ever more distant and uniform in hue. 'Twas when passing over tracts of open farmland that I was most sensible of our ascending. Then, as it seemed, an invisible hand impelled my ship upward. Over woods this impulse was less. I knew (recalling so much of Gault's prating) the balloon, when once at its highest point, would begin slowly to descend. But I knew not how soon that point of equilibrium might be reached. The whole was planned for the weight of the pendant rudder as well as a man's, so that I feared without that added drag I must fly high indeed. Gault meant to regulate his descent by means of what he called the *valve* at the top of the envelope, a contraption with a double gate opening to the pull of a rope; constructed to snap shut again by means of metal springs—this, when sufficient gas had escaped. That rope dangled ready to my hand. Yet did I fear to risk such a move, all ignorant as I was of the violence of effect to follow. And what if the springs did not work? Again I felt nausea, at the thought of the long, plummeting drop to follow.

No, I would let the *Liberty* take me down at her pleasure. 'Twould be by good luck—or the mercy of God—did I plant my feet again upon the earth unscathed. Dimly I heard Gault speaking of possible explosion, fire . . . I thought it had to do with the landing. But rack my brain as I might, I could recall no more. Such fragments of recollection served but to stir more ferment of alarms within me.

So for the nonce I put aside all thoughts of descent and abandoned myself to the joys of flight. Since he was created, has not man yearned to share the happy lot of the birds? There came in my ears a buzzing and in my soul a sense of rapture that led me to sing snatches of Billings' *Chester* hymn, and:

Then join hand in hand, brave Americans all;
By uniting we stand, by dividing we fall; *(Not fall, O Lord!)*
In so righteous a cause let us hope to succeed
For Heaven approves of each generous deed.

Something after eleven it was when I began my ascent. The sun now hung west of the zenith, and the shadow of the envelope lay upon the basket. I was amazed to find my watch read past two. Truly, that silent aerial world had about it a sort of timelessness. Only my stomach spoke of the passing dinner hour.

I had somewhat overcome my initial fear of moving about. Aunt Deb's handiwork was stout, and I found that with caution I could shift my position without causing any unpleasant dip or sway. I found among the sandbags Gault's instruments and log book, also a sack containing bread, cheese and a bottle of madeira. So, ignoring the scientific gear, I seated myself and made short work of the victuals—and of a good third of the bottle. This last rendered me more easy than yet I had felt aloft. Indeed, I have never enjoyed a meal more. Nothing brings the flavors of God's bounty sharply to a man's palate like the lurking knowledge, the meal may be his last. 'Tis a painful kind of pleasure, however, not one I am like to hanker for again.

Our course altered through the afternoon to due west. Far upon my right hand the mountains of New Hampshire were clearly visible, and below me a blue-grey ribbon of river winding southeast. For that it looked so neat and narrow, I could not guess its name. (I think now 'twas the Merrimack south of Nashua, where New Hampshire and Massachusetts meet.) How beautiful, its curves and wanderings. Indeed, all of Nature, oft so random and unkempt, now showed herself in patterns hitherto unrevealed; the fields a checkerboard of greens and browns; roads running with visible purpose and intent 'twixt village and village; the softened woods shapen in pleasant lappings upon the shoulders of the hills. 'Twas like seeing Earth not *as through a glass darkly,* but as its Creator first thought on't—a flowering design.

One hour after, a white veil passed below me. 'Twas the vanguard of a sea of cloud approaching from the southwest, toward which my balloon now drifted. Soon I saw but little of my native earth, for that slow flock, milky-white under the sun. Ere another hour passed, there lay a hundred feet below the basket a solid floor of cloud. The *Liberty* and I moved in celestial solitudes. So near and compact looked that pearly floor, it seemed I could safely step over the side and drop down upon it (though I had to be sure no mind to assay such a move). And ever dark behind, glided the *Liberty's* shadow, skimming now upon the sea of cloud.

Whatever the cause—my late, sleepless night, the madeira or the unwonted purity of the air—drowsiness so o'ercame me that down I curled like a cat into the basket, pillowed my head upon my arm—and slept. E'en now it boggles my mind to think on't.

June 27, 1794

Last night weariness and pain forced me to break off writing. Wrist, arm, shoulder—all made querulous demand that I tax them no further. Today I take up my account of that flight and how I slept whilst hung 'twixt Earth and Heaven.

I woke mortally cold to find the balloon sunk into the midst of the clouds. All about swirled the grey veiling mists, here light, there dark, but with no rent in their texture. 'Twas like the thickest fog that ever I was in, twice compounded. My skin and raiment were covered with droplets. I could see naught below; even the topmost part of the envelope was vanished and the ropes glistened with wet. A wretched situation.

Still the balloon descended (no doubt the faster for the weight of clinging moisture). Whilst still I rubbed my numbed joints, cursing the clouds, I glimpsed earth again; and, through ever thinner veils of mist, the *Liberty* broke into the clear. Below lay the country, unobscured; burnished (for the western sky was cloudless) in the long light of the setting sun.

That I lay in deadly peril, I forgot. That I was hungry, cold, and cramped, I forgot. Such a dream-like spell did that vision cast . . . My *Liberty* seemed a ship indeed, with her great tricolor sail belling overhead. Steadily and with no sound her invisible prow cut the air. The clouds above gleamed gold, and under, the darkening land rolled endlessly on.

All else sank clear out of mind and heart. Gone the injustice, the petty spites and sorry passions of earth. Fears, vain longings—all lost. I was uplifted in the spirit by a sense of mystery, of foretokening; almost, like Saint Paul, snatched out of the body; held fast in all my being to the grandeur of the land, my land, *America.* My heart with love for her waxed fierce and hot. Never will I forget that vision of her lakes and fields, of her vast still forests. Not since certain night watches of the War have I seen her so plain in her majesty and promise—and in the western sky the sun, like the Idea that gave her birth, touched her with glory.

How long I stood rapt by that spectacle I know not. But as the earth fell into twilight beneath me, I shook myself awake and bethought me how to get down before dark.

Under, moved deeply wooded hills. Now came a high ridge I felt I could lean out and touch ere it dropped away to a valley of farms. A village stood at the western side.

(This was Ashburnham, I since have learned.)

In a pasture below me stalked a huge shadow herd, followed by a shadow herdsboy; his mile-long legs scissoring an acre at each step. I needs must strain my eyes to make out the real boy and cattle, so small and dim were they—dwarfed by their own shapes dark fallen upon the grass. The sight of them, and of candlelight in the village, gave me a pang of loneliness. Waving my hat, I halloaed at the boy, but he never saw me.

From the village, however, I was sighted. 'Tis amazing, how swiftly—as if conjured up, indeed—a crowd can gather. The faces turned upward, the arms gesticulating, the shouts and cries—so long I had been hearkening to the celestial silences, I felt as one deaf whose ears suddenly are opened. Their voices clearly reached me as I drifted over the rooftops at a height twice that of the meetinghouse belfry.

"*I want to light down!*" I roared, cupping my hands toward the sea of faces. "*I want to light down!*" No one could hear, for the clamor; but I was something heartened that a number among them mounted horses and set out in pursuit of the *Liberty.* One green-coated fellow in especial leaped his mount o'er a wall by the roadside and tore with whoops across a cornfield in my wake. At the same time an upward draft of air pushed me higher till I could scarce see him in the dusk.

I was in a quandary. Should I risk the valve, for the chance of a timely landing in these hospitable fields? Or sail onward, hoping to come down in the natural course, before dark? The thought of drifting through blackness, unable to see the perils I must encounter, was terrible to me. Though the trees looked soft almost as clouds, I knew I was in a fair way to perish, did I come down amongst them. Had I fully understood the valve's operation, I might have trusted to it; but all ignorant as I was, I could not bring myself to pull that rope.

So it was that once more I miscarried. I found myself beyond the ploughed fields, passing ridge after ridge of wooded hills, and the *Liberty* still two hundred feet aloft. Light was failing, there seemed no end to the forest ahead. It near broke my heart—but will-he nill-he, Josh Medley must bid adieu again to earth and course aloft to safer heights. With shiverings and forebodings I cast loose all but three of the sandbags. Lightened, the ship soared upward till the horizon was again an unbroken circle, the black earth a featureless saucer under.

The hardships and terrors of that night are beyond the powers of my pen. I was mortally cold, wetted with invisible cloud; and suffered both from hunger and thirst. 'Tis true, I slept fitfully; but ever waked with a jerk, my heart pounding. Nary a star could I glimpse. The blackness had a look of black marble, a solidity that threatened resistance. I could scarce credit the balloon's power to cut a passage through it.

Ah, what vain regrets did I suffer, that I had not used the valve—were it only to perish at once. Better a swift death (as I thought) than these hours of cold, anguish, and dread. But I fortified myself by prayer and was much the better for't; feeling a drowsy peace creep o'er me and a warmth I can in no way account for but as God's mercy upon His wretched servant. In His respite I fell at last into grateful slumber, huddled in that basket where (it seemed) I had spent already nine lifetimes.

'Twas dawn when I awoke. The envelope hung suspended against a cloudy sky. I thought, 'Tis day, I must be on the descent once more; 'tis time to get my wits about me and see to a landing. So painfully I got to my feet, hoping to find not cloud below me but fields and trees. What did mine appalled eyes behold—not two hundred feet below—but the grey rollers of the sea.

Struck stupid, I gaped. Naught to the horizon but the heaving waste of waters. The new sun was but a white spot in a bank of low cloud. In the night the winds had shifted northwest; bearing the *Liberty* (as I now know) back along a course something to the south of yesterday's route; bearing her faster and farther, off the coast and out to sea, where her unhappy passenger must meet with certain death.

Turning, I saw land behind me—beach, marsh and, upon one rocky promontory a squat brown house that seemed to stare hard after me. Its windows reflected the dawn, a cloud of birds brushed the sky behind it, but all shrank visibly as I gazed. Strong, those winds bearing me from life!

Gault's valve now was useless quite; nor could I spy a single sail upon that ocean. This peril was the greatest I had yet faced. But strangely (not to brag but to record the curious fact) I felt grimly calm; resolved to save myself an' I might, or—if the worst came—to die with fortitude as became a Christian. I said a few brief prayers, keeping a sharp lookout for a sail.

I had, indeed, three sandbags left me; but those could win me but a brief respite. The balloon was sagging less than a hundred feet above those seamed and hissing waves—I made sure I must presently die.

So passed a shivering hour. Clouds covered the sky; and I felt it hard that I must drown without one last glimpse of sun. As was natural, I had much in mind those near to my heart. I pictured my mother, my aunt, Will—e'en Socrates, the rogue—and in especial Her of Portsmouth, and wondered how sorry she might be. For the first time I spoke her Christian name aloud, thinking I might make so bold when I would ne'er look upon her in this life again.

As I turned and turned in the basket, seeking some hope, I noted that the coastline was dwindling no further. With a leap of heart I minded that a sea breeze in summer often follows a climbing sun; that could I stay aloft so long, the hours of ten or eleven might send airs to waft me again toward shore.

I had been calm in the face of a death that looked certain. This forlorn hope of a sea-turn set me all a-quiver. By my watch 'twas but six-twenty, almighty far from those magic hours of late morning—and the *Liberty* hung but fifty feet above the sea.

Three hours crawled by. The land slowly drifted north; showing that the wind was shifting the balloon to southward. I waited till I could feel the spray blown back upon me from those long rollers passing under, black and glossy like the backs of great eels. Then out went a sandbag, and upward sprang the balloon to seventy-five feet.

Five minutes after, I espied on the horizon the topsails of a large vessel. She was of no earthly good to me. Soon indeed she vanished, swallowed up (as it seemed) under the sea; as I would presently be. I remember gazing ruefully down at my ruffled linen and thinking (what seemed monstrous and wrong) that 'twould soon adorn a corpse. I held my watch in my hand and wondered if that ticking or my own beating heart would first be stilled.

At nine-forty I passed a pinkie laboring in the swell, three men on board of her. Statues for stillness, they stared upward at the balloon. But when I hailed them (roaring, *Help!* as the message best conveying in brief my situation) they began to shout and run about the deck. One, who wore a red knitted cap, gave a mighty upward heave of a line. If I could have reached it, they might have contrived a rescue; but the line fell short by fifteen feet. Then I was past them, still heading south. I saw them hauling on their sail to put about in pursuit. But soon they were but a whitish speck, and by ten I saw them no more.

Down again, to forty feet. No darkling or ruffling of the sea eastward to denote a sea-turn. The water was oily in texture. A mile and a half off (alas, I could no more hope to make that swim than if 'twere twenty miles) the pale land drifted northward. Once a river mouth, with eight or ten small craft struggling on a course to the northeast. They were too distant for hailing, nor could I guess what those mariners made of the *Liberty's* bright globe, did they espy it. Human life so nigh me yet so helpless (or oblivious) in the face of my desperate need made Death that comes to one sick abed—friends and mourners about him—seem a happier thing than e'er I dreamt it.

At eleven the basket was but twenty-five feet from the waves. I lightened it, insofar as was in my power without sacrificing my last sandbags. All of Gault's equipment went into the sea. Over went my hat, coat, shoes. Yet I did not shed more garments. A kind of pride or shame withheld me. A man should have some dignity in death; such was my thought.

'Twas after rising a few feet by these means that I spied a line of land ahead. Not the mainland—that lay beyond, more and more distant. This was an island or a considerable reef, and I saw well that I must reach it or abandon hope.

As I approached that precious morsel of earth, it broke into two islets, a widening channel of water between: the nearer high and rocky, showing two lighthouses and a small dwelling; the further island of low elevation and desert.

I passed the first helplessly two hundred yards to seaward and with the basket ten feet in the air. (I glimpsed no life about the buildings.) The reflection of the envelope glimmered brokenly over the swells, presaging the fate now hard upon us. So low it hung, its speed seemed near doubled. Sagging, it leaped forward, as if expending its last strength to reach the second island.

A check and shock as a wave caught the basket. With no thought but to keep aloft at all costs for another quarter-mile, I let go the last two sandbags. Fool, I proved myself! I should have kept the one—I should have slit it with my penknife and, by judicious pouring out of its contents, kept the balloon at an even height of twenty feet or so. Instead, I allowed panic to rule me. Too late I perceived my error, as the balloon lifted up, up . . . back to sixty feet. I saw my last chance, the second island (with a sudden astonishing pond in its middle) laid out below and, sweeping toward me, the open sea beyond.

My hand grasped the trailing valve rope. I pulled (having now no other course) in desperate haste; fearing to miss the island altogether. Down dropped the *Liberty* with terrible swiftness. At the same time she seemed to gather forward speed until we fairly flew. I clutched the basket and braced myself. A flash of beach sand, a gleam of breakers, and then a crashing shock that hurled me clear out of the basket. I lay stunned, scarce feeling the basket as it was dragged across my back, to be caught wedged betwixt two granite boulders.

Slowly—with much pain—I found Josh Medley to be yet alive. I was, I fear, too shaken and dazed to feel rightly thankful for that great mercy. My left shoulder was come loose of the bone socket and pained me much when I assayed to move. Before me, half upon the rocks and half in the sea, the envelope rose and sank upon the swells.

Oh, 'twas good, good, good to feel once more the Earth under me. Despite the hardness of her initial greeting, I could have kissed the barnacled rock whereon I lay. Bruised and a-tremble, I struggled to my feet and managed after much trouble to haul the greater part of the silk to shore. Then—with an ingenuity that Consider Gault himself must have admired—I made use of the valve spring, attaching the rope to my left wrist, and snapped my shoulder back again into its socket.

This operation wrenched a cry from my lips. Astounded, I heard my noise echoed by another voice. In my swift passage over the island it had appeared altogether desert.

From atop the dunes a man peered at me.

"Who be ye?" he cried; and as I took one step toward him, off he darts like a rabbit.

I followed, making but slow headway from my bruises and exhaustion. He was headed at a hard run toward the far end of the island, where I made sure he had a boat. I feared I would be left upon the place and tried to run after; but without shoes in the scrubby furze I made poor work of it. Then up he pops from the brush, a musket levelled straight at me.

I stopped dead. ('Twas a grateful sensation.) "Have no fear," says I, raising my empty hands.

His eye gleamed ominously at me along the gun. "Afeared?" says he. "I bean't afeared. Ye're the one best be afeared, without ye give account of yeerself, *Mister.* Who be ye then? What are ye after with that infernal flying car ye come in?"

"Balloon, man, balloon," says I, impatient of his ignorance. "My name is Medley, Joshua Medley, conjuror of note. I made an ascent—"

But he interrupted me. "—Medley?" he cries; and takes one step closer, peering at my face. "That's so, then," he says at length. "Lawful heart, I scarce knew ye. I saw ye at Gloucester six months agone make the card fly into the box." His face became stern as judgment. "I thought 'twas but a cozening trick—not devil's work."

"And so it was, man," I shouted. "A balloon is but a natural phenomenon. The gas within the envelope is lighter than the air surrounding—" I broke off. "Surely you have heard of the *Liberty*," I says. "You have read of the balloon ascent last year at Philadelphia at which President Washington was in attendance? No devil's work, I assure you. And you will oblige me" (I spake testily) "by pointing that gun at me no more."

Grudgingly he lowered the muzzle; not without muttered grumblings concerning sinful presumption in the face of God's laws, &c., &c. But he lent me an arm to lean on, for which I was grateful.

We were on the Island called Milk, he told me, off the back shore of Cape Ann. Sheep and cows are set out there to graze in the summer and autumn months. My farmer had fetched him over three trussed ewes bought of a Hamilton drover. He consented to take me back with him. So am I come here to the very Gloucester tavern where last February I played; to fill my famished belly and sleep away two days and a night.

June 28, 1794

Reunion with Will unmanned him quite. Once I was sighted out to sea, he mourned me as dead till word came to the happy contrary.

So it seems we are rich men all, or near to't. But Gault will not forgive my free flight without his rudder.

July 4, 1794

Bonfires, bells and celebration with bells ringing all along my route, for joy of independence. A great day. With Socrates I came to Boston to make certain of my affairs, and then shall to Portsmouth, to win or lose for good and all. Found no letter waiting upon arrival here.

July 5, 1794

I must have a new suit for Portsmouth. —Ready-made, alas! For there is no time for measuring, cutting, stitching, &c. But I will have it of Federal Blue or Independence Green (how grand a ring to these shades of fashion!) with linings of white silk.

'Tis true I shall love her till I die. Yet does there seem more of philosophy in me now. Today, for the first time, I was able to speak of Sir William Buckland to Will—e'en to laugh at a certain proud and clumsy conjuror's visit to that worthy. Yes, something has come to Josh the passionate, the touchy, the proud—God grant it be a lasting influence! I have in this journal set down all my aerial voyage—yet do I know what vision will outlast the terrors and discomforts herein described.

July 7, 1794

Moths are got into my horsehair trunk. Where, O Medley, is your philosophy now?

'Tis shrunk small and brown and flitters about the room.

July 9, 1794

New suit packed away in my trunk. The stage leaves at two, so I must to bed, where Socrates keeps a warm spot for my feet. He comes to Portsmouth—for did he not win smiles when I could not?

July 12, 1794

The Inn crowded, but I am given a private bedchamber —see what a reputation for wealth can do!

Tomorrow decides my fate. Called this morning and engaged to take Mistress Emery for a drive if the day prove fair. Then must she tell me the best or the worst.

I found them in a sad way indeed, with scarce a stick of furniture remaining—it has all been possessed for the creditors, and soon the house itself must go the same way. Then must they seek meaner quarters.

Mistress Atwell is in pitiable state, turned almost silly with fear at finding herself suddenly so poor. Her niece, when her aunt is present, puts a better face upon it, affecting to laugh at the bare rooms; insisting she looks forward to a change of residence. "It may prove best to leave Portsmouth altogether," she says.

Privately, she told me her aunt will scarce go out, for shame of meeting old friends; and at home does little but weep and berate her niece for refusing offers of assistance.

"For we are not friendless," says she. "My aunt declares I am much too proud."

Here I became (as I think) more of a sly dog than often I manage, with the ladies. I made as if I feared her too proud, indeed; too proud to be seen out a-riding in a hired chaise with a conjuror. I put on quite an injured air about it, with the result that she agreed (nay, insisted, her eyes snapping with anger) that we ride out tomorrow. A grim ride of it I may have, too, poor lass! For I made her very cross.

For Mistress Atwell I feel pity and disgust. She has no use for me, as she has more than once made plain. Yet am I a small something better than their present poverty. Were I Old Scratch himself (and is he not called in local parlance *The Black Man?*) come as a moneyed suitor to her niece, she would smile upon me with the same pained resignation. In truth, did her prejudice o'ercome her poverty, rather than the reverse, she would have more of my respect.

From the papers they knew somewhat of my late exploit and congratulated me upon my daring. I look forward to telling all the tale to her tomorrow as we ride. Her adventurous young heart will delight to hear, and the recounting will carry us out of the town, where amidst rural delights I will speak of dearer concerns.

The countryside is burgeoning into summer. Journeying north from Boston, I thought New England had ne'er appeared so fair. The weather was fine and cool, the scent of pine strong under the sun. The west wind gusting over the fields bore the odors of new hay, wild strawberries and the farm flower gardens. Clove pink and Sweet William and roses—even lilac late to bloom. Hollyhocks nodded at us o'er many a stone wall. I rejoiced to hear the rattle of wheels beneath me, the beat of the horses' hooves. E'en the taste of dust did not offend. I was rapt alike by the local history dished up by our driver and by the political arguments among my fellow-passengers. Indeed, they must have thought me silly, for the way I beamed at every man and object before me. I felt a thankfulness for mere living that makes me almost sanguine for success tomorrow.

I have out the new suit. I now something regret having settled on the Independence Green. But the white silk lining looks well.

July 14, 1794

Yesterday. Sorrow in sweetness, joy in pain.

The gist: —She has shown me such tenderness as proves she can—nay, does—care somewhat for me. Yet, yet, she will not wed me. What can a man do with this?

She did indeed propose a course whereby we might resolve this sad puzzle. But her expedient is one no man of honor could consent to. —But to set down all in order.

After such fine weather, the day threatened rain. I feared our ride must be put off and my suspense prolonged. But I found her dressed to ride out, eager (as she confided in the hallway) to escape the desolate rooms and her aunt's complaining. So off we went, clattering through the town, neither at ease with the other. She sat very straight at my side; awaiting always the first salute from acquaintances along our way, which she then cordially acknowledged. Some stares we drew, indeed; a number of folk recognized Medley the Conjuror. And we were both so distracted by Portsmouth (or, as it were, the World) we spoke scarce at all till town and bridge were passed. I took the river road toward Eliot. Now we were at our ease, and she did indeed desire an account of my journey through the air.

Before I finished, a fine soft rain commenced to fall. 'Twas scarce enough to wet us; yet I drove beneath the sheltering boughs of a massive oak at the side of the road and twisted the reins about the whip holder.

'Twill soon stop," says I.

"There are breaks in the clouds yonder," she says. (There were none.) "How strange to think you have been above them!"

"To view them from below likes me better," says I. And then we both fell silent. From the thicket a catbird rejoiced at the rain.

She turned and looked at me. So then I broke silence and told her, how my heart was unchanged; that 'twas for her sake I had made the balloon venture and increased my assets by half again. "I never meant to fly in her," says I. "That was done upon impulse and in anger. Though indeed—I do not boast—for your sake I could dare it in cold blood—or any other thing."

"I do not doubt it," says she, low.

"Thank you for that word," says I. "If you can say nothing further to my advantage, I shall be grateful still. —You were most patient at Boston. I made my suit as badly as a man could do, and took my disappointment with groanings and complaints, like to one cursing an east wind. I am in frame to do better now, *Mistress Dorothy*—for by that name I called to you when death was close at hand. You shall, if you must again refuse me, find me no such peevish Grumbletonian as at Boston. —Only, think not from that" (and my voice sank) "think not from that, my heart is any the less yours. For it is yours, all yours, and shall be, whilst I live."

She sat flushed, her eyes cast down upon her lap. "The

honor you do me I have already thanked you for," says she faintly. "Such devotion I do not deserve. Indeed, 'tis—a marvel and a trouble to me."

I started to speak, but she stopped me, with her hand upon my arm. "I will tell you all as it is," says she. "I think such a love as mine for Mr. Emery comes but once. —At least I am persuaded 'tis so with me. One can give that girl's heart but one time for all. But Mr. Medley, I cannot be indifferent to your manliness and generosity. I have no choice but to esteem—to love you for those things." She brushed somewhat impatient at her face. "I do not say clearly what I mean!" says she then. "But if you understand —if you can content you with such a love . . . then will I be your wife and, if Heaven please, the mother of your children. —Attend, Sir, I have not done!" (For, transported by her word, I had made to embrace her.) "There is one condition I must set." She looked me frankly in the eye. "You will not like it, as I think," says she. "Yet Sir, without it I will not wed you or any man."

"Your aunt will be welcomed under our roof," says I.

She shook her head and laughed, blushing a little. "I meant not that," she says. "Look you, how I presume upon your generosity—I never doubted you would love my aunt for my sake. —No, 'tis the matter of my debts. Knowing your considerable means, knowing your liberality—still I cannot bear to come bringing you such a burden. And I think I have found out a way for us. You shall wed me in my shift, and I can then be yours with a free heart. —Mind you!" she cried, for she saw my face, "I will be wed no other way."

"My dearest love," says I. (What balm to my heart to address her in such terms.) "'Tis like your generous valorous nature. But I would be a sorry creature indeed, were

I to agree. No. —'Twas ever a barbarous custom, performed but seldom in these enlightened times. —I would rather ten times the debts you owe, than to be freed of them by exposing you near naked to the public eye. What sort of man could countenance such a humiliation for his chosen bride! I cannot conceive of such a mercenary wretch."

"As you know, there have been many such," says she. "Though the custom has fallen something in abeyance, 'twas but four years back, one Colonel Moses so wed a widow at Newfane, in Vermont. A friend of ours, on business at Brattleboro at the time, wrote us of the affair. I had forgot it till lately whilst racking my brain for some escape from the debts. —I believe the Vermont lady made use of a closet rather than the public highway; and after she had stood naked within and reached her arm through a hole in the door to wed her Colonel, she emerged gaily clad. But that was to cheat her creditors, as I think. I would feel honester, did I display my self shorn of all worldly goods on a public way."

"God forbid!" I cried.

"—Nay, but *Joshua,*" she urged (with a sweetness that shook me with yearning for her), "you would do me a great kindness by consenting. 'Twould take such a burden from me."

"Yours are shoulders that should never have felt such a load," I said heartily. "Put it all upon me, my love, my back is stout."

But she shook her head. And by her folded lips I could see the thing came near to her indeed, and that I would be hard put to dissuade her. "You may make up your mind, I am dead in earnest," says she.

Then I began to argue and to expostulate, of all courses the most foolish I could have chosen. All my words accomplished naught but to set her lips tighter; and when I paused for breath,

"Ah," says she sadly. "I feared you would not hear of it. How little we can agree, even on this day when we have come near betrothal."

"You break my heart, to speak so," I cried. "In all else, in all else, command me! But this, mine honor can ne'er agree to."

"But I too am proud," says she. "And as strong-willed as yourself, Mr. Medley. One of us must sacrifice his pride to the other's. 'Twould be chivalrous to let me have the choosing of my bridal."

"I could not hold my head up," I cried. "What, *you* to stand in your shift, barefoot, out upon the public highway? Have you thought what such exposure—"

But she interrupted me.

"Then I think, Mr. Medley," says she in a dead, small voice, "you had best take me home."

"Have you no heart?" I cried, and I was near weeping. "One minute ago, I was the happiest of men—would you leave me wretched because of my tender care for your honor?"

"'Twas of *Mr. Medley*'s honor I think you spoke," says she. "I see no dishonor in a clean shift—I can devise one ample as any tent, I promise you. —I have given much thought to the whole matter. I have thought for the creditors, even, though by their greed for the last drop they have somewhat chilled my concern for justice there. I think they must content them with the house; for, whatever the law may declare, I do not see you under moral obligation to them." She reddened. "The debts were none of your making."

"But your debts should be my debts," I cried. "Our two

honors must be one. What injures one must injure the other."

"Since we are not wedded, that is not yet the case," says she. "And I have sworn to live single all my life if I cannot marry debtless." Then she laid her hand upon mine. "O but 'tis not what I would choose," says she. "I would rather, far rather, be your wife. A shift wedding I fear not a whit. — Since first I thought on the expedient, it has been the wish of my heart." She lifted my hand and held it to her cheek. "You must deny me nothing today, Mr. Medley," she murmurs.

"My dearest love," says I, and my voice shook. "You must cease to press me for what my honor cannot give."

That word was the finish of our ride. She put my hand aside as 'twere a dead kitten, and coldly asked once more to be taken home. I could read hurt and reproach in her countenance—had she looked into mine, she would have found despair. But she turned away and spoke no word, for good or ill, till I pulled the horse up at her door.

"Good day, Mr. Medley," says she then, in a voice tight with tears.

As I handed her down; "May I wait upon you tomorrow?" I asked; but with little hope.

She laughed cheerlessly. "After refusing to have me as your wife," says she, "'twere kinder, as I think, to stop away."

"You are wrong, wrong to mock me so!" I burst out. "Knowing my love—"

"—Ah, yes," she flashed. "You men and your *great loves.* You make very pretty talk of love. 'Tis our mistake, ever to push you to the proof."

"Indeed," I cried, "I think I prove it well, sacrificing your good will and every hope of happiness to preserve your dear dignity. Would a father show love, who allowed a child to tease from him what was to the child's hurt?"

This proved the most unfortunate word of all I spake. With cold, white face, she curtseyed to me. "This *child* will tease you no more, Sir," says she. And off she sweeps into the house without another look.

What, what am I to do? What can I do? One of us must surely yield, or there can be no future for us two. Valorous she is, but of will as stubborn as mine own. 'Tis unbecoming in a woman, as I think. Could two such live together in harmony?

Yet my heart breaks. To lose her when just I won her. God help me to bear it.

December 6, 1794

Extract from the records of the Town of Alstead:

These are to signify unto all ministers of justice and whomsoever it may concern that Joshua Medley of East Alstead in the State of New Hampshire did meet with Dorothy Emery, widow of the Town and State aforesaid on October 24, 1794 after she had gone four times across the Highway in only her shift and hair lace and no other clothing, without housing or lands or any personal state whatever; and on said Highway I did join together in marriage the above said Joshua Medley and Dorothy Emery on the day and year abovesaid, in the presence of Priscilla Atwell, Elizabeth Poole, and Hannah Aikens, as witness my hand and seal hereto affixed. John Hassard, Minister of the Gospel

Blessed are the meek, for they shall possess the land.

But not Ohio land. The change from town lady to farmer's wife is sufficient without haling Mrs. Medley off to the frontier. Purchased from Silas Burnley, these 400 acres of good land betwixt East Alstead and Marlow with standing crops of oats, rye, and corn; the corn in tassel.

A journal is the occupation of solitary men. Of late my hours have been too full for record-keeping. Our house is near finished—though indeed, my wife says it ne'er will be finished for the cause of my adding wings, ells and adornments without end. 'Tis a mansion, in very truth! That she shall grace as its Mistress. Meanwhile we live snug enough in the Burnley homestead, purchased with the acreage.

I love to see my wife seated by the fire sewing, an adorable picture of domesticity, her *spectacles* upon her nose! Indeed, 'twas the first word (a merry one) I spake to her after our marriage. "Now, must we haste to get you dressed, Mrs. Medley," I told her, "and I beg you—put on your spectacles. I fear you have never yet seen plain the man who is now your husband." I laughed when next I beheld her to see those spectacles upon her nose. She made as if examining me minutely, and then,

"Well, Sir," says she. "I have seen likelier men. But I fear you must do." Saucy minx!

In February I go out upon the road, as far west as to Albany. My wife agrees I should conjure for a part of the winter, to defray a portion of our building expenses. Indeed, I would keep my hand in. The thought of letting my name fall altogether into obscurity mislikes me. Socrates will accompany me, and Mrs. Medley will have her aunt to visit. This suits both that poor lady and myself—she can never abide her new nephew, and I would rather miss than enjoy her visits. That she will not consent to live with us, I count as a great blessing. Yet does she *condescend* to accept my provision for her wants at Portsmouth.

March 2, 1795. At Albany

I must give over this journal. I am become a sad dog at writing when I must catch it up after a lapse of months. I write tonight because I am in the dumps at bacheloring it again. I shall make this journey as short as may be.

Profits good, last night. We have taken, Socrates and I, 78 dollars in two days.

How used I write such long entries on the road? Answer: You did not lavish time on tender, witty, sprightly, gossiping letters to your wife.

March 9, 1795

At Haverhill. A good crowd. Performed the trick where the chosen card leaps from the pack and runs upon the table.

My volunteer was an old soak whom I had earlier observed about the taproom cadging drinks. Having met with no success, he presumably was sober; but childishly eager to choose a card. He was well known to the crowd, who cheered him on, with cries of, "Old Bart! —To it, Bart!" &c., &c. I hastily selected another man at the front, but he, with a, "Here, take Bart Pecker," left me no choice.

After he took his card, I placed it in the pack (so as to find it again) and shuffled. I had already the piece of wax under my thumbnail and a longish hair from my head attached to it. So I had but to stick the other end of the hair to the card before spreading the pack face down upon the table.

"Sir," says I, "If you be an honest man, your card will leap out of the pack."

Affronted, he was beginning loudly to insist upon his honesty when out leaps his card to dance a step or two upon the table.

"Sir, you are indeed an honest man," says I. "Is not this prancer the card you chose?"

A look of foolish cunning appears upon his face. "No," he says coyly.

At this, the crowd roars with laughter. I foresee total failure for my trick if I cannot swiftly change his word.

"Come, Sir," I say quietly. "Your card and I declare you honest. Your reply, I see, was but jest. Now we need to know the truth of it. Is not this your card?"

"—Yes, 'tis the very one," he declares firmly; and I breathe easier.

He returned to his place, to great applause, and I thought no more on him. But after my performance, as I refreshed myself in the bar, comes Bart Pecker again with a footstool and plumps himself down next my chair.

"Mr. Medley," says he. "They say you were in the War, Sir."

"Indeed," says I.

He brightened. "I am rejoiced to meet a fellow veteran. Will you treat an old soldier to one glass of rum, Sir? And join me in a toast to General Washington?

From his breath, I judged the General to be already well toasted; but I agreed to one glass. Solemnly he proposed the toast, with rheumy moisture in his eyes.

"And what was your unit?" I asked him.

He lifted his chin. "The Washington's Life Guards," says he.

"Were you indeed of the Guards?" says I; scarce crediting the word as I looked at the scarecrow of a man. "Every man knows of that unit's fame."

"Ay," says he. "We were a pretty body of men, the Life Guards." And he began to run on concerning the glories and vicissitudes of his military service, whilst I gave him but half an ear, having fallen into thoughts of my own about the War. In this way we downed our drinks and I bought him another—that he scarce needed.

After, I made excuse to retire. He rose, bowing—when down falls from somewhere within his disordered attire a handkerchief, itself a veteran of long and arduous service. Out of it rolls a gold piece and clanks into the fender.

I retrieved it for him; smiling wryly to myself to see how he had wheedled rum from me when well supplied with money.

He read my thoughts, as it seemed; for he held up the coin close before my eyes. "D'ye see that?" he whispers. "Uncommon bright, is it not?"

"It has a pretty shine," says I.

He blew tenderly upon it; and rubbed it on his well-rubbed sleeve. "That goes to the grave with me," says he.

I observed that it would furnish fine obsequies.

"No, no," he cries. "'Tis to be buried with me, is what I mean. In the coffin, upon my breast. —I am fallen into hard days, Mr. Medley—Haverhill must find me a pauper's place in the ground. But I will not part with this coin. It goes with me—I have so wrote instructions for when I die. —D'ye recall the General's tour? (He be President Washington now, but I call him my General still.) Mind ye the General's tour in '89 round New England?"

"Ay, I mind it," says I.

"He came to Haverhill!" Pecker cried with rising excitement. "He stayed one night here at Harrod's before he took the ferry on to Andover for his breakfast. He said Haverhill was the pleasantest village he had passed through." Then his countenance fires with outrage. "They would not let me get nigh him!" he cries, thumping his fist upon his knee. "I told the Committee, for days before I told them, 'I'm well acquainted with the General—the General knows me.' But would they let me near? They tried to hide me away, like something shameful. Though I wore my uniform up to the very door of Harrod's—though I followed that morning down to the ferry—they still would keep me off. Stuffed politicians who ne'er shouldered a piece! 'Twas, *Have Pecker out of the way, for God's sake!* Though I pleaded with 'em, pleaded, Sir, for but one word of greeting to the General!"

"You did not speak to him then?" I asked.

"Yes, Sir!" Again he thumped his knee. "He had already set foot upon the ferry—the carriage and horses were on, and Mr. Lear, his Secretary—and then says I to myself, *It's your last chance, and an't you as good as any of 'em?* So I shouldered my way pretty supple. 'I *will* speak to the General!' I says. . . I could be heard, I guess over in Bradford. I pushed right up to where he stood. —They was just casting off—and I put out my hand. 'General, General,' I says, 'How d'ye do?'

"Well, Sir, I'm some altered since the War—no man need tell me I've altered and not for the better. But he knew my voice, Mr. Medley—he takes my hand and looks into my face—surprised to see me—something sad, too, for the old days. *Bart, Bart* says he, *Is this you?* as the water 'gins come betwixt us. He slips this piece to my hand. *Goodbye, goodbye!* he calls. And I watch the ferry all the way cross river."

April 11, 1795. At Hancock

Home tomorrow by suppertime. I burn with impatience.

August, our child is due. May it prove the first of many small Medleys! She gave me the glad news before my departure, as she said, to rejoice me on the road. Yet did it make parting from her more tender, difficult. I shall travel no more this year. She has plenty of help in the house, and Trask looks after the farm. But she will do too much, and laughs at me for remonstrating.

My mother must come on again by mid-July and stay two months.

The Reverend Smiths to dine again on Thursday se'ennight, the Martins and the Todds. —It seems we have naught but good neighbors. Not one hard or guarded look have I received from any around Alstead. To this happy fact, prickly Josh will himself attest.

The dream, last night. I have ceased to rack my memory. That hill never belonged to my early life, as now I think. Nor was it a foresight of this farm. I spend hours of delight riding over my acreage and its fertile beauty rejoices me at any season. (Note: Remind Trask we must add more lime to the compost.) But nowhere within its boundaries stands such a line of hill, just such lofty trees. If a part of the future, 'tis far, far beyond the length of my days in the land, as I believe. Those trees are no more than dark seeds of promise still hid in our American earth.

For the rest, 'tis mystery, and must remain so.

HB10H